The Hemlo

1 pretty little to

1 picturesque inn

2 talented sisters even better at solving crimes
than they are at their day jobs

1 (or more) murders . . .

A WINNING RECIPE FOR MYSTERY LOVERS!

Don't miss these Hemlock Falls Mysteries . . .

A Taste for Murder
One of the year's biggest events, the History Days
festival, takes a deadly turn when a reenactment
of seventeenth-century witch trials leads to twen-
tieth-century murder. Since the victim is one of
their guests, the least Sarah and Meg Quilliam
could do is investigate . . .

A Dash of Death
The Quilliam sisters are at it again, this time
trailing the murderer of two Hemlock Falls
women who won a design contest. Helena
Houndswood, the celebrated expert on stylish living, was furious when the small-town women
won. But mad enough to murder?

A Pinch of Poison
Hedrick Conway is a nosy reporter who thinks
something funny is going on with a local devel-
opment project. But nobody's laughing when two
of his relatives turn up murdered. For Hedrick,
and the Quilliam sisters, this could be one dead-
line they'll *never* meet . . .

MURDER WELL-DONE

Claudia Bishop

BERKLEY PRIME CRIME, NEW YORK

MURDER WELL-DONE

A Berkley Prime Crime Book / published by arrangement with the author

PRINTING HISTORY
Berkley Prime Crime edition / July 1996

The Putnam Berkley World Wide Web site address is
http://www.berkley.com

ISBN: 0-425-15336-3

Berkley Prime Crime Books are published
by The Berkley Publishing Group,
200 Madison Avenue, New York, NY 10016.
The name BERKLEY PRIME CRIME and the BERKLEY PRIME CRIME
design are trademarks belonging to Berkley Publishing Corporation.

PRINTED IN THE UNITED STATES OF AMERICA

10 9 8 7 6 5 4 3 2

For Harry and Jenn,
"a love story with detective interruptions"

The Cast of Characters

The Inn at Hemlock Falls
Sarah Quilliam—owner-manager
Margaret Quilliam—her sister, gourmet chef
John Raintree—their business manager and partner
Doreen Muxworthy—head housekeeper
Dina Muir—receptionist
Kathleen Kiddermeister—head waitress
Mike—the grounds keeper
Bjarne—a Finnish sous-chef
Claire McIntosh—the bride, a guest
Elaine McIntosh—Claire's mother, a guest
Vittorio McIntosh—Claire's father, a guest
Alphonse Santini—the bridegroom, former senator
Tutti McIntosh—Vittorio's mother, a guest
Evan Blight—world-famous author, a guest
Nora Cahill—TV anchor, a guest
—various bridesmaids, groomsmen, and aides to Senator Santini

Members of S.O.A.P.
Elmer Henry—mayor of Hemlock Falls
Dookie Shuttleworth—minister, Church of the Word of God
Harland Peterson—a farmer
—among others

Members of H.O.W.
Adela Henry—the mayor's wife
Marge Schmidt—owner, the Hemlock Home-
   town Diner
Betty Hall—Marge's partner
Esther West—owner, West's Best Dress
   Shoppe
Miriam Doncaster—a librarian

The Village Officials, and others
Frank Dorset—the sheriff
Davy Kiddermeister—Kathleen's brother, a
   deputy
Dwight Riorden—the bailiff
Bernie Bristol—the town justice
Myles McHale—a citizen
Howie Murchison—a lawyer

The opinions expressed by some of the characters in this book are peculiar. The author disavows all of them.

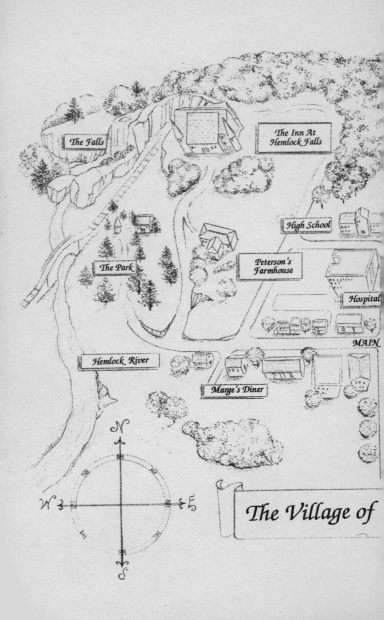

The Falls

The Inn At
Hemlock Falls

High School

Peterson's
Farmhouse

The Park

Hospital

MAIN

Hemlock River

Marge's Diner

The Village of

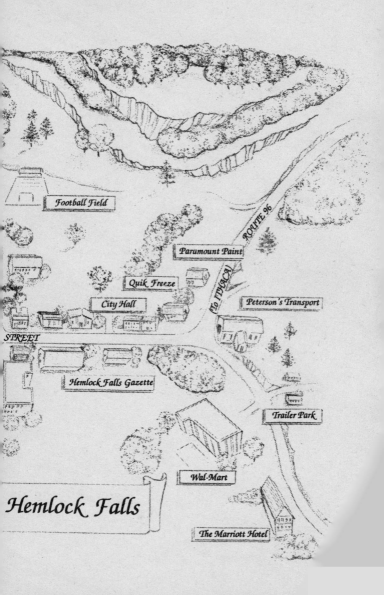

Football Field

ROUTE 96

Parumount Paint

Quik Freeze

To ITHACA

City Hall

Peterson's Transport

STREET

Hemlock Falls Gazette

Trailer Park

Wal-Mart

Hemlock Falls

The Marriott Hotel

CHAPTER 1

"You've sure got one heck of a life-style," Nora Cahill said enviously. "Your Inn is gorgeous, your sister's food is terrific, and your business manager is the best-looking guy I've seen since I nailed an exclusive interview with Kevin Costner after his divorce. I've heard that little boutique restaurant you've invested in got a franchise offer. Even the show of your paintings last month got great reviews." Resentment crept into her voice, souring its carefully cultivated modulations. Pensively, she shoved her sour cream crepe with her fork. "No offense, but if you tell me you've got your love life socked, too, I'm going to hit you with a stick. I haven't had a date for eight months."

Sarah Quilliam set her cup into her saucer in awkward silence. Nora had checked into the Inn the night before and asked if she could speak to the owner. Quill, with a jammed schedule, had suggested an early breakfast. She was curious about Nora, one of Syracuse's most popular television anchors. They'd met at seven in the Tavern Lounge of the twenty-seven-room Inn Quill owned with her sister Meg and their partner, John Raintree. Nora was smaller-boned than she appeared on television, and her hair was darker. She was tall for a

1

woman, about Quill's height. She had the well-buffed perfection characteristic of the very wealthy or the fairly famous: short, precision-cut hair; skin like the outside of a choice fruit; clothes that were so expensively made they never wrinkled. She was probably in her early thirties—about Quill's own age—and the six o'clock anchor for a Syracuse network television affiliate.

Quill, not sure how to respond to Nora's slightly rancorous catalog, said vaguely that she hoped she liked the Inn.

"Perfect," said Nora. Then, "I hope nothing happens to spoil it for you. You did all the decorating in here yourself, too?"

The Lounge was a pleasant room, although during those times when Quill's work as a painter wasn't going well, she tended to avoid it. At her sister's insistence, the deep teal walls were hung with Quill's own acrylics from her award-winning Flower series. Sometimes, Quill would look at her work with deep—if slightly guilty— pleasure. More often she despaired of ever achieving that height of line and intense color again. This morning, if the staff hadn't been setting up a fund-raiser brunch for the Inn's most prominent guest, Senator Alphonse Santini (R., New York), she would have taken Nora Cahill to the dining room; her painting hadn't been going well at all. Not for the last few weeks. Not since the trouble with Myles. Which was going to be resolved once and for all at lunch in Syracuse today.

"Was the breakfast okay?" asked Quill. She looked dubiously at Nora's half-eaten crepe Quilliam. It was a specialty of Meg's, cheese soufflé with sour cream and caviar wrapped in a thin Cointreau-flavored pancake.

"Fine," Nora said absently. "Too fine. I've got a lot to accomplish while I'm here. I don't know now if I want to do it. The whole place is so seductive I just want to sit and stuff myself.''

A fire snapped warmly in the stone fireplace. The air was filled with the fresh scent of the pine wreaths over the mantle. The long mahogany bar gleamed with lemon-scented polish, and Nate the bartender whistled under his breath as he restocked the shelves. To Nora, here for a week's stay while she covered the Santini wedding, it must have seemed like a refuge. To Quill, who was facing the emotional equivalent of a train wreck—in the middle of the busiest holiday season the Inn had ever had—it felt like jail. She resisted the impulse to run shouting into the snow, and asked again how she could help make Nora's stay at the Inn more comfortable.

''I don't see how you could make it more comfortable.'' Nora tucked one long leg under the other.

Quill watched Nora's show on the rare occasion when she had free time in the early evenings. Nora had brains and style underneath the glamour. The stories the station permitted her to cover on her own were pungent and well-balanced. ''I liked that story you did on teen mothers,'' Quill offered. ''Every time the station lets you do investigative reporting, the show is wonderful. Are you working on anything in particular now?''

Instead of answering Quill's question, Nora admired her teacup. ''Even the china's terrific. I've never seen anything like it. It's like that Wedgwood pattern Kutani Crane, only the birds are more vibrant.''

''It's a rose-breasted grosbeak,'' said Quill. ''The design was created right here in Hemlock Falls by some friends of ours. They made the Inn a present of a service for twenty-four. I use it a lot.''

''Heaven,'' said Nora, waving a well-groomed hand. ''This place is absolute heaven. From the plates to the location. And so peaceful. All this snow and the gorge and the waterfall—it's like something out of a fantasy.''

"There are drawbacks," Quill said.

Nora's eyes, which were black and uncomfortably sharp, flicked over her, but she said merely, "Oh, right. Your sister's a three-star chef, the rooms are stuffed with some of the most gorgeous antiques I've seen outside of a museum, and in case you get bored, you can chat up the famous people who stay here." The corners of her mouth turned up. "Of course, I've heard about the ones who come to stay and leave in body bags. You've had more than your fair share of murders in your swell little village, haven't you?"

Quill rubbed her nose. "I suppose that's true."

"Well, it all sounds like fun. Frankly, a nice little domestic murder'd be a welcome change from the stuff I've got to deal with. Ten-car pileups on Interstate 81, teenage hookers, kids who've been beaten to death."

Quill made a noise in protest. Nora shrugged dismissively. "Life of a small-town anchor."

Quill, who'd been reacting to the listing of society's horrors rather than the impediments to Nora's career, glanced at her in surprise.

"So I'm egocentric," Nora said in shrewd response to Quill's expression. "It doesn't take long to knock compassion out of you—not in my business. Too few plum assignments and too many hotshot kids waiting to take your place if you screw up. Nice guys finish last. If they even get in the race at all."

Quill, despite the press of her schedule for the day, was genuinely curious about a life so different from her own. "Why did you choose it as a career?"

"I could say: You don't know how many journalism students get inspired by the Woodward and Bernstein affair. I could tell you: I got suspended from school for staying home to watch the Watergate hearings when I was sixteen. But the truth of the matter is, I like to bug people. I like to get in their faces.''

"Watergate?" said Quill. "Surely not."

"Oh, yeah, I'm a lot older than I look, Quill. A large part of my salary goes to what's euphemistically known as aging face procedures. I had my first lift at thirty-seven. Which was two years later than Mrs. Kennedy had hers." She grinned abruptly. "You know, kiddo, come to think of it, I can see where you might have big-time problems as an innkeeper. Anybody could read your face like a book. How do you keep your guests from finding out how you really feel about stuff like face-lifts?"

Quill blushed so hard she felt warm. "I don't . . . I mean, if a face-lift's what you want—" She abandoned this defense, which sounded lame even to herself, and stood up. "Would you like a few more of these pastry bows? I'd be happy to send Kathleen for some. Unfortunately I've got a full morning and I have to get to Syracuse this afternoon, so unless there's something specific we can do for you, I'm going to have to excuse myself."

"Sit down and don't mind me, Quill. I'm in the business of needling people. What I'd like is a tour of the Inn. Officially, I've got two days vacation before I go back on duty to report on the senator's wedding—"

"Ex-senator," Quill said automatically.

"And thank God for that, right?" said Nora. "I mean the dirt I've got on that guy. I wish I could broadcast the half of it, but I can't. Not for a while yet. It'll curl your toes when I do, cookie, let me tell you." She examined Quill thoughtfully, and a catlike grin crossed her face. "You might find out yourself, soon enough. Anyhow, as one of the few members of the media brotherhood to be allowed to cover the Santini wedding, I'm

practically guaranteed a network feed, but I might as
well see what other programming I can scrape up while
I'm here. The Inn'd be just right for a little Christmas
Eve spot—you know, as background for the station's
Christmas message. Maybe a ten-second spot on holiday
food or child carolers. Too much to hope you've got a
local bunch of photogenic carolers, I suppose.''

''Carolers we've got. The Reverend Mr. Shuttleworth's children's choir from the Church of the Word
of God, the Women's chorus from H.O.W, and I'm
pretty sure the volunteer firemen are—''

''Wait, wait, wait, wait, wait. H.O.W.? H.O.W.
what?''

''The Hemlock Organization for Women,'' said Quill.
''Most of them are here at the Inn right now. Mr. Santini's organized a series of fund-raisers involving some
of the local groups. H.O.W. was the first to accept.''

''A feminist organization? In a country village the
size of what—three thousand and something? And here
I thought the happy villagers were farmer's wives and
quilters. Well, I'll be dipped. How long has this been
going on?''

''Just a few weeks,'' Quill said uncomfortably. ''And
it's not anything really radical. At least, they aren't violently radical.''

''There's that readable face again.'' Nora almost
purred. ''Come on, cookie, there's a story here. Give.''

''There's nothing to give.'' Quill stood up again. (*And
this time*, she thought, *I really mean it.*) ''I love the idea
of the Inn as background for the station's Christmas
message. John's always after us to be more public-
relations oriented. We used to use a small advertising
agency here in town for P.R., but the guy moved on to
New York a few weeks ago. So I've sort of assumed the
responsibility. What about collecting the staff around the

Christmas tree in the foyer? Or the dining room. We put pine garlands around the windows overlooking Hemlock Gorge every year. That'd make a great backdrop, especially if it snows. *When* it snows, I should say, since it always snows up here in December.''

Nora closed a cool hand firmly around Quill's wrist. "Just call me Bird Dog. What about H.O.W.?"

Quill sat down at the tea table again. The table was a drop leaf, made of cherry. She'd found a set of four fan-backed chairs in the back room at a farmhouse auction and refinished them to go with the table. She looked at the empty chair opposite Nora with critical attention. The cotton damask upholstery wasn't wearing well.

"Quill?"

"Hmm?"

"The investigative reporter thing is in my blood. If you don't tell me, I'll just ask somebody else. Like that Mrs. Muxworthy, your housekeeper?"

"Doreen," said Quill. She bit her finger nervously, then folded both hands firmly in her lap.

"That's the one. She looks just like somebody who'd know everything about everybody in a town this size. Kind of like a nosy rooster."

Quill was conscious of exasperation. "Doreen's a friend of mine," she said stiffly, and then immediately regretted it. The most irritating thing about Nora was her gift for backing people—okay, her, Quill—into defensive positions. And for demanding and getting sententious responses. "There's nothing special or unusual about H.O.W."

Nora picked up a pastry bow, inspected it, took a large bite, and set it back on the plate. Quill tugged at her hair in irritation. Who was going to eat a half-bitten pastry bow? The recipe was one of Meg's best. And it was expensive to make. And it wasn't just the one mangled pastry bow, there were three half-eaten ones abandoned on Nora's plate as well as the half-gutted crepe. This was significant of Nora's attitude in general. Mentally she counted backward from five, then said, "H.O.W.'s not a story, really. Just an incident in the life of a small town. We had village elections this year in November and in the general upset—"

"All of New York's Democrats lost their seats. I wouldn't call it a general upset. The whole thing was a rout."

"Well, we both know a lot of incumbents lost their seats. And not just the governor and Alphonse Santini. The Village of Hemlock Falls town government toppled, too. Our justice of the peace has been replaced." Quill hoped her smile wasn't too stiff. "And so was our sheriff, and a couple of other officials."

"The sheriff, yeah," said Nora, clearly bored, "so what kind of job does a small-town sheriff get after he's been dumped?"

"A pretty remunerative one. Myles, that is, Sheriff McHale had been one of the top detectives with the N.Y.P.D. before he retired here. After the—um—upset, he took a job with one of those global investigative bureaus. They made him quite an offer. They're sending him overseas for a year." Quill carefully pulled the mint out of her grapefruit juice and set it on the rim of her saucer. Her hands were steady.

Nora lifted a sarcastic eyebrow. "Wow. So what was the reason behind this political cataclysm?"

Quill breathed a little easier. Evidently her readable face was in a foreign language, for once. "Our party lines were gender-based this year. No special reason, really," she added hastily, "I mean, none at all. It started with a marital spat between our mayor and his wife and kind of escalated from there. The women lost, the women voters, that is, and the male voters won, and so the Chamber of Commerce split up.''

"What does the Chamber of Commerce have to do with the price of bananas in Brazil?" There was an impatient edge to Nora's voice.

Quill offered her the last intact pastry bow, grateful that she'd escaped interrogation about the gender wars, and even more grateful that she didn't have to attempt indifference about Myles McHale. "I'll get to that. You'd be amazed how labyrinthian small-town politics can be.''

"If you think that life in Syracuse is any different, think again. It's just a bigger small town, that's all.'' She dug into her purse for a cigarette, lit it, and blew the smoke upward. "I'm not going to be around that hick town for long if I can help it, or this one either, for that matter. So what about the relationship of the Chamber of Commerce to H.O.W.?"

"The Chamber of Commerce had always been the focal point of social and political village life. Not anymore. The men have formed their own organization and the women have formed theirs, and they meet separately instead of together. It's kind of stalled civic events. So I don't know how successful you'd be in finding a newsworthy story to add to your coverage of the Santini wedding. We have almost no crime here. Just a little shoplifting and that's mainly kids. And, as I said, village activity is at a temporary standstill. So,'' finished Quill, getting up from her chair with a decisive movement, "that's about it. I've got to get going, Nora. Between the wedding and Santini's entourage and their fundraiser and Christmas, I don't know which end is up today. I can ask one of the staff to take you around the Inn if you want to scout locations for a possible background tape. Or I can call Reverend Shuttleworth and you can listen to the children's choir rehearse this afternoon. Or . . ." Inspiration hit. "You can go listen to Alphonse Santini in the dining room, talking to H.O.W. Maybe there's a story there."

"The camera crew won't be up until tomorrow. And I've listened to that fathead more times than I can count."

"I'd have to agree with you about the fathead part," Quill said incautiously. "Well, you'll let us know if there's anything we can do to make your stay more pleasant."

Nora grinned and brushed crumbs from her wool trousers. They were white wool, beautifully tailored. Quill was immediately conscious of her own calf-length wool skirt (which had never really recovered from an encounter with a damp paint palette) and the small hole in the elbow of her sweater.

"There's one thing you can do to make my stay more worthwhile." Nora cocked her head. With her long nose and high cheekbones she looked like an elegant heron. "I need the guest list for the Santini wedding."

Quill, with six years innkeeping experience behind her, had long accustomed herself to the necessity for small social lies. She shook her head regretfully. "We don't have it, Nora. I'm sorry. But I'm sure the senator does. Why don't you ask him?"

"Quill!"

Quill turned. Dina Muir, full-time Cornell graduate student and part-time receptionist at the Inn, stood at the Lounge entrance waving a sheaf of papers.

"Mrs. McIntosh just called. There's a new guest list for the wedding, she said. What do you want me to do with this one?"

"Um," said Quill.

"I think the new one is much longer than the old

one.'' Dina hesitated. ''But before you take a look, I think you should know that there's some kind of problem in the dining room. With the fund-raiser buffet. Maybe you better take a look.''

Nora swept past Quill like the bird she resembled and dived for the list in Dina's hand. ''I'll throw this out for you, kid.''

''Nora,'' said Quill. ''I don't think—''

''Phooey,'' said Nora, ''I can get it from Al anytime. I just want to see what good old *paesanos* the father of the bride's invited before I actually cover the damn thing.''

''*Paesanos*?'' said Quill.

Nora hummed a few bars of the theme from *The God-father*.

''McIntosh,'' Quill said faintly. ''The bride's family's name is McIntosh. That's Scot.''

''You've met Vittorio McIntosh?''

''Claire's father? Well, no, I—''

''Surely you've *heard* about Vittorio McIntosh.''

''Quill!'' Dina said. ''Honestly, I really, really think you should check out this breakfast thing.''

Quill, who'd been aware of a rising hum from the direction of the dining room, rather like the distant sound of a very large wave offshore, resisted the impulse to clutch her head with both hands. ''What's the prob—never mind. Nora, it was . . . it was . . . inappropriate,'' Quill concluded lamely, ''that's the word, inappropriate, to grab that list. Even though you have been invited to the wedding. Could you please give it back to me?''

''Wow!'' said Dina. ''Hear that?''

''Shouts!'' said Nora, with a pleased air. ''Damn. And I don't have a camera with me. Excuse me, guys.''

Quill took a deep breath and followed Nora through the lounge, past the foyer, and into the dining room at what she hoped was a casually unobvious pace: rapid but unworried.

The dining room was one of Quill's favorite spots at the Inn. In the mornings, sunshine streamed in the floor-to-ceiling windows overlooking Hemlock Gorge, flooding the room with light. In summer, the light was freshly gold; in winter, the snow and icebound Falls were a crystal prism, refracting white sunlight across the deep mauve carpet and the round tables. Quill especially liked the room just before they opened for meals with the deep wine carpet glowing and the glasses and cutlery sparkling. Even now, as a fork caught a shard of sunlight as it flew threw the air and landed in front of (ex) Senator Alphonse Santini, Quill found time to appreciate the beauty of the room.

He flung his hand in front of his face and ducked. An ominous grumbling filled the ranks of women seated before him. H.O.W.'s membership numbered around forty; forty annoyed women, Quill realized, made quite a formidable audience. She was the one who'd suggested that eight tables of five women each be arranged in a circle around Santini, his two blue-suited factotums, and his fiancée Claire McIntosh. Claire, blond hair stiffly teased in a sunburst around her angular face, sat pugnaciously silent.

"If I've offended any of you ladies, you certainly misunderstood my little joke." Santini raised his hands to either side of his ears in an eerily Nixonian gesture. Like Nixon, he had jowls that were rapidly moving from the incipient to the pendulous. Unlike Nixon, he was short, with a basketball-sized belly.

"Put a sock in it, Al!" yelled one of the supervisors from Paramount Paints.

"So we can boot your behind!" shrieked somebody else. Betty Hall, Quill thought, although she wasn't sure.

She hoped not. Betty was the best pitcher in the Hemlock Women's Softball League. If Betty threw forks, they'd hit the target.

"You gonna take one percent outta *my paycheck* to fee-nance your next campaign?" roared a familiar foghorn voice. "Outta that paycheck you just tole us should go to some outta work man?!"

"Doreen!" said Quill.

"Finance," Claire McIntosh said in a nasal Long Island accent. "It's FI-nance. Not fee-nance. Huh!"

Doreen rose furiously from her seat, bristling, skinny neck thrust out. "I got just as much right to work as anyone else."

"Hoo!" said Nora, clearly delighted. "Quill! You don't think he pulled that conservative bullshit about women staying home to take care of their men with this group, do you? Santini Screws Up Again!" She dug a notebook out of her purse and began to scribble.

"Or maybe you could send me somma that there federal housing money that built your fancy home in Westchester!" Doreen, gray hair frizzed to a righteous height, pitched a spoon after the fork. This piece of silverware struck Santini's right arm and bounced into Claire McIntosh's lap.

"Eeew," she said.

Quill turned to Dina, eyebrows raised. "How did this start, anyhow?"

"He asked for questions from the floor, or something. Doreen asked about that business of his appearing as a character witness for the Mafia—sorry—alleged Mafia guy," Dina said in an undertone. "Then she went on about how he let his own brother use his name in that deal with the Pentagon, and that Santini should be ashamed of himself, and then Claire McIntosh said Doreen should stay home and take care of her family instead of taking up a paycheck that should go to one of the unemployed male heads of households inflicted on us by our Democratic president, then Senator Santini sort of smirked and said, 'Power to the little woman,' or something like that, then Doreen said her political movement—Doreen's, I mean—''

"Doreen's into politics?" said Quill. She swallowed twice. Doreen's transient fancies had always involved the entrepreneurial before this. "She's into politics when we've got a senator's wedding here in four days?"

"Ex-senator," Dina said. "And it's not just Doreen; basically he's insulted all the ladies in H.O.W. WIND-BAG!" she roared suddenly.

"Dina, for heaven's sake!"

"Greedy guts, Al!" shrieked Miriam Doncaster, Hemlock Falls' blue-eyed blond librarian.

"Get yer snout outta the public trough, Al!" shouted Marge Schmidt. (Hemlock Hometown Diner. Fine Food! and Fast!)

"Yaaaahhh, Al!" chorused various members of the Hemlock Organization of Women.

"Ladies, ladies, ladies." (ex) Senator Santini's rather watery blue eyes gleamed angrily behind thick-lensed spectacles. Quill had met him several times over the course of his stay at the Inn. It was a curious fact that although he sent his shirts out to be laundered every day (valet service courtesy of the Inn at Hemlock Falls) his shirts always looked as though they had been slept in. "If you'll bear with me just a moment, I'd like to point out that not once, I tell you not once, have I been convicted of any of these alleged crimes."

"They aren't alleged crimes," Dina shouted indignantly. "They ARE crimes."

"Dina!" Quill whispered. "Hush! Let's give everyone a chance to quiet down."

"Not once have I even been indicted for a crime . . ."

"It's a fine state of affairs," Miriam Doncaster said tartly, "when the best that can be said of a politician is that he hasn't been indicted."

A chorus of rumbles from the assembled women suggested a fresh outbreak of cutlery casting was imminent.

"What are you going to do?" Dina hissed. "He'll be pitching stuff back at 'em in a minute. The way he did at that press conference in Queens when he conceded the Senate race."

"Is John in yet?" Quill asked in a cowardly way.

"Not till eleven or so. He drove Mrs. McIntosh to the florists in Ithaca to check on the roses for the reception. LOBBYIST!" she screamed suddenly.

"Senators can't be lobbyists," Quill said, exasperated. "It's illegal."

"There you are," Dina said mysteriously.

Quill cleared her throat and, holding her hands up, wound her way through the tables to the mahogany sideboard where Senator Santini had fled, rather like Robert De Niro at bay in *Frankenstein*. He was gesturing forcefully at Nora Cahill, his voice an angry mutter.

"Marge. Adela." She nodded to Marge Schmidt and Adela Henry, president and vice president of the Hemlock Organization for Women. "How are you guys this morning?"

"Just fine, till this bozo started in on disintegration of the American family," snorted Marge. Her keen little eyes, buried in an impressive amount of muscular fat, bored in on Santini. "Seemed to think it was wimmin's fault."

"I'm certain you misunderstood, Mrs. . . . ah"—Santini ducked forward to glimpse at Marge's name tag—"Schmidt. If any of you ladies took any offense at what was simply meant to be a joke—"

"It's Miss," Marge said shortly, "and I take offense where offense was meant." She rose to her feet, a truculent bulldozer, and gave Quill a friendly punch in the arm. "Good food, as usual. Tell Meg I like the idea of saffron in the scrambled eggs. Ladies, let's beat it."

There was a general scraping of chairs. Adela Henry (who up until the disastrous elections of November 8 had been more widely known as Mrs. Mayor) nodded graciously to Quill. "Have you made a decision about joining our organization, Quill?"

"Innkeepers," Quill said firmly, "should be apolitical."

"It is not possible to be apolitical in these times," Adela said darkly. "A woman has to stand for something."

"Right on," said Doreen, veering in their direction. "Power to the oppressed."

"Amen," said Mrs. Dookie Shuttleworth, the minister's wife.

Adela elevated her chin to a DeGaullean height. "Those who are not with us, must be against us. We will expect you, Quill, at the next meeting."

"Can't we just have the Chamber of Commerce back?" Quill said plaintively. "I enjoyed the Chamber meetings. I *liked* the Chamber meetings. The Chamber meetings accomplished a lot of good. Things like Clean It Up! week, and Hemlock History Days, and the boutique mall where our restaurant . . ." She trailed off. Each of these events, in one way or another, had ended in some degree of disaster. "Um," said Quill. She thought a moment. "Did I tell you I checked the Innkeeper's Code of Laws?"

"You did not. I was not aware there was any such institutionalization of innkeeping behaviors."

There would be by nightfall if she had a few minutes

with her computer and printer. Quill gestured vaguely. "The code bars me from any political affiliation. Sort of like judges, you know." She gave Doreen a meaningful stare. "It bars housekeepers, too."

Doreen made a noise like "T'uh!"

"I see." Adela regarded Al Santini, who was shaking hands with as many departing H.O.W. members as would allow it, with disapproval. "We've determined, as you may know, that the fourth Thursday of every month shall be the official H.O.W. meeting date. That's the day after tomorrow, assuming that the conference room here will be free at that time. The Innkeeper's Code cannot possibly bar political meetings of ordinary citizens."

Quill tried to concentrate. There was something about that date . . . She shook her head. "I'll have to check the calendar. I think it will be okay, but I'm not altogether certain."

"I will take that as a yes. Come, Marge, Doreen. We'll retire to Marge's diner. I have a few ideas about the protest that I'd like you to hear."

"Protest?" asked Quill. "Wait a minute. What protest?"

"Never you mind," said Doreen. "I'll see ya later."

"Doreen!" Quill yelled in frustration at their retreating backs. "Are you planning to come into work today, or what?!"

"Labor troubles?" asked Al Santini in passing. "You should vote Republican."

"It's not going to affect the wedding, is it?" Claire, tagging behind her betrothed like a dingy caboose, clutched Quill's arm. She demanded in her nasal twang, "Daddy'd be *reee*ly upset if anything affected the wedding."

Quill opened her mouth to assure Claire of the absolute integrity and quality of the Inn's level of service, but Claire rolled on, "You go ahead, Al. Quill? We need to talk. Where can we talk?"

Quill surveyed the dining room. It had emptied with dismaying rapidity. Even the nosy Nora had gone—before, Quill hoped, she'd heard any intimations of a political protest to be staged by H.O.W. "Of course, Claire. Let's sit down here."

"The tables haven't been cleared," Claire said. "I hate it when the tables haven't been cleared. You're sure that your staff is up to this? I mean, I've had my doubts about this little backwater even though Mummy said your sister is absolutely famous. But, I mean, my *Go*-od, there's nothing here. It's all very well for you. Mummy said everybody who's anybody knows about your painting, although I never heard of you in my art appreciation classes, and I guess you can paint on the moon or anyplace like that if you want to."

"Claire," said Quill. "Follow me over here. To the window."

Claire trailed Quill like a quarrelsome duckling. Quill pushed her gently into a chair at table seven, sat down opposite her, and fixed her with a firm—yet friendly—glare. "Now. How can I help you?"

Somebody, Kathleen the head waitress, most likely, who had been taking evening courses at the nearby Cornell Hotel school, had folded the crisp white napkins into elaborate tulip shapes. Claire picked one up, unfolded it, tried to refold it, and blew her nose in it. "Sorry. Allergies. Look. You've got to think of some way to keep my grandmother out of this wedding."

"Excuse me?"

Claire frowned. She was a natural blonde, in her late twenties, with the dry papery skin that affects thin women who spend too much time in the sun. In a few

years, she was going to need the services of Nora Cahill's plastic surgeon. "Tutti," she said impatiently,
"Daddy's mother. My *grand*mother."

Quill tugged at her hair, examined a curl, then said,
"You don't want your grandmother at the wedding?"

"Of course not. She'll spoil everything!"

"This is just a little case of nerves, Claire. You'll be
fine. I can't imagine how your grandmother could spoil
your wedding. Is she ill? Are you afraid it might be too
much for her? We have an excellent internist here, and
a very fine small clinic. If she needs medical help, we'll
be happy to make arrangements for a nurse."

"She doesn't need a nurse. She's crazy," Claire said
resentfully.

"Oh, dear. Is it Alzheimer's? I'm so sorry, Claire."

"Good grief, no. She's not certifiable. At least a judge
wouldn't think so. Stupid jerk."

Quill wasn't sure if this last referred to her, to the
unknown judge, or to Tutti, and she wasn't about to
inquire. Her own grandmother had been an elegant,
forceful lady whom she had loved very much. "Gosh,
Claire. I don't think I can do too much about your guest
list. That's really the province of, um . . . the family.
What does your mother say?"

"You know Mummy. She doesn't *inhale* without Daddy's okay."

"And this is your father's mother."

"My *grand*—"

"Yes," said Quill. Her temper—not at its equable
best in the past few weeks—suddenly snapped. "I can't
imagine how in the world I would prevent her from
coming. Even if I wanted to. Which I don't."

"You could tell her the Inn is full. You could give
her room to somebody."

"No," Quill said flatly. "As I said, we can suggest

a good nursing service, if you really find it necessary . . ."

Claire sniffed scornfully. "A nurse for Tutti? Tutti can flatten a nurse in two seconds. Maybe less." She blew her nose once more in the napkin and dropped it disdainfully on the table. "All I have to say, if this wedding's wrecked . . ." She stood up, leaned over Quill, and hissed, "It'll be all your fault!"

CHAPTER 2

Margaret Quilliam tucked a sprig of holly under the pig's ear and stepped back to regard her work.

"Guy I knew in the old neighborhood looked a lot like that after he welshed on a bet," said Alphonse Santini. He flung both hands up and cowered behind them in mock self-defense. Quill, who'd fled into the kitchen in search of respite, hadn't been pleased to find him there. "Hands out" was a gesture she was becoming all too familiar with, since Al had spent a large portion of the last three days harassing Quill and her sister Meg, when he wasn't aggravating the citizens of Hemlock Falls. The gesture always accompanied his notions of what was funny. Al considered himself quite a humorist.

"I'm sorry," she said, "about the fund-raiser. You've arrived at Hemlock Falls at sort of a peculiar time in the town's political history."

"That bitch Cahill," he said without rancor. "The press. Go figure."

"I don't think . . ." Quill paused. For all she knew, Nora may have prompted the H.O.W. revolt at breakfast, although to be fair, she couldn't see how.

"So. This roast pig's for a special occasion? Or what? Kinda early for Christmas."

The pig contemplated the ceiling. Meg contemplated the pig. Quill, whose testiness was increasing as the time for her lunch with Myles drew nearer, drummed her fingers on the butcher block counter. She stopped, not wanting to be rude. Ex-Senator Santini hacked into a well-used handkerchief, wiped his nose, and repeated his question about the roast pig. One of Meg's sneaker-shod feet began to beat an irritable tattoo on the flagstone kitchen floor. Quill held on to her own temper firmly and said in as diplomatic a tone as she could manage, "It's a special order for a men's organization in the village. Now, to get back to your wedding reception, Mr. Santini."

His eyes slid sideways at Quill. "I keep the title Senator, you get my drift? Even though I lost this time around. Most of my compadres call me Senator Al."

Quill, who'd been refusing Mr. Santini the honorific out of nothing more than perversity, decided to relent. For one thing, Senator Santini did have a miserable sloppy cold—or allergies—and he wasn't complaining about it. In Quill's opinion, far too many people with colds made their misery yours. For another, he was short for a man, about her own height, which made his frequent demands for attention more understandable, at least to Quill.

Quill had never gotten used to the fact that celebrities in person looked smaller than they did on television. This shrinkage made her sympathetic. Or maybe, she thought, they weren't smaller than they appeared. Maybe she'd only met celebrities who were smaller than the average person. The alternative was that her subconscious enlarged public figures based on the size of their reputations, which still didn't explain why she'd expected Senator Al to be bigger than he actually was, since his politics were so awful.

He certainly wasn't conventionally good-looking. He was balding, with lank brown hair that flopped over his ears. He had small, rather watery blue eyes and a pot-belly. None of this explained his undoubted appeal. Despite his height and rather flabby appearance, ex-Senator Al Santini definitely had charisma. The charisma might have been due to his voice, which was deep and resonant. Since he had a heavy Long Island accent, Quill didn't think so. It'd be a challenge to paint his portrait. She'd have to capture the charm and still get across the greed, vulgarity, and boys-in-the-back-room politics that had—finally, after three terms—lost him the race for the Senate.

"Quill?" Santini rapped his knuckles on the butcher block counter. "I got snot on my face or what?"

"Sorry, Senator," Quill said. "You were saying?"

"We got a few more people coming than we'd planned on."

Meg clutched her forehead, groaned, and said mildly, "Your mother-in law—prospective mother-in-law, I should say—has been taking care of everything just fine, Senator. Did you check this new number with her?"

Senator Al waved largely. "She's busy with the other stuff. My guys've been on the horn. I'm telling you, we've gotta be prepared for a crush."

Meg and Quill carefully avoided looking at one another. Senator Al had been unseated in a rash of very bad publicity six weeks ago; *Newsweek*'s editorial on the demise of his career had been scathingly final. Earlier in the week, they'd wondered if anyone would show up at all.

Meg said patiently, "Your fiancée Claire booked our Inn in April for a December wedding. In May you gave us the count for the reception—small, you said, since you didn't want a media circus. Forty, you said. Twenty of the immediate family, and twenty of your nearest and dearest friends. In the last few days you've gone from twenty to forty to seventy. Now, four days before the wedding, you want to bounce it to two hundred!?'' Meg's face got pink, which made her gray eyes almost blue. Her voice, however, remained soft, although emphatic. ''Our dining room won't *take* two hundred. I can't *cook* for two hundred. Not in four days.''

Al Santini waved expansively. ''Hire all the help you need. Money's no object.''

This blithe disregard for the fiscal gave Quill a clue as to a possible reason why the senator's campaign finances had occasioned such investigative furor from the national media.

Meg stared at him expressionlessly. ''If I could hire somebody else to do what I do, do you think *I'd* be doing it?''

''Say what?''

Quill, grateful for Meg's unusual equanimity, and not too sure how long it would last, interrupted, ''My sister's a great chef, Mr. Santini. A three-star chef. There aren't a lot of people who can cook with her style. I know that's one of the reasons your fiancée and her family wanted to have the wedding here. And, honestly, this last-minute change just isn't possible. You can't expect Meg to do a five-course dinner for two hundred. Not with this kind of notice. And not in our dining room. We don't have the space.'' Especially, she added to herself, for a guest list that was unlikely to materialize.

Senator Al put a large hand on Meg's shoulder and bent down to look her earnestly in the eye. ''Five-course dinner? Am I asking you for a five-course dinner? Absolutely not. No question. But I got a problem here, you understand that? I got a hundred, maybe two hundred people that are going to be coming to my wedding."

"Which is it?" Meg asked patiently.

Santini shrugged. "Who knows? All I'm saying is we gotta prepare for the contingency."

"Contingency," Meg said. "Right."

"I got a couple of Supreme Court justices, a couple a guys from the Senate, ambassadors, and what all coming to this shindig. Important people, you know?"

Meg rubbed her forehead and squeezed her eyes shut.

"Which is how come I can't give you an exact count. If there's a war, or something, or like Bosnia heats up again? You gonna tell General Schwarzkopf he can't hightail it to the action on account of he's supposed to be at my reception?"

"General Schwarzkopf's coming?" said Quill.

Senator Al shrugged. "He got an invitation. I expect him. Look, I don't want to say too much, okay? But there's something of national significance coming down pretty soon. And the eye of the nation is gonna be on Hemlock Falls."

Meg rolled her eyes at Quill.

The double swinging doors to the dining room banged open. One of the blue-suited men from the Santini entourage stuck his head inside the kitchen, a portable phone in one hand. Quill couldn't remember which of the men it was; they all looked and sounded alike. "Senator? We finally got Nora Cahill to agree to the interview. We have her in the conference room."

"Yeah, yeah, yeah, I'll be right there. You see? It's starting already. Now we got the media. So we bag the five-course dinner for seventy. We do heavy hors d'oeuvres. Stand-up. A buffet, like. The dining room can handle that if you take out the tables. So, Meg, dolly. No dinner."

"Dolly?" Meg said blankly. *"Dolly?"*

"We're looking at serving two hundred, right? If we can't seat 'em, let 'em stand. That pig, there?" He flicked his finger at the holly under its ear. "You roast a couple of those, we're all set."

"Heavy hors d'oeuvres for two hundred," Meg said stonily, "means a steamship round, pasta and shells, and baked BEANS!" She planted both hands on either side of the pig and drew breath. If one didn't know her very well, the expression on her face might pass for a smile. It put Quill herself, who knew her sister better than anybody, in mind of the wrong side of an outraged baboon. To Quill's amazement, Meg swallowed twice, and said merely, "Why don't we take the change in the menu up with Mrs. McIntosh?"

Santini, clearly unaware he'd escaped a verbal tsunami, continued, "So, no roast pig. I can live with it. If the food's a little less fancy than we planned—don't sweat it." His pat on Meg's shoulder was dismissive. "I gotta take this interview. So, look. You got more questions about the menu? Talk to the ball and chain."

"The what?" Meg demanded.

"Claire. My fiancée. Or her ma. Either one. Same-same." He waved at Quill, gave Meg the high sign, pointed a pistol-like forefinger at them, and went *pow!* "Catch you all later."

The double doors swung shut behind him.

"I don't believe it," said Meg. "Ball and chain? Dolly? Oh, *God*. I can't *stand* it!" She ran her hands through her short dark hair.

"Steamship round?" said Quill. "And pasta and shells?"

Meg grinned. "It's tempting, isn't it? That idiot."

"That's all you've got to say? That idiot?"

Meg shrugged. "Why should I waste my breath? It's

kind of pathetic, thinking that all these people are show-
ing up for this party. Mrs. McIntosh told me herself that
one of the reasons they picked our Inn is because it's so
hard to get to in the winter. He's got a guaranteed excuse
for nobody accepting the invitations. I have no idea
where all this last-minute *agita* is coming from.''

"Maybe he's nervous about getting married," said
Quill.

"Whatever. Anyway, Claire and her mother have had
seventy acceptances. Almost all relatives. Five-course
dinner with no expenses spared. That's what the McIntoshes are paying for and that's what they'll get. General
Schwarzkopf, my eye.''

Quill twisted a strand of hair around one finger and
tugged at it. "You don't think . . .''

"That two hundred politicians, ambassadors, and the
President's cabinet are going to show up for this wedding? On Christmas Eve? In central New York?'' Meg
gestured toward the window. The kitchen faced the vegetable gardens at the back of the Inn. Quill could barely
see the tops of the brussels sprouts for the snow.
"They're predicting four inches more by this afternoon.
If the rest of the wedding party doesn't get here by tomorrow, we'll have to cancel the reception and eat each
other like the Donner party since we'll undoubtedly get
snowed in. Which reminds me. I thought you were going
to have lunch with Myles in Syracuse. You better give
yourself plenty of time to get there.''

"I'll be fine," Quill said. "I told him two o'clock."

"You're sure about it," Meg said, after a pause. "I
mean, this business about it being the last lunch."

Quill nodded. "This relationship is just—not going
anywhere."

"You want to talk about it?"

"No."

"You're sure?"

"I'm sure."

"Well, at least it should end all this angst."

"What angst?" Quill demanded.

"The angst that's kept you functioning at half speed for the past couple of months. Good grief, Quill, you haven't even gone through the mail this past week."

Quill, who absolutely did not want to talk about her farewell to Myles until it was all over, changed the subject abruptly. "What's with the pig? It's down on the schedule as a delivery before noon. It's half past eleven now. Would you like me to take it somewhere before I leave for Syracuse?"

"One of the *sous*-chefs should be here soon. Unless the snow gets worse." She pulled the clipboard that held the day's rota from the wall by the small TV and studied it. "Bjarne's on today. He's a Finn and they're used to the snow. I'll get him to do it." Meg moved the roast pig into one of the aluminum pans they used to transport food and looked at it with a frown. "Do *you* think the holly's too Christmassy?"

Quill vaguely recollected Santini's offhand comment. "On the pig? Maybe a little."

"The holly's not in celebration of Christmas. It's a subtle reminder of the Druid influence on the S.O.A.P. rituals. Not that those idiots would know a Druid from a downspout."

Quill looked doubtful. "Suckling pig only serves twelve to fourteen, doesn't it? Last count, actual S.O.A.P. membership was thirty-two."

"The meeting this afternoon isn't the whole membership. It's just the executive committee. Elmer Henry, Dookie Shuttleworth, Harland Peterson, and those guys."

Quill sat in the rocker by the cobblestone fireplace,

propped her feet on the hearth, and rocked back and forth. Menu planning had been a lot simpler before the Chamber of Commerce had split into two rival factions. S.O.A.P. wanted earthy, primitive fare with a gourmet touch, and H.O.W. was seriously considering vegetarian. She had a vague recollection that holly had something to do with Druid rites, but she wasn't sure what. "I don't think that S.O.A.P. is based on Celtic mythology. I think it's AmerInd."

"Do American Indians strip to the waist, paint themselves blue, and stick stones in their hair?"

"Is that what they do at those meetings?"

Meg grinned. "So I've heard. But it's just gossip. The men won't talk about it, and the women don't know anything because the men aren't talking." She began to pack the pig in aluminum foil. "It's all Miriam Doncaster's fault, anyway. She never should have let the mayor have a copy of *The Branch of the Root*. It's a stupid book."

Quill's mood wasn't improving, and wouldn't, she knew, until the final lunch with Myles was over. She said crossly, "How do you know it's a stupid book? Have you read it?"

Meg raised her eyebrows. "See this look on my face?"

Quill shoved the rocker into motion and muttered, "Never mind."

"Cheerful sarcasm," Meg said, "that's the look on my face. We're still recuperating from the Thanksgiving rush. We're headed into even worse chaos between Christmas and the most boring wedding of the decade, and you want to know if I've found time to read a seven-hundred-page book that's supposed to get white guys in touch with their maleness, for Pete's sake?"

"Good point."

"You betcha." She glanced at her watch. "You go on to your lunch in Syracuse."

"I've got lots of time." Quill wriggled her toes in the warmth of the fire. The kitchen was redolent with cinnamon, sage, and garlic. Meg had left the Thermo glass doors to her grill open when she'd removed the roast. Every now and then a bit of cracking fell from the rotisserie spit onto the flames with a hiss. The smell of seared pork and the warmth of the fire contrasted pleasantly with the wind-whipped snow outside.

The back door banged and Bjarne the Finnish *sous*-chef burst into the room.

"I am late," he announced. He was very tall—as most of the Finnish students seemed to be—and had a ruddy, hearty sort of face with bright blue eyes.

"So you are," said Meg. "Don't take off your coat. I want you to deliver this pig."

"It is a beautiful pig," said Bjarne. "A prince of a pig."

"It is, isn't it?" said Meg, pleased. "It's for the S.O.A.P. meeting."

"Ah," said Bjarne, with an air of enlightenment.

"You've heard about them, too?" asked Meg.

"Oh, yes."

"Have you been to a meeting, Bjarne?"

He shook his head.

"Well, take this pig and see if you can crash it. Then report back to us. Quill and I want you to be a spy."

"*I* don't," said Quill. "Who cares what goes on at those meetings?"

"I do. Ever since the Chamber of Commerce split into these two factions, the village hasn't been the same. It's depressing. It's depressing me and everyone else. Although, to be fair, it's not what's depressing you. This business with Myles is what's depressing you."

"Stop," said Quill.

"It's not that the women aren't incredibly curious about S.O.A.P. Marge Schmidt thinks they hold sacrificial rites under the statue of General Hemlock in the park. Betty Hall thinks they toss the bodies into the gorge because Esther West told her she's heard weird noises at night near the waterfall."

"Esther thinks *The X-Files* is based on factual information from the FBI," Quill pointed out. "She's not what I'd call a reliable source."

"*The X-Files* is what's going to happen now that the Republicans have been reelected," Meg said darkly.

"I know what happens at the men's group," Bjarne offered, to Meg's surprise. "There are drums. Drums are an important part of the ritual. *The Branch of the Root* connects the hand and the heart and the"—his pale blue eyes looked wistfully down at Meg—"male root. Through the drum. The root of the primitive puts us in touch with ourselves. They chant. They eat. And beat drums."

Meg, who was short, bent her head back to look Bjarne in the eye. "How do *you* know? Nobody's even sure what the acronym means."

Bjarne shrugged. "I hear. From the other students. At the hotel school. This S.O.A.P. is the Search for Our Authentic Primitive. It is perhaps based in a true Norse heritage. The heritage of the dominant, all-conquering male. There is a warrior code, involving this pig. Pigs are well-known hunter-gatherers of the animal kingdom. They are a forest animal, living off of roots and berries. There is a spiritual link to the earth when you eat a pig. This is not merely a pig. This is an emblem for the wild boar. Wild boar is warrior food. The strong, the heroic, the conqueror warrior male is very Finnish. This S.O.A.P. search is a familiar one to us Finns."

"*We* Finns," Meg said, a little testily. "Norse. Indian. Druid. Whatever. It's hooey. If I catch you joining these bozos, Bjarne, I'll turn you blue myself. With a rolling pin."

Bjarne grinned. Meg's temper was a matter of legend among the Cornell students who apprenticed in her kitchen.

"Besides, in this weather you'll catch cold and sneeze all over the sauces."

Bjarne frowned. "This cold, it is nothing. You should be in Helsinki in November. Besides, Finns don't catch cold. We are quite tough."

Meg planted her wooden spoon firmly in the middle of Bjarne's chest. "Wrap the pig. Then deliver it to the park. To the statue of General Hemlock. And forget spying and get back here fast. We've got a lot to do today."

Quill looked past Meg, Bjarne, and the pig to the mullioned windows. One of the big advantages of the location of the twenty-seven-room Inn she owned with Meg and their partner John Raintree was the sprawling grounds and the room for a good-sized vegetable garden. Quill could see most of this garden from her seat by the fire. The snow was falling faster than ever and the parsnips weren't visible at all. She said aloud, "It's going to be cold and miserable in those woods. Maybe we should add hot coffee to the delivery. Those S.O.A.P. guys will freeze their blue-painted chests off. Or what about some mulled cider?"

"Nothing but what the woods provide," said Bjarne. "They cannot eat or drink food from unauthentic civilizations."

"Unauthentic?" asked Quill.

"Any culture that's been afflicted by technology."

Meg snorted. "Well, this pig's the product of some of the best farm technology around." She leered like

Jack Nicholson after his wife in *The Shining*. "It was a happy pig. A clean pig. A pig with buddies. A pig that never even knew the end was coming."

"Cut it out," Quill said testily.

"Anyhow, this pig came straight from the Heavenly Hoggs farm yesterday morning. They're not only the best pork producers in central New York, they're the most up-to-date. This pig's never even seen a tree, much less rooted in the mud for grubs. Half the guys in S.O.A.P. know this. So, phooey on this authentic wild man stuff, and phooey on thinking it's a stand-in for a wild boar."

Bjarne frowned again, then gazed at the pig with a fond expression. "Perhaps I am wrong about this being a boar. Perhaps it is a representation of a poem," he said to Meg, his pale blue eyes alight with passion. "Yes! This pig is an epic poem. An *Edda*."

"It's not a poem, it's a pig. Headed for a party in the woods. 'The woods.'" Meg added, with inspiration if little accuracy, "'are lovely dark and deep/ and we have promises to keep.'"

Quill smiled. "What part of the cold and snowy woods does this get delivered to, Meg?"

"Just to the park. Mayor Henry will be there at noon to pick it up." Meg looked at Bjarne in an abstracted way, as if calculating his market weight. "I'd almost sell my Aga stove for a chance to see what those guys really do in the woods. Myles has got to know where they meet. He was the sheriff, for goodness sake. I don't suppose you'd want to ask him about it at—never mind. I'll join the women's group and bring it up at the next H.O.W. meeting. We'll find out. Nothing can stop a bunch of women with their minds made up."

Quill set her feet on the hearth with a thump. "Why don't you just leave the poor guys alone? If they want to meet in the woods, let them. And let's stay out of this whole village contretemps. We've talked about that before.''

Meg gestured grandly with the wooden spoon. "Because the village is falling apart. We don't have a Chamber of Commerce anymore. We've got the Search for Our Authentic Primitive instead and their archrivals the Hemlock Organization for Women and goodness knows what else. Now, I don't care that Elmer and those guys bounce bare-naked around the statue of General Hemlock in twenty-degree weather. But I do care that what passes for town government and plain old social intercourse has come to a screeching halt. Not to mention other kinds of intercourse. Most of the members of the rival groups are married to each other, and nobody's speaking to anyone else. Ever since Elmer started S.O.A.P. and Adela Henry started H.O.W. it's been chaos. Total chaos. Look at what happened with the town elections. Howie and Myles are right out on their kiesters. And we've got some weird new guy in charge of the sheriff's office that gives me and anyone who gets a traffic ticket the creeps. It's not just that S.O.A.P. is ridiculous. It's that something is going on in those meetings that's a threat to comfortable community living.''

"I am going now," Bjarne announced. He picked up the foil-wrapped pig. "You will come with me, Meg?"

"No," Meg said. "Don't go out without your hat and gloves. It's freezing out there!"

"I am not so cold," Bjarne said stubbornly.

"You just think it's not so manly to protect yourself against the snow. Wear a hat. And if you drop that pig or join that men's group, don't bother coming back!" She scolded him out the back door, then returned, accompanied by a swirl of cold air. "Now, where was I?"

"You were giving a Margaret Quilliam lecture, 'The

Decline and Fall of Hemlock Falls.' We'd be better off planning the Santini wedding.''

"Let me tell you something about the Santini wedding. I've decided we can't plan it until after it's over."

"You might have something there," Quill said.

"So, since we can't plan the Santini wedding, we can plan your love life." Meg settled on a stool behind the butcher block countertop and tugged at her short dark hair. She was wearing a fleecy green sweatshirt with the emblem of the Cornell medical school, a red bandanna around her forehead, and her favorite fleece-lined jeans. She looked about sixteen. "How come you've decided to whack Myles around? I thought things were going relatively well. A couple of months ago, you two were talking marriage. Does he even know you're planning on dumping him this afternoon?"

"I'm not planning on dumping him," Quill said indignantly. "I'm terminating the relationship with tact and affection. And does he expect it? Probably not. This new job keeps him on the road. I don't have a chance to see him."

"I can't believe we lost the election," Meg said, momentarily diverted. The results of the town elections in early November had been the topic of exhaustive, repetitive discussion for weeks. Myles had been replaced as sheriff by newcomer Frank Dorset. Howie Murchison was no longer town justice. Bernie Bristol, a retired Xerox engineer from nearby Rochester, had campaigned successfully for Howie's job. The only member of the Old Guard left was Elmer Henry who was the founding father of S.O.A.P. The mayor had retained his job by the merest margin, since H.O.W. sympathizers represented slightly less than fifty percent of the voting population. While most townspeople put the election upset down to what Howie Murchison called the gender wars,

Quill herself wasn't so sure. Meg was right. Something very peculiar was going on in the village.

Meg dropped the perennially promising discussion about town politics and bored back in on Quill. "So what are you going to tell him?"

"I haven't thought about it."

Meg went "Phut!" and sprayed Quill.

"Don't go 'phut'!" said Quill.

Meg appeared to be honestly startled. "I went 'phut'?"

"Yes. Do you go 'phut' all over Andy?"

"I don't go 'phut' over anybody."

"You just went 'phut' all over me."

"I give up. Sit there, be a jerk, and just forget it." Meg began to hum through her nose with an elaborate air of indifference.

"And while you're at it, don't make kazoo noises, either."

"All right," Meg said with a deceptive assumption of amiability. "Why don't I just wrap my emotions in Ace bandages like a certain red-haired, straightjacketed, uptight, rule-abiding lady manageress—"

"Lady manageress?"

"Victorian enough for you? Yes! *Lady manageress* who can't stand it when the seas aren't calm." Meg set her hands on her hips, leaned forward, went "Phuut! Phut! PHUT!" and started to hum a Sousa march through her nose so unmelodiously Quill couldn't tell what it was.

" 'Stars and Stripes Forever'?" asked John Raintree, coming through the doors that led into the dining room. Doreen stumped in after him.

Meg grinned and increased her volume.

"Has Meg got a new idiosyncrasy?" John guessed. "I liked the socks."

"This one sounds like two cats fightin' over a back fence," Doreen grumbled. "Whyn't you go back to them colored socks? At least they was quiet."

"Doreen," said Quill. "About this protest you mentioned at breakfast . . ."

Doreen glared at the grill sizzling in the fireplace, grabbed a pot holder, pulled the spit free with a sniff of disapproval, then disappeared out the back door, holding the spit. Quill gave it up. She'd find out only when Doreen was ready to spill it, and not before.

John frowned. He had an attractive frown. He was three-quarters Onondaga Indian, and his coal-black hair and coppery skin made him attractive altogether. He was a big success with a substantial portion of the Inn's female guests.

"What's wrong?" Quill asked. "There's no problem with the florist, is there?"

"No. We've got three thousand sweetheart roses arriving early Friday morning and a whole crew of Cornell students to drape them all over the Inn. The flowers are fine. But on the way back from Ithaca, Lane mentioned that she's made a few changes in the reception." John swung his long legs over a stool at the kitchen counter and drew his notebook from the breast pocket of his sports coat.

"We've got a final count?"

"One hundred and fifty. And she's changed to black-tie."

Meg shrieked. "It's for real!?"

Quill sat bolt upright. "One hundred and fifty?! You mean the senator was right?"

"This was supposed to be a small informal ceremony!" Meg yelled. "What are we going to do with one hundred and fifty guests? In evening dress, yet. That means champagne, salmon, the whole high-ticket lot."

"The ceremony's still small. It's the reception that's gotten bigger. So, no dinner, just heavy hors d'oeuvres."

Meg clutched her hair, muttered, and began scribbling frantically on her memo pad.

Quill took a deep breath. "Where the heck are we going to put them all, John?"

"The dining room will hold a hundred and fifty."

"The fire code's for one hundred and twenty. And I hate crowding guests."

A cold eddy of air from the back room announced Doreen's return, minus the spit. "Snowbank," she said in response to Quill's raised eyebrow. "Freeze that grease right offen it. And it's snowing a treat out there. You going to Syracuse, you better get a move on."

"You knew Lane McIntosh in school, didn't you, Doreen?" asked Meg.

"Wasn't Lane, then. She was Ee-laine. Elaine Herkemeyer. Daddy owns that there dairy farm up on Route 96. Marge Schmidt knew her, too. Marge says she's done pretty well for herself, marrying that Vittorio."

Marge, owner and senior partner in the Hemlock Hometown Diner (Fine Food! and Fast!), was probably the wealthiest (and certainly the nosiest) citizen in Hemlock Falls. Lane McIntosh was a former Hemlockian; Marge would know the McIntoshes' balance sheet to the penny because Marge knew every past and current Hemlockian's net worth to the penny.

"I like her," said Meg, although nobody'd said anything derogatory about Lane.

"I like her, too," said John. "But she is ... ummm ..."

"Nervous," Quill supplied.

"A little dithery," Meg offered. "Now, that Claire ..."

"Ugh," Quill agreed.

"That Elaine's gone crazier than an outhouse rat," said Doreen. "Didn't used to be. Always full of piss and vinegar, that one. And now look at her. Worrit about keeping holt of all that money, I shouldn't wonder."

"Well, I think it's very nice that she wants her daughter to be married in Dookie Shuttleworth's church," said Quill. "She told me that's where she married Vittorio, twenty-five years ago. Did you go to her wedding, Doreen?"

Doreen snorted. "Me? Not likely. Marge didn't go neither. On'y ones ast to that weddin' were Vittorio's fancy friends from New York City." Her beady eyes narrowed in recollection. "Elaine tolt you twenty-five? That was thirty years ago, or I'm a Chinaman. Elaine shaving a few years off herself?" She eyed Quill from beneath her graying frizz. "There's plenty of us remember how long ago it was. So. I don't expect to get invited to this one, neither. This Alphonse Santini's some hot-shot senator, ain't he?"

"Was," said Quill. Santini's defeat in the recent elections had revived her somewhat shaky faith in the electorate. "He lost. By the way, who gave you all that information about him?"

"Hah?"

"Don't 'hah' me. All that stuff about Mafia hearings and kickbacks you were hollering about at breakfast. Did you read it somewhere?"

Doreen gave her an innocent blink. "I'm a citizen, ain't I? I can subscribe to *Newsweek* like anybody else. Thing is, Santini never shoulda bin elected in the first place. Stuffing the payroll with his sisters and his cousins and his aunts. Bein' bought off by fat-cat political interests."

"Allegedly," said John. "Nothing was ever proven. The official line is that Santini was defeated in this year's general ousting of incumbents, Democratic *and* Republican."

Doreen's snort, honed by years of use against those guests she felt to be both intemperate and obstreperous (Quill surmised this was approximately ninety percent of the Inn's registry at any given moment) had the force of conviction behind it. "Ha!" she said. "And ha! I bin readin' about conspiracy ever since Sheriff McHale and Mr. Murchison got their asses booted out of office six weeks ago. Conspiracy's behind this whole crapola about S.O.A.P., too."

"Conspiracy?" asked Quill. "What conspiracy?"

"On account of Al Santini."

"Doreen, Al Santini lost the election," said Meg. "This is a good thing. He was a bad senator. I voted against him, and I assure you, I am not part of any conspiracy. The election for the Senate has nothing to do with the town elections. Although the town elections may have a lot to do with S.O.A.P. That's a possible conspiracy, I admit it."

"There's a pile that goes on that us citizens don't know nuthin' about. I ast Stoke to look into it on account of it's time he did an editorial."

Doreen's husband, her fourth, was Axminster Stoker, editor and publisher of the *Hemlock Falls Gazette*. The *Gazette* specialized in weddings, funerals, lost dog reports, and, in February in central New York State, a "Notes From Florida" column, which consisted of chatty notes from those residents of Hemlock Falls fortunate enough to afford to escape the brutal winters.

Quill, conscious of foreboding, asked anxiously, "About this protest, Doreen? And this political group?

Did you mean H.O.W.? I didn't know H.O.W. considered itself a political group as such.''

''Depends on what you mean, 'groups.' ''

This was ominous. ''Citizen committees. Or antifederalist committees. Or, you know,'' Quill floundered for a moment, ''activists.''

Doreen was a joiner. Her joining proclivities could be relatively innocent—like Amway—or on more than one occasion, riot-inducing, like the Church of the Rolling Moses. Up until now, her intentions had been good—even worthwhile, but with Doreen, one never knew for sure.

Meg, her attention drawn from her menu planning, looked up. ''You signed up for the NRA, Doreen? Or maybe with those guys who dress up in camouflage on weekends and mutter about the FBI planting transmitters in their rear ends?''

Doreen's expression brightened at the mention of gluteal implants.

''Never mind,'' Quill said hastily. ''Just *please*, Doreen. No more throwing stuff at the guests. No forks. No spoons. Got it?''

Doreen grunted. Quill couldn't tell if this signaled agreement or indigestion.

Meg scowled. ''We've got a final count for the Santini reception, Doreen. It's a lot larger than we'd thought, so we may be looking at more overnight guests. That's going to affect your maid staffing. What about registration, John? How many people will actually be staying? And for how long?''

John scratched his ear. ''Slight overbooking problem.''

''That's terrific,'' Quill said warmly. ''I mean, usually we're scrabbling for guests in the winter months. And we've got too many? We can just send the overflow to the Marriott. I've already discussed that with Lane Mc-Intosh, anyhow. She won't mind.''

''It isn't overnight guests. It's the conference room. Mrs. McIntosh would like Santini's bachelor party to be held the night before the rehearsal dinner in the conference room. They—er—would prefer not to have to drive after the event.''

Doreen sniffed.

''Well, that's okay, isn't it? I mean, ever since the Chamber of Commerce breakup over S.O.A.P., we haven't had any meetings scheduled there at all. I mean, the only thing all December is . . .'' She faltered. ''Damn and blast. The S.O.A.P. meeting. On the twenty-second. The day before the rehearsal dinner. *That's* what I was trying to remember this morning.''

''Right. So?''

''So Adela wants that date for a H.O.W. meeting. And if I tell Mayor Henry and the guys we need them to cancel the S.O.A.P. meeting, they'll be totally bummed, and if I cancel H.O.W., Adela Henry's going to have my guts for garters. She's mad at us already for allowing the men to meet here last month. I can't break my commitment to either one. Now if I ask them to reschedule, she'll think this is a direct shot at H.O.W.''

''Right again,'' John said.

''Ugh.'' Quill slid down in the rocker. ''Ugh, ugh, ugh.'' Meg was right. The dissolution of the Chamber of Commerce and the formation of the rival rights groups had done a lot more than affect the election for sheriff and town justice.

''Nuts,'' said Quill. ''Any suggestions?''

''Let's lay out the options,'' John suggested. ''We can cancel both and have Adela Henry *and* the S.O.A.P. membership really annoyed at us. This is not a good idea. Village meetings account for a large portion of revenues in our off-season. We can tell Mrs. McIntosh that we can't handle the stag party and risk having her move the whole wedding party to the Marriott.''

"There's a good idea," Meg muttered. "Seventy extra people. Three days to prepare. Phuut!''

"Or?" said Quill.

"Or what?''

"There's got to be another option!''

John grinned. "The only other thing I can think of is to disband S.O.A.P.''

"There's another good idea." Meg tossed her pencil onto the butcher block countertop. "You're just full of good news, John. I don't suppose there's anything else to gladden our hearts and minds?''

"Not," John said, "unless you count the warrant out for Quill's arrest.''

CHAPTER 3

"Jeez," Doreen said into the silence.

"Good grief," said Meg.

"A what?" said Quill. "A warrant?"

John smiled. "Follow me."

Quill got to her feet and followed John through the double doors to the dining room. Winter pressed in on them from the floor-to-ceiling windows overlooking Hemlock Gorge, dulling the mauve and cream of the walls. The wind had risen; swirls of snow the width of a hand slapped against the glass with a sound like shifting sand. Quill glanced at the familiar view, so welcoming in spring, and was oppressed.

"A warrant?" she said feebly to John's back.

Kathleen Kiddermeister, dressed in the fitted mauve jacket and slim black skirt of the dining room staff, sat at the table Quill permanently reserved for Inn personnel. She was sipping coffee. Otherwise, the dining room was empty. John, maddeningly, slowed to talk to her. "Any lunch reservations, Kathleen?"

"Not yet. The weather's too punky. We might get a few drop-ins, though. There's an RV convention at the Marriott, and those guys are nuts for snowmobiles. Big tippers, too."

"If no one's here by one-fifteen or so, why don't you take the rest of the afternoon off. I can handle any late lunches."

"You sure?"

Quill fidgeted.

John smiled, and continued, "Absolutely, Kath. You know what things are like this time of year."

"Uh, John," said Quill.

"Why don't you go ahead to the office, Quill. I want to talk with Kathleen about scheduling for the wedding reception."

"John!"

He feigned surprise. "And while you're at it, why don't you go through the mail."

"The mail?"

"Yeah, you know. Little envelopes with stamps on them? Letters. Bills. Communications from the Justice Department?"

Quill blushed. "You mean the mail that's been stacked up on my desk for the past week? That mail?"

"That mail."

"There was," said Quill, "a parking ticket. Last week. I sort of forgot about it."

"Parking ticket?" John looked politely skeptical.

"Well, that's all Davy said it was. Actually what he said was that it was the *equivalent* of a parking ticket."

John's teeth flashed white in his brown face. "Take a look."

The foyer seemed less welcoming than usual. The fireplace was cold and the four-foot Oriental vases flanking the registration desk were empty. Quill, never too enthusiastic about mail to begin with, paused to consider the vases. She was never entirely certain how soon the bronze spider chrysanthemums she used at Thanksgiving should be replaced by pine boughs. She usually waited until the 'mums began to droop. The shipment this year hadn't lasted long, and the first week in December was too early, she'd thought, for pine, so she'd waited, and now it was practically Christmas. She kicked disconsolately at the vase.

Dina Muir, their receptionist, was yawning her way through a textbook at the front desk. She looked up.

"Whoa," said Dina. "You're still here? I thought you were going to lunch with the sheriff. Anything wrong?"

"Not really."

"That's just what John said when he stomped out of the office a few minutes ago. I asked him, 'Anything wrong, John?' 'Not really, Dina,' he said back, when it was perfectly clear that something was really, really bugging him just like it's perfectly clear something's really, really bugging you. Is it the lunch with the sheriff?"

"Did he say anything to you?"

"John? Yep. I just told you. He said not really."

Quill, putting off the inevitable, was glad, for once, that Dina was inclined to chatter. "How are things?"

"Fine," Dina said brightly.

"School going okay?"

"Yep."

"Dissertation coming along? Are you reading a text for it?"

Dina lifted the book in her lap. "You mean this? No. I figured I'd better take a look before he got here, is all."

"Before who got here?"

"Evan Blight. He wrote this book that's made everyone so mad."

"You're actually reading it? *The Branch of the Root?*"

"Well, sure."

Quill took the book. The cover was a painting—a bad

one—of a dark tree with the kind of roots found on a banyan. The leaves were vaguely oaklike. The branches were widely spaced and symmetrical, like a Norfolk pine. The title, *The Branch of the Root* by Evan Blight, was metallic, in Gothic type. Inside, the typeface was small, the paragraphs dense. The chapters had subtitles like "The Father-Spirit" and "The Soul of the Tree." Quill flipped to the back leaf. Evan Blight looked like Robertson Davies. Quill was conscious of a spurt of annoyance. She liked Robertson Davies a lot. She didn't want somebody who wrote a book that had caused as much trouble as *The Branch of the Root* to look like one of the better writers of the twentieth century. "Can I borrow this after you've finished?"

"Sure. But I'm only halfway through and it's due back at the Cornell library next week. Mrs. Doncaster at the library here said the waiting list is two weeks for the Hemlock Falls copy. You could buy your own copy. The Wal-Mart's carrying it. It's been deep-discounted to twenty bucks."

"Twenty dollars? I'll get on the waiting list at the library."

"That won't give you enough time. You want to read it before he gets here, don't you?"

"Before who gets here?"

"Evan Blight."

"Evan Blight? Evan Blight's coming to Hemlock Falls?"

"Well, sure."

"Wow."

John, walking into the foyer, shook his head, gave Dina a pat on the back, and opened the office door, gesturing Quill inside. "After you, you felon, you," he said, and shut the door in Dina's interested face.

Quill walked over to her desk and regarded the pile

of mail stacked in her In-box. John settled into the
leather chair behind the desk. She tugged at her hair and
attempted unconcern.

"Quill. Some of this mail has been sitting here for
two weeks."

"Hmm," Quill said. "Anything urgent?"

"If you mean are we going to get the phones cut off,
like the last time you let the mail sit, no. But there's
this." He waved a scarlet envelope at her.

Quill sank meekly into the chair in front of the desk.
"What?"

"It looks like a bench warrant."

"A what?"

"A warrant for your arrest. For a speeding ticket."

"Me? I didn't get a speeding ticket." Quill took the
envelope with a strong sense of indignation. "I would
have remembered getting a speeding ticket. Now the
equivalent of a parking ticket, yeah. I remember that.
Last week."

"You didn't remember the phone bill last year," John
said mildly. "And the phones were shut off for three
hours."

"Yeah, but." She opened the envelope and took out
a piece of cardboard marked **Bureau of Traffic Violations, Village of Hemlock Falls, Notice of Violation
and Impending Default Judgment. This is your final
notice.**

"I never got a first notice," Quill said indignantly.

John waved a second, unopened envelope at her.

Quill ignored it and stared at the warrant. "We don't
have a Bureau of Traffic Violations in Hemlock Falls."

"We do now. Sheriff Dorset and Bernie Bristol arranged for it last week. Don't you read the *Gazette*? It
was part of their campaign platform."

Quill turned the cardboard over. "It says here I can

plead not guilty by requesting a hearing Wednesday morning at nine a.m. Which Wednesday?''

"Any Wednesday."

"But I didn't get a speeding ticket!" She read it again. "This says I got a speeding ticket last Friday. Davy Kiddermeister stopped me near the school. He gave me a warning and the equivalent of a parking ticket. But he didn't give me a speeding ticket."

"You'd better give Howie a call and get on down to the courthouse tomorrow to get it straightened out."

"I won't. This is ridiculous!"

"Then they'll come after you."

"Who's going to come after me?"

"Deputy Dave, most likely. Maybe Dorset himself."

"I'll just call Myles. Oh. I can't call Myles, can I? He's not sheriff anymore. And besides . . ." She trailed off. John's eyes were uncomfortably shrewd.

John held one hand up and took the phone with the other. He dialed, waited a moment, got Howie Murchison on the line, described the situation briefly, then said, "I can't, Howie. I've got a meeting with some suppliers. Meg will have to do it. You want to talk to Quill? She's right here."

He held the phone out.

"Do what?" asked Quill, hesitating to take the receiver. "What will Meg have to do instead?"

"Just talk to him, Quill. He's agreed to represent you in traffic court tomorrow, but he wants more details."

Quill put the receiver to her ear. "Howie?"

Howie, who was one of the most patient, equably tempered men Quill knew, was admirably calm and agreed to meet her at the courthouse the following morning. He asked her questions about the ticket. Quill expostulated, Howie demurred; Meg, he said, would be needed as a character witness. He'd heard odd things about this sheriff. Quill thanked him, hung up, and looked at John. "Are you still upset?"

"About the mail? No, Quill. I know about you and mail. About the traffic ticket, yeah. It's dumb. Meg's told me often enough about you and traffic tickets. When you offered to take care of the mail last week when I was finishing the year-end accounting, I should have followed up. But this ticket stuff isn't anything to mess with. I've heard funny things about this new sheriff."

"What kind of funny things?"

John shrugged. "Nothing specific. But the town's changing."

Quill made a face. "Everything's changing." She brooded a moment, shook herself, then said, "About the mail. I'm sorry, John. I booted it."

He reached over and squeezed her hand. "It seems to be taken care of. And you've had a lot on your mind lately. I thought you were going to Syracuse today."

"Yep."

"You'll feel more like yourself after you've settled things. Weather's getting bad. You want to give yourself enough time. Just let me run over a few of the arrangements for the rest of December, then I think you should get on the road early. You know this is the first year we're totally booked through the holidays."

Quill nodded. "Dina told me. I hadn't heard about Evan Whosis. When is he coming to Hemlock Falls?"

"Day after tomorrow."

"Two days before the wedding? He's not staying here, is he?"

"Yes, he's staying here."

"I thought we were booked up for the Santini wedding."

"I moved one of the bridesmaids to the Marriott instead." He leaned forward and flipped through the registry. "A Meredith Phelan. I called to ask about the change. She was charming about it."

Quill put her head in her hands. "Why here!?"

"Elmer Henry wrote to him. He's a guest of S.O.A.P."

"Are they paying for him?"

John nodded again. "We received a deposit check from Harland Peterson in yesterday's mail. He's the treasurer. I thought it'd be better to have Blight here—it's good for business."

Quill exhaled. A long, long sigh. She'd always thought John's pragmatic approach to celebrity guests rude. It wasn't right to exile poor Ms. Phelan to the Marriott in favor of a more prominent guest. If she protested, John would merely point out that the Inn was making money.

But the implied insult to a prospective guest paled beside the public relations problem she was going to have. When word got out that they were the hosts for Evan Blight, proponent of manly men, Adela Henry would blow a gasket. The H.O.W. membership was furious with S.O.A.P. and all it stood for. Quill's imagination rioted. The foyer would be yet another scene of confrontation between agitated people of varying age, sex, and gender. Elmer, Harland, Dookie, and the other earnest disciples of primitive man (or whatever the heck Blight called it) would show up half-naked and painted blue right in the middle of the Santini wedding. Alphonse, his prospective in-laws, and Claire, the bride-to-be, would be furious. They'd all be furious.

She'd spend Christmas like a gerbil on an exercise wheel.

Her face got warm. She realized *she* was furious. She had a sudden, overwhelming urge to throw something. "You know this is going to create more hassle for us.

Why didn't you just tell the stupid jerk to STAY HOME!''

John looked sympathetic, but firm.

Quill took several deep breaths, tried to calm down, then said gloomily after a long pause, ''Everybody's paying for my bad mood.''

''Not everybody.'' He laughed a little. ''Me, maybe. And Meg. And Myles, of course.''

She stretched her legs out, folded her hands over her middle, and leaned her head against the back of the sofa. The office had a tin ceiling which she'd never really liked. The stamped ivy design marched from molding to molding in regular patterns. She'd always found this regularity, this dependability that one square looked exactly like the next, a little depressing. ''You know what?''

''What?''

''It's people I want to be dependable. Not art.''

John blinked.

Quill sat up. ''I've been thinking about this a lot, John. I mean, I'm thirty-four years old and I just realized I don't like people to be . . . to be . . . well, people. Normal, rowdy, un-self-controlled. That artist's retreat I went to? Just before Thanksgiving? For a bit after I came home, I was painting really well. Then I stopped. When Myles asked me to change my whole way of life and marry him. He wants children, John, companionship every day, someone to be there when he comes home at night. I can't do it. It freezes me. I want all the randomness, all the ambiguity, all the uncertainty of life in my paintings. And yet, not in people. And I don't know if I'm right or I'm wrong. Meg just told me I've got my emotions all wrapped up in Ace bandages. People like Meg may be right. If I don't allow that . . . that . . . *direct* sort of messiness of emotion into my life, it can't get back to my work.''

Quill fiddled with a sofa cushion. It was a wild iris in needlepoint, the gift of one of their regular guests. "I don't want to talk about it anymore. I'm sick of thinking about it. I'm so tired, John."

"You can, you know. Talk about it. I'm always here."

Quill took a breath. "You are. And I'm taking advantage of it. I swear as soon as—I mean after I get back from Syracuse you are going to see a new reformed Quill. I'll go through the mail. Remember to pay all my parking tickets. Be diplomatic to all the guests." She groaned suddenly. "Nuts. What am I supposed to do about this stupid bachelor party for Santini? Tell me you really don't want me to kick S.O.A.P. out and cancel H.O.W. and get everyone mad at me."

"Why don't we put the Santini bachelor party in the dining room, H.O.W. in the conference room, and S.O.A.P. on the terrace?"

"In winter?"

"Sure. We'll get some smut pots from Richardson's apple farm and line the terrace with nice primitive light and a modicum of warmth. They'll love it."

"A modicum," muttered Quill. "The warmth will certainly be less than a modicum. What's less than a modicum?"

John shrugged. "I don't think they'll complain. From what I can gather, the rites of passage involve exposure to extremes. They're spending all day in the woods barbecuing a steer the day of the meeting, and Elmer said they'll be bringing it with them. They don't want service or food—just the space. I'll get Mike to bring up the barbecue spit from the shed. And we'll put the bridal shower in the lounge. So all you have to do is let everyone know the schedule."

Quill sighed and looked at her watch. "I could catch Elmer in the park if I hurry. They're meeting there today. Meg roasted them a pig. And I'll tell Doreen about H.O.W. And I'm meeting with Senator Santini and Claire at five o'clock to get the particulars about the bachelor party and the shower and the rehearsal dinner. I wonder if he has any idea of the number of men that are going to show up."

"You'll meet the Santini party after Syracuse?"

She nodded, feeling that internal shift that meant her hesitation was over. She said goodbye, left the office, and went into the foyer to get her coat and boots. She'd been meaning to replace the coat, which was a tattered red down, and her hat, which was ugly but warm, but had been too depressed to do it.

"You're seeing Sheriff McHale?" Dina asked as she crossed the foyer to the coat closet.

"Just lunch," Quill said with an airy wave of her hand.

Dina's large brown eyes were moist. Quill, to her alarm, detected sympathy. Nothing, absolutely nothing was private in this place. "Well, be careful. And, Quill?"

Quill paused, her coat slung over one arm. "What!"

Dina quailed. Twenty-four-year-old graduate students spent a lot of time waiting for opportunities to quail and made the best of it when the least little chance happened by. "Nothing. Just. Ah. Watch for icy spots."

Quill carried her boots through the dining room. Kathleen had gone, so Quill couldn't ask her why her crazy brother thought he'd given her a speeding ticket when he hadn't. A faint sound of singing came from the back of the kitchen. Meg, with a particularly tuneless version of "The Boar's Head Carol." The sound was too muffled to be coming from the kitchen itself. If Meg were in the storeroom, Quill could sneak out without a lot of last-minute questions.

Quill edged the swinging doors open a few inches. She could see part of the birch shelving, a few bundles of dried red peppers hanging from the beams, and a copper saucepan bubbling on the Aga. Quill pushed the doors open. Meg was nowhere in sight.

" 'The bo-o-a-ar's head in hand bear I/ Bedecked with bay and rosemareee . . . ' "

Quill winced. Meg's music suffered more in minor keys for some reason. But it tended to deafen her awareness of the outside world. Quill made it to the back door and stopped to pull on her boots.

Meg popped her head out of the storeroom. "Off to Syracuse?"

Quill jumped.

"You're wearing that ratty down coat? And that fur hat?"

"What's wrong with this coat?" Quill asked defensively.

"It's ugly," Meg said frankly. "It's so ugly you can tell it a mile off. And that fur hat with the flaps? And to think some poor rabbit died for that hat. Yuck."

"It's warm," Quill said stubbornly.

"Leaving without saying anything?"

"Um," Quill said. "You were right. John is right. The weather looks a little stormy and I thought I'd get an early start."

" 'Don't know why' " Meg sang, " 'There's no sun up in the sky/ Stormy weather . . . since my man and I . . . ' "

Meg dropped the egg whisk she'd been using as a microphone. "Oh, Quillie, don't. I didn't mean it about the coat and the hat. Well, I did, but who cares? Don't cry. It's not . . . it's not like he's dumping you. You're dumping him.'' She set the box of onions she was carrying on the butcher block and approached Quill rather warily. "I'm sorry. But you're right to push off the dock like this. The relationship just isn't going to work."

"There's no reason why it shouldn't," Quill sobbed, amazed at her own tears. "He's a great guy . . ."

"A terrific guy."

"And he's been absolutely wonderful, and patient, and so . . . so . . . calm. And steady."

"I know." Meg patted her on the back. "Do you want a glass of sherry or anything?"

"And this is going to hurt him so much."

"I know. What about a cup of—"

"You know!? And you're just going to let me go off like this and do it? Tell him I want to break it off? That I've really, really tried, but I just can't. I just can't. It's just . . ." Quill, convinced she was looking too piteous for words, scrubbed at her face with her scarf and made a conscious effort at coherence. "I don't like tin ceilings."

"Of course you don't."

"I need more than a tin ceiling. Not that tin ceilings aren't good for some people. Just not me."

"You're absolutely right."

"Do you think he'll do something?"

"Like what?"

"I don't know. Yell. Or cry." Quill began to take off her coat. "I can't do it. I can't do it to him now. Not so soon after he's lost the election. It's like kicking him when he's down. I'll call the restaurant and tell him I have the flu."

"Quill, this detective agency he's joined is one of the best. They're sending him all over the world. Do you know how much he's making? If you're going to tell him, tell him now, while he's up about this job. He's off to the U.K. this afternoon, isn't he? You don't want to wait until he gets back. That'll be weeks. And,'' she added frankly, ''no one around here is going to be able to stand it if you don't get this over with. Soon.''

''I know. And I know about the European assignment.'' She put her coat back on. ''But I didn't know about the money. Of course, I know it has to be a lot better than that ridiculous amount he was paid as sheriff. How much is he making?''

''Seventy-five dollars an hour. After the agency cut.''

Quill felt better. ''Wow. Who told you that?''

''Marge Schmidt, of course. To tell you the truth, Quill, I don't think Myles would have stuck around Hemlock Falls as long as he has if it weren't for you. I mean, this isn't exactly a hotbed of crime. Although,'' she added reflectively, ''we do seem to have an unusual number of murders per capita. But honestly, Quill, do you think a guy like Myles should waste himself on being a county sheriff?''

''He wasn't wasting himself.'' Quill, not sure if she was indignant on behalf of Hemlock Falls or Myles, or herself, kicked off her shoes and pulled on her boots. ''So. It's my fault he's been stuck in this backwater, huh? I'm going to be doing him a favor by dumping him, as you so charmingly phrased it?'' She straightened up. ''Okay. I'm going. But don't you dare hum one note of 'Release Me.' ''

''It's going to be fine. Well, not fine. But you'll get through it.''

''I thought I'd tell him how much I admire him.''

''That's good.''

''And that somewhere there's a wonderful woman who's not as tied up in knots as I am about commitment.''

''That's okay, but I wouldn't dwell on it.''

"And that I'm not worth it."

"Self-abasement, in these situations is usually not ef-
fective." Professional curiosity entered her voice.
"Where are you meeting him?"

"That Italian restaurant just off Exit 56." Quill
tugged at her hair. "It's called Ciao."

"Oh, God." Meg swallowed a chuckle. "It's a New-
Ager. Sort of self-consciously healthy while slipping you
all the fats and carbohydrates a bottled salad dressing is
heir to. Not too bad if you stay away from the pasta.
They precook. Try the wood-smoked pizza. Don't stay
too long, okay? This weather's turning nasty."

"I'll be back around four-thirty. I've go to talk to
Santini and Claire about the pre-wedding parties." Quill
made a face.

Meg made a face back.

Quill, driving south on Route 15, was actually grateful
for the storm. The plows had been through earlier in the
morning, and at least three inches had fallen since then.
The roads were slushy with packed drifts concealing
stubborn patches of ice. Her Olds was a heavy car, with
front-wheel drive, but it was slippery. She concentrated
on driving until she hit the Interstate.

I-81 to Syracuse was clear and fairly dry, and Exit 56
came up too fast. She glanced at the little battery-run
clock John had stuck on the dash when the car clock
had died several years ago. One-thirty. She'd be early.
She was never early. One of Myles's few complaints
about her had been about her lateness. Myles was always
spot on time. Maybe she'd order a glass of sherry while
she waited.

She looked at the sky, pregnant with heavy clouds.
No sherry. She'd order hot tea, to keep her head clear
for the drive back and her emotions under control. She

parked. The lot was crowded, but she noticed Myles's Jeep Cherokee right away.

She sat in the car. Her toes got chilly as soon as she turned off the heater.

Myles would be civilized. He was always civilized. But anxious. If he was here early, it meant he was anxious. But civilized, Quill reminded herself.

The very first thing, she'd order a glass of wine, not tea. For both of them. He rarely drank during the day; a glass of wine might help both of them through this. And the order for wine would be a subtle signal, a flag that bad news was coming. Maybe without even having to say it.

Halfway across the parking lot, Quill paused in mid-slush. She knew, all too well (at least from watching Gerard Depardieu movies) the leap in the heart when a lover caught sight of his beloved across a crowded room. She could spare Myles that leap by going in the back way, scanning the crowded room for him, and quietly walking up behind him. A discreet touch on the shoulder, a welcoming but suitably depressed "hello," and then a few well-chosen sentences of farewell.

Quill resumed her march across the parking lot and went in the door marked exit. She'd find Myles. Walk up unnoticed. She'd sit. Raise her hand to forestall his kiss of greeting. Hope that the waitress would be quick, and not too perky, and not named Shirelle. Or call her honey. Then she'd order, quickly, two glasses of merlot. No. Not merlot. Not from a restaurant that had a sign in the back room—"We Value Your Patronage—Thank You for Not Smoking." Any restaurant that valued your patronage before they got it probably bought merlot in plastic bar bags. And Meg avoided smoke-free restaurants on principle, a consequence of a year's study in

Paris, where tobacco was considered a civilized finale to a meal. She'd ask for an Avalon cabernet sauvignon. It was great stuff. Not spectacular enough to make up for devastation, but it'd go a long way to assuaging what they both had to know was an intolerable situation.

The restaurant wasn't crowded at all. Of the maybe sixty tables scattered across the bleached oak floor, ten were filled. Myles saw her as soon as she walked down the hall leading to the restrooms and into the Euro-Tech ambiance of Ciao.

The blonde that was with him saw her, too.

And not just a blonde, Quill thought, suddenly conscious of her own hair, her snow-splattered boots, the muddy hem of her skirt, and, worst of all, the coat, conspicuous for its ugliness. A sophisticated blonde. With large breasts, tastefully presented behind a scoop-neck silk T. A slouchy Armani jacket. And, as she rose from the table, one of those boyishly hipped figures that made even jeans look elegant. Much less the bottom half of the Armani suit. She wasn't pretty, Quill thought. She was distinctive, with a decided aquiline nose, well-defined lips, and direct gray eyes.

Myles rose and waved. Quill crossed the floor. He introduced the blonde with a slightly apologetic air.

"Quill, I'd like you to meet Mariel Cross, my partner on the U.K. assignment. Mariel, this is Sarah Quilliam."

Her handshake was firm, decisive. "I won't interfere with your lunch. The Bureau got a fax Myles had to see. That's the only reason I'm here. The Brits need an answer by seven o'clock tonight. And with the time change, that's two o'clock here in Syracuse." She smiled. "I'm glad I've met you, though. I've heard a lot about you. I've seen your work. I like it very much."

Quill, who knew herself to be graceless whenever dis-

cussion of her painting came up, blushed and looked at
her feet. Her boots were leaving muddy puddles on the
polished floor.

"Well." Mariel hesitated, a behavior Quill instinc-
tively knew was uncharacteristic. The woman oozed
self-confidence. "I'll fax this back to the client, Myles."

"Fine. I'll meet you at the airport around six."

Quill sat down in Mariel's place. Myles covered her
hand with his.

"I don't need to say anything, do I, Myles?"

"It's awkward," he said.

"She's really attractive. She has . . ." Quill paused,
searching for the right word. "Presence. A lot of presence."

"You're beautiful," Myles said. His hand tightened
on hers. "But yes, she has presence."

She was back at the Inn by four.

"There you are," John said as she walked in the back
door. Meg raised her eyebrows. Quill gave her a half-
hearted wave. "Santini wants to push the meeting up.
Can you see them now? I've got to check the wine shipment."

"Sure," Quill said listlessly.

"Are you all right?"

"Fine. Where are they?"

"Having tea. At the regular table."

Quill removed the coat, swearing to purchase another
as soon as the damned Christmas rush and the stupid
wedding and the barbaric rites of Santini's bachelor
party were over. She grabbed the planning clipboard
from its hook on the wall and pushed through the swinging doors into the dining room. There were six people
at the table, Claire and a pretty girl whom Quill hadn't
met, and the senator and three of his aides.

The youngest aide got up as she approached and pulled a chair out for her.

"You know Frank, Marlon, and Ed," Santini said breezily. Quill nodded. "And the ball and chain, of course."

"A—al!" Claire protested in her nasal voice. "This is Merry Phelan. One of my bridesmaids."

"Meredith," she said in a self-possessed voice. "How do you do."

Quill shook her hand. "I'm awfully sorry about switching you to the Marriott."

"Not at all a problem. As a matter of fact, I'm off there now. Elaine and I are planning a little shower for Claire Thursday night, and I want to check over some details."

Santini saluted as she left the table. She gave Quill a wink, and proceeded demurely out the entranceway. Santini waited until she was out of earshot, then hunched over the table.

"So," Al said, "glad you could make it a little early, Quill. I've got a good opportunity in the park around five. A fund-raiser with this men's club. Crazy assholes wanted to meet in the dark, but hey, no problem. I'm adaptable."

"S.O.A.P.?" asked Quill.

Frank—or maybe it was Marlon—consulted a thick notebook. "Right. Men's organization. Acronym for the Search for Our Authentic Primitive. Chief is Elmer Henry. Mayor, and a Republican. He's fifty-six. Married, to Adela Henry, aged fifty-eight. One of the Walters family, Senator. Used to be money there but not anymore. First Brave is Harland Peterson, big farmer around these parts, net worth in the (he named a figure which astonished Quill), a Democrat, unfortunately, but maybe he can be persuaded. The sheriff, Dorset, is a member and so is the justice, Bristol.''

''Stop already.'' Santini swallowed a scone whole and said through it, ''How much time I got with them?''

''Half an hour. Our data suggests that the hearth and home speech should be appropriate.''

''Got that one socked. Okay. So, Quill, dolly. I got more time for you than I thought. The bachelor party Thursday night's for twelve. You got that?''

''One of these gentlemen . . .''

''Ed,'' said Ed, giving her a toothy smile.

''Yes, Ed, gave us the count several months ago. But no guest list.''

''In the interests of security,'' Marlon, or maybe Frank, said smoothly, ''we'd prefer to be circumspect.''

Santini snorted. ''With that Cahill bitch sniffing around, you can bet we have to be careful. The thing is, Quill, dolly, we need to get her out of the way for the evening.''

''Out of the way?'' Quill repeated.

''Couple of these guys, they can't make it for the wedding. Christmas Eve and all. But they can make it Thursday. They want maybe to make a little contribution to the cause. You know what I mean?''

Quill, uncertain, nodded in lieu of doing anything else.

''You don't get it, do you?'' He leaned forward and mentioned a Supreme Court Justice noted for his aggressive—and mean-spirited—decisions on Affirmative Action, a congressman who'd been indicted—but not convicted—twice for money laundering scams, and two names even Quill recognized as having been involved with illegal gambling activities.

''Senator,'' warned Ed.

''Yeah, yeah, yeah. So. We're giving these guys the best, right? Sirloin. Baked potato with all the trimmings, lotta good whisky, the works. But we don't want this Cahill broadie to give them the works, you catch my meaning?''

"Yes," said Quill. ''But I'm not sure what I can do about it.''

''She wouldn't do a thing about Tutti, either, Al,'' Claire complained.

''Your gramma's still coming? Shit!'' Santini sat back with a shake of his head. ''That's not till tomorrow, right? So we worry about it tomorrow. Hey!'' He snapped his fingers. ''That's from some book, right? Now, Quill. What are you going to do about Cahill? I figure it's your problem, see what I mean? She's a guest here, got that? And you're in charge of the guests.''

''Could Claire take her to the shower at the Marriott Thursday night?''

''A-al!'' said Claire. ''It's my very closest friends at this shower!''

''It could work,'' said Ed. ''Yes, Senator, it could work. You could give her an exclusive, Claire, couldn't you? Your father's notor—I mean well-known for avoiding interviews with the press. You could give her some safe inside dope, like where you and the senator will make your home, the place you're going to buy in Georgetown. Those sorts of things.''

''Part of the political life, baby,'' Santini offered.

''All *right*. But I'm going to want something very, very nice to make up for this, Al. I'm warning you.''

''S'all right. You get your nice little butt in gear, dear. Catch Cahill before she starts sniffing around about the party and nail her down. Quill, dolly, good work. You ever think about getting into the game, you let me know.''

''Game?'' asked Quill.

''Politics, baby. Politics. It's the only game there is.''

• • •

"And that was it?" Meg exclaimed, much later, when they were sitting in Quill's room discussing her shortened lunch. "Myles didn't say, 'Let's keep in touch,' or better yet, 'You'll always have a special place in my heart'? 'It's awkward'? 'You're beautiful'? And 'She has presence'? That was it?! And you went straight from that to loathsome Al?"

"Well, sure there was the keep-in-touch speech, and the never-forget-you speech. But I think, Meg, he was relieved. I think I'm too complicated, or too independent. Or too—I don't know."

"You poor thing," Meg said with deep affection. "How do you feel?"

"Chagrined."

"Because of all the rehearsing," Meg said shrewdly. "You should know by now, Quillie, never rehearse. Other than chagrined, how do you feel?"

Quill swirled the last of her wine in her glass. "I think my heart's broken."

Meg shook her head, jumped off the sofa, and marched to the small kitchenette where they sometimes prepared meals. She didn't have a kitchen in her rooms, which were one floor down from Quill's. The last thing Meg wanted to see at night, she'd told Quill and Doreen, was a stove or a refrigerator.

"No paper towels?"

Quill wiped her cheek with her hand. "Cloth ones."

"Here." Meg tossed her a dishtowel. "Are you sorry you broke it off with him?"

"He broke it off with me!"

"Do you want to make up?"

Quill shook her head.

Meg sat down next to her and announced, "This is absolutely the last pat of the day," and rubbed her back.

Quill cried, Meg patted her back, and then the room was quiet. They sat on the cream sofa in front of her French doors, feet propped on the oak chest Quill used as a coffee table. Quill drank another glass of the cabernet. Outside the French doors, the snow knocked against the window like a soft white cat trying to get in.

Quill's easel stood in the corner, half-hidden by the tea-stained drapes. A half-finished charcoal sketch—Doreen, laughing with a cup of coffee in one hand. Quill looked at it and felt the familiar clench of muscles in her right hand.

"Meg. Remember that taxi driver?" she said suddenly.

"The one that picked us up at the train station ten years ago? The day we arrived in New York? Me off to Paris, to learn to cook, you off to paint great things?" She laughed. " 'The great thing about dis job, goils? Ya never know where it's gonna take ya.' " She smiled. "And he took us for a ride, all right. That was the wildest taxi ride I've ever been on before or since. To this day, I don't know why he didn't get a ticket."

Quill sat bolt upright. "Traffic court!"

"He didn't take us to traffic court. He took us to that cool little apartment in SoHo. Actually, it wasn't all that little . . ."

"I have to be in traffic court tomorrow morning. Nine o'clock. And you have to come with me."

"Why do I have to come with you?" Meg demanded indignantly. "I'm not the one who got a speeding ticket."

"I didn't get a ticket. Dave Kiddermeister stopped me and told me I was going a little fast past the school. But he didn't give me a ticket."

"How much over the limit were you?"

"I don't know. He didn't write me a ticket," Quill

said patiently. "It's some screwup. Howie Murchison's going to represent me."

"Howie? Over a speeding ticket you didn't get?"

"Well, there's this thing called a bench warrant or whatever."

"Quill." Meg's voice was ominous. "You know exactly what a bench warrant is. You used to get them all the time."

"I swear to God, Meg. I've reformed. No speeding. No unpaid parking tickets. Honest."

"If they pulled your driving record from New York City, you could be in big trouble."

"It's been years," said Quill, "and if I have to tell you one more time that I didn't get a ticket, I'm going to scream. I talked with Howie on the phone today and he said just to be safe I should bring a witness."

"A witness to what?!"

"My general honesty, I guess. I mean, what if Dave says he gave me a ticket? He won't. Or he shouldn't. It'll take two minutes, Meg."

"Not necessarily," Meg said darkly. "And if they want me to witness what kind of driver you are, you're in big, big trouble. And anyway, what can I say? That I've never witnessed you getting a ticket?! That's bull. I've seen you get parking tickets, speeding tickets, every kind of ticket."

"Howie just said to bring you so you can testify as to my probity."

Meg shrieked, "I'm your sister. They aren't going to believe a word I say."

"Well, you have to come anyhow."

"Well. Okay. Since you've got a broken heart. But you better get over this broken heart fast." She grinned suddenly. "Howie's divorced. And I think he's pretty neat."

"The last thing I want is to jump into any kind of relationship with anybody. I'm going to be an aunt. A professional aunt."

"A professional aunt?"

"Yep. You're going to marry Andy Bishop sometime next year and have zillions of children, and I'll sit and rock them to sleep and look melancholy, and everyone will wonder about my tragic past." She started to hum a version of "Melancholy Baby" that was so repellent Meg threw a pillow at her and stomped off to bed.

Quill slept and dreamed of empty canvases, stacked in abandoned warehouses.

CHAPTER 4

Meg threw back her head and caroled, "Top of the world, Ma!" Then conversationally, "You're going to get sent up the river. To the big house. Yep, you're looking at hard time."

"Oh, shut up." Quill twitched the modestly tied scarf at her throat. She wasn't sure about the scarf; her hair was red and the scarf was a brilliant gold and teal. She felt tired, after yesterday's confrontation with Myles. She felt conspicuous. She didn't know if her anxiety was over the way she looked or the fact that she was in the Tompkins County Courthouse waiting to be arraigned for a nonexistent traffic ticket. She'd never actually been in the Tompkins County courtroom before. She wasn't surprised at how intimidating high ceilings, butternut paneling, and the musty smell ordinarily common to attic closets could be. "Other voices, other rooms," she said obscurely. Then, "It's only a traffic ticket. And it's my first traffic ticket. . . ."

Meg, startled out of her Cagney imitation, went "Phuut!" which in turn startled Howie Murchison, who'd been sitting quietly next to them.

"In Tompkins County," Quill amended. "And that means it's my first for seven years at least. And they

71

take them off your what-do-you-call-it after three years anyway.''

"Your MV104," Howie said with a faintly surprised look. "You've had priors, Quill? In some cases the court can pull your records all the way to the beginning. They don't dump old information. It just doesn't relate to most of the within-eighteen-months laws, so it isn't listed on current requests. You didn't tell me you had priors.''

"She didn't, huh," said Meg. Her gray eyes, clear and limpid, met Howie's wary gaze head-on.

Quill pulled at the scarf around her throat again. "This darn thing is stifling me.''

"I must say that suit and little bow don't become you," Howie said thoughtfully. "No offense, Quill, but I'm used to seeing you more—how should I put it?— loosely dressed.''

"Loosely?" Quill demanded, slightly affronted.

"Casually," Meg supplied. "You mean casually dressed, Howie.''

"You said to dress discreetly, Howie." Quill stuck her thumbs in the waistband of her tailored wool skirt and jerked at the material. "I don't understand why the heck this thing is so constricting. I haven't gained any weight since the last time I wore this.''

"You wore that suit to interview for the graphics job at Eastman Kodak company," said Meg. "Which means you last wore that suit when you were nineteen. Which makes it a B.T. suit. Ha! That's why you're wearing it. For luck.''

"B.T.?" said Howie.

Quill jerked the skirt over her knees and glared a warning at Meg.

"B.T.?" Howie repeated. "What's B.T.?"

"You haven't gained weight," Meg added. "It's just that a person sort of settles around the middle, Quill, after fifteen years. Or is it seventeen?'' She counted on her fingers, her lips moving. "Nope, fifteen. You're thirty-four.''

"Before Taxes?'' Howie said, and sighed. "I don't get it. But then, I never get half of what you girls are talking about anyway.''

"Girls?'' asked Meg, eyebrows raised.

Quill wriggled her shoulders against the high-backed seat and slid down so that she couldn't see over the top of the bench in front of her. "Howie, is this going to be over soon? I've got so much stuff to do back at the Inn that I haven't even opened my mail for a week. Which is why I'm here in the first place.''

He peered at her over his wire-rimmed glasses. In his late forties, Howie had settled into a comfortable, slightly paunchy middle age that Quill found very appealing. His well-cut Harris tweed sports coat was worn at the cuffs, the knot of his striped tie was skewed to leave his shirt collar loose, and his black wing tips had been resoled at least twice, not, Quill knew, because he couldn't afford another pair, but because he didn't want to break in new shoes. Like Myles (now on his way to London, with that perfect-looking woman!), Howie had his own kind of stubborn integrity. "Hard to say. I haven't been up before Justice Bristol yet. As you know, I'm accustomed to being on the other side of the bench.''

"Well, *I* voted for you, Howie,'' said Meg, with an emphasis that seemed to imply Quill hadn't.

"*I* voted for Howie, too,'' said Quill.

"Of course you did. So did John. So did Doreen and Axminster. So did Marge Schmidt. Why are you acting like I didn't vote for Howie?''

"You're the one that's acting as though *I* didn't vote for Howie.''

"I am NOT. Howie was a *great* town justice. And he's Hemlock Falls' best lawyer."

"I'm Hemlock Falls' only lawyer," Howie pointed out dryly.

"Whatever." Meg's cheeks were still pink from the cold outside; she rubbed them vigorously and made them even pinker. "The thing is, Howie, with everyone so mad at the President and the governor, *all* the incumbents in *all* the elections in New York State got kicked out six weeks ago. Myles isn't sheriff anymore. You're not town justice anymore. And it's not your fault. It's not Myles's fault. It's nobody's fault. It's democracy. It's the voice of the people. Just read the newspapers. Of course," Meg continued sunnily, "the other fact is that you sentenced the mayor and the Reverend Mr. Shuttleworth and practically the whole male side of the Chamber of Commerce to three months of community service for public rowdiness. *That* may have had some . . ."

Quill, exasperated, poked Meg into silence. Hemlock Falls tended to lag behind fashionable trends, but eventually caught up to such contemporary issues as male emancipation. S.O.A.P's first meeting, in the back room of the Croh Bar on Main Street, had ended in a public display which violated town ordinance 2.654 (prohibiting total nudity and drunkenness in public) and 4.726 (vandalism). Outraged citizens unsympathetic to the Men's Movement (Adela Henry and the members of H.O.W. mostly) had demanded their pound of flesh. Howie had reluctantly bowed to the legal demands of the aggressive plaintiff's attorney Mrs. Henry imported from Syracuse just for the occasion, and sentenced S.O.A.P. members to several weekends of highway cleanup. Reprisals had been effected at the polls in November.

Meg tapped her fingers against the wooden bench and ruffled her short dark hair. "Is this Bristol ever going to show up? You said it'd take a few minutes. It's been more like an hour. We're booked for the holidays and the rest of the McIntosh family is coming in this afternoon and I've got to get back." She looked at her watch, scowled, and rose to her feet. "As a matter of fact, I should be at the Aga right now."

"You can't leave. You're my witness." Quill shoved her back into her seat.

"Quill, it's just a lousy ticket. I wasn't even there. You just want me here as a character witness, and Howie doesn't even think I need to be here, do you, Howie?"

"I'd like it. Just as a backup."

"And besides, you always get tickets. There's not a thing I can do about it. There's never *been* anything I could do about it." Meg began to edge her way out.

Howie stirred uneasily. "Maybe you ought to hang on a little while longer, Meg. This won't take long. It's a matter of routine. We'll plead Quill guilty, have her throw herself on the mercy of the court to get the fine down, and that will be the end of it."

"I didn't get a ticket," Quill said. "I told you. It's a frame. Meg? Where are you going?"

Meg paused at the end of the row. "Honestly, Quill, I'm busy. Mrs. Whosis is coming in this afternoon to begin planning the food for the reception and I told her I'd have some samples."

"Mrs. McIntosh," said Quill. "It's not Mrs. Whosis, it's Mrs. McIntosh. For the Santini wedding," she explained to Howie. "He's already here."

Howie nodded. "I've heard."

"Have you met him?"

"Mm-hmm."

Meg jiggled impatiently. "Right. I'm suggesting pork

tenderloin in persimmon sauce. If Santini wants pasta, I'll black his little eye.''

Quill, still feeling pitiful, gave her a woebegone look.

Meg edged back along the bench and hugged her. ''You'll be fine. Howie, tell her she'll be fine.''

''As long as there aren't any surprises, yes, Quill, you should be fine. You're sure about no priors?''

Quill made a face in the direction of the judge's bench. She had a sudden, passionate regret that Myles was out of her life. Then, just as passionately, she decided she could save herself.

''So, there.'' Meg avoided her sister's eye, edged her way along the wall to the aisle, waved, and jogged toward the back doors, looking both innocent and ingenuous in her wool leggings, scarlet knitted cap, and droopy scarf.

Quill sat back, unknotted the silk scarf at her neck, and retied it.

The courtroom was as cavernous as a church, and as sparsely populated. The jury box and the judge's bench were segregated from the spectator pews by low spindled railings. The prosecutor's desk, Howie had told her, was typically to the left in front of the raised judge's dais, the defense to the right. The desks resembled library tables; long, broad, and made of a hardwood stained an ugly coffee color. The whole arrangement was stark, putting Quill in mind of some strict and unforgiving religious sect.

Pictures of the incumbent President and the governor of the state of New York flanked an American flag on the front wall. Quill wondered where pictures of the new governor would come from in January when the new governor took office and what would happen to the old ones. Were former gubernatorial pictures destroyed thoroughly and with precision, like worn-out money sent

back to the mint? Or did cartons and cartons of them
get returned to the loser, who was probably in a severely
depressed state to begin with and shouldn't have to deal
with fading portraits of a vanished career? Quill had
liked this governor, who'd forgone a presidential campaign because he didn't want a greedy, self-aggrandizing
media poking around his family any more than they had
already. As far as Quill was concerned, at least at this
specific minute, a person's private history should remain
private history.

A door to the left of the flag opened. A figure dressed
in black judicial robes stumped into the room. Hemlock
Falls' new justice, Bernie Bristol, was round and jowly
and wore the dopey, happy look of a hound getting its
ears scratched. An engineer retired from Xerox Corporation fifty miles away in Rochester, Bristol had bought
a small farm south of the village in September, and run
a well-financed campaign for the justiceship. Quill had
met him, once, when he'd stopped by the Inn for dinner.
He'd been rather endearingly innocent of enough French
to order his entrée. On the other hand, Quill hadn't been
surprised to discover he was a lousy tipper.

"All rise!" roared Dwight "Run-On" Riorden, the
bailiff.

"All what?" said Howie, nonplussed. He got to his
feet, muttering, "This is justice court, for God's sake,
and we're all supposed to *rise*?" and stepped into the
aisle, ushering Quill in front of him.

"Murchison?"

Howie turned, his eyebrows raised in polite inquiry.
A brown-haired man carrying an expensive leather briefcase walked rapidly past the two of them, clapping his
hand on Howie's shoulder in passing. It was, Quill saw
in mild surprise, Al Santini.

Quill smiled and asked if he was looking for Meg.

His eyes ran over her without a flicker of recognition.

"Al?" Howie's voice was wary and tinged with surprise. "What brings you out this way?"

"Good to see ya, buddy." Al grinned, revealing teeth like a picket fence in need of whitewash. He looked different. Quill looked at him carefully. He looked—almost senatorial. His scanty hair was moussed to an illusion of fullness. His dark blue pin-striped suit (cut to conceal the concave chest and his little potbelly) was so determinedly well-pressed it seemed to wear him. His watery blue eyes flicked over Quill like a pair of clammy hands. "This the perp?"

"The perp?" said Howie.

"The miscreant. The malefactor. The culprit." Al delivered a professional grin. "And a beaut she is, too, Howie." He clicked his tongue against his teeth, banged the briefcase playfully against Howie's knees, and loped up the aisle.

"What the heck?" said Quill. "Howie! He's acting like he's never seen me before! He's been a guest at the Inn for three days! He . . ." She subsided, muttering.

Howie frowned. "Now what the hell is he doing here?"

Santini stopped just short of the bench and appeared to be opening shop. He thumped his briefcase on the prosecutor's side of the bench, snapped it open, and spread a sheaf of legal-sized papers on the desk top. Above him, Justice Bernie Bristol polished his gavel with a spotless white handkerchief.

Quill looked around the courtroom. There were five—no, six—alleged traffic violators besides herself. At least, she assumed they were alleged traffic violators; all were probably as innocent as she was. She gave a sudden sigh of relief. "Howie. We won't need Meg as a

witness after all. There's Betty Hall. I didn't know that
she got pulled in, too, but I know for sure she saw me
get stopped. And she knew I wasn't speeding. I mean,
she's been driving school bus part-time for months and
ought to know a speeder when she sees one. She'll be
glad to testify to the fact that I'm a totally law-abiding
citizen. She'd parked her school bus right on the side of
the road where I got picked up. She even gave me this
sort of sympathetic wave when Davy pulled me over.''

Howie pursed his lips. ''I don't like this. No, I don't
like this at all. Quill, about those other tickets Meg mentioned. The ones from New York?''

''Oh, dear.'' Quill fidgeted with her scarf. ''Um. It's
like this. I thought that all that stuff would have disappeared by now. I mean, it's been seven years.''

''B.T,'' Howie said thoughtfully, ''B.T. Meg meant
. . . Before Tickets?'' he hazarded. He looked at her over
his wire-rimmed glasses. ''You mean you've been getting tickets since you were nineteen? How *many* tickets,
Quill?''

Quill twirled a piece of hair around her ear. ''It's not
the tickets, so much. More like the totals.''

''The totals?'' Howie's eyes narrowed. ''You don't
mean totals as in total wrecks? Tell me you're not re-
ferring to total wrecks.''

''All this happened years ago, Howie. In another life.
I drove taxi while I was trying to make it as an artist.
In New York City, for Pete's sake. And you can just
imagine . . . I mean, Howie, most of them weren't my
fault. Well, half of them weren't, anyway,'' Quill said
generously. ''Meg knows all about it. So did Myles.
Kind of.''

Howie, if he picked up on the past tense, made no
mention of it. ''*Half* of them? How many . . . ? Oh,

boy.'' He rubbed his nose. ''I just need to know one thing. You haven't had so much as a parking ticket in the last seven years?''

''Not so much as a broken taillight,'' Quill said virtuously. ''I mean, Deputy Dave did issue a warning last week—but that's all, honest.''

Howie smiled. He had a very attractive smile. ''Then we'll find out what's going on here. It's probably nothing. Can you handle Run-On's conversation for five minutes?''

''Sure. I mean, if anyone would know what's going on, he would.''

Howie raised his voice slightly and called, ''Dwight?''

Dwight ''Run-On'' Riorden had combined courthouse maintenance with the duties of bailiff ever since the Tompkins County Board of Supervisors had decided neither was a full-time job. Dwight wore a suit coat over his coveralls and white athletic socks with black lace-up oxfords, a mode of dress which seemed to accommodate both occupations. He gave Howie a high sign and ambled over. ''Ms. Quilliam? Mr. M.?''

Quill extended her hand. Dwight's palm was calloused. ''Hi, Dwight. I haven't seen you at Marge's diner on Sundays for a while.''

''Nope. Been working weekends, Ms. Quilliam. Mr. Hotshot Bristol there got his knickers in a twist over the state of the courthouse. Day after the election returns come in, Mr. Murchison, Bristol there wants to know how long's it been since it's been painted. Long enough, I say, and it's going to be a sight longer. Don't have a budget for painting walls that don't need paint. The boiler now, I tell him, that boiler she could use a valve job. Place where I'm going to be judge got to look better than this, he tells me. The hell with the boiler, he tells me. The hell with you, I tell him. Course, after he goes to judge's school you'd think the son of a gun would know better than to tell people he's a judge. He's not a judge, he's a justice. But no, he's an elected official of the people, he tells me, and things been too slack around here. But judge or justice those walls don't need paint. So I tell him that and he tells me—''

Howie interrupted. Most people talking to Dwight interrupted. Those who couldn't made a practice of avoiding him. "Dwight, when did Bristol get back from judge's school?"

Responding like a rudderless boat to a brisk breeze, Run-On's conversation tacked amiably in a different direction. "Before Thanksgiving, it must a been when we got that couple inches of snow. Didn't think I was going to have to get the blower out till after Thanksgiving, but some years I just don't—''

"Is this the first justice court session he's held?"

"Nossir, held four Fridays ago, it was, just after Thanksgiving. You were on that cruise and then out to your sister's in Rochester, and everybody knew they couldn't get hold of you so nobody tried.''

"I just got back yesterday," Howie agreed absently, his attention on the back entrance to the courtroom. "There were a lot of phone calls waiting for me. Thought most of the callbacks could wait. . . . Riorden, who are those people?''

"Them?" Run-On craned his neck. "That's press. Media people. Judge Bristol told me to be sure and save seats for them, so I did. I roped off seats by the fire extinguisher, although I roped off enough for a dozen, judge said, and it don't look like to me that there's more than four, counting the guy with the camcorder. Hey!''

His furry eyebrows rose in mild excitement. "Hey! That's Nora Cahill! She's on the news from Syracuse when I eat my supper."

Quill waved hello. Nora ignored her. Maybe, thought Quill, there was some kind of cream she used that gave her complexion that flawless even tone. If there was, she wanted some.

A somewhat embarrassed-looking figure in trooper gray edged in behind Nora Cahill's camera crew. "There's Dave Kiddermeister, too," Quill whispered, as the deputy eased into the courtroom. "You know, Kathleen's brother. She's one of our best waitresses. Davy's the officer that flagged me down. And, Howie, I wasn't speeding, honestly. What the heck's going on?"

Howie took her arm and pressed her into her seat. "Stay there. Stay quiet. Don't say anything unless I ask you a direct question. And when I do ask you a question answer yes, no, or I don't know."

Quill bit her thumbnail nervously.

"Bailiff!" said Judge Bernie Bristol. "Can you come up here?" He took a deep, happy breath and thumped the gavel. "This court is now in session." Bristol thumped the gavel again and kept on thumping with an air of mild pleasure. After some seconds, Al Santini reached up, removed the gavel, and laid it to one side.

Run-On Riorden ambled back up the judge's dais and laid a stack of files in front of the justice, who regarded them with confusion.

"The people call Sarah Quilliam," Al Santini prompted after a long moment.

Howie rose to his feet. "Your Honor," he said, in dramatically sarcastic tones, "I was not aware that my learned colleague had been elected to the bench. I object to this disruption of proper courtroom procedure. It is the right and proper role of the bailiff to perform the roll call.''

Quill blinked, her anxiety somewhat allayed; she'd never seen Howie in court before. He was impressive.

Bernie took a moment to digest the objection, then turned anxiously to Al Santini. ''Well, I guess I object, too, Mr. Santini.''

Al spread both hands in a deprecatory gesture. ''My apologies to the court, Your Honor.''

''Oh, that's okay,'' Bernie said generously. ''No harm done. Let's see.'' He shuffled through the files, took the topmost one, stared at it, set it down, stood up, and hitched up his judge's robes. He was wearing the kind of red plaid trousers popular with stockbrokers at Christmas parties. He drew a small black notebook from his trousers pocket, shook out his robes, sat down again, and opened the notebook up. The silence stretched on, broken only by little hisses and sighs as Bernie read aloud under his breath. Howie cleared his throat. Al Santini sighed elaborately. Quill, feeling obscurely uneasy again, looked over her shoulder. Nora Cahill, the Syracuse anchor, was standing behind her, microphone at the ready.

''There it is, right here, got it,'' said Bernie.

The man holding the camcorder behind Quill switched it on. Bernie squinted a little in the sudden flood of light. ''You are Sarah Quilliam, of One Hemlock Road, Hemlock Falls, New York?''

Quill looked at Howie, who nodded.

''Yes,'' said Quill, much more loudly than she'd intended.

''You are charged with violation of section 11.74A of the Vehicular and Traffic Code.'' He beamed at her. ''That's passing a stopped school bus, Miss Quilliam.''

"A stopped school bus?" asked Quill, bewildered.

"One moment, Your Honor." Howie folded his arms and regarded Al Santini with a steady and disapproving eye. "The violation listed on Miss Quilliam's traffic ticket is 9.32C, speed in excess of five miles over the posted limit . . ."

"Well, according to the deputy over there, she was only going a couple miles over the limit and there's no news in that," said Bernie, clearly in the spirit of help-fulness.

"Of course there's no news in that," Howie said evenly. "And if there's a new charge, Your Honor, neither I nor my client has been notified . . ."

"Oh, yeah, she has. She's been notified. Got sent a letter after we got the computer readout on the camera. Sent the ticket through the mail. This school bus thing is valid, you know. Because of the camera."

"The camera?" said Howie. "What damned camera?"

"Counselor, Counselor," Al Santini said reprovingly. "The hidden intersection cameras. You're familiar with those, Murchison."

"You mean the cameras they've put up in New York City to catch people running red lights at intersections?"

"Uh-huh," said Al.

"There's one in Hemlock Falls?"

"Put up last week. Came out of the sheriff's budget. Lot of traffic violators out there, Murchison, so Judge Bristol kept it very quiet. Have to keep the streets safe for the kiddies. These little towns are laboring under the burden of high taxes paid to Albany and have little or nothing to show for it in the way of improvements to local government. When monies are made available to the hundreds of towns like Hemlock Falls across this great state of ours for the express purpose of saving lives, of making the streets safer for our little ones—I say it's money well spent.''

Howie cast a sardonic glance at the running cameras. Nora Cahill smiled at him like a cat who'd had baby birds for breakfast. Quill took several deep breaths and retied the bow around her neck.

"Your Honor," Howie said, "I make a motion to dismiss.''

Bernie cast a benign eye around the courtroom. "Do I hear a second?''

"A second what?'' asked Howie.

"A second to the motion," Bernie explained with a kindly air. "If I hear a second, I have to consider dismissal, don't I?''

Howie spread his hands and looked up at the ceiling. His lips moved.

"Well,'' said Quill, more to break the stunned silence than anything else, "there was a school bus there, as a matter of fact. Betty was in it. She saw me, and she knows absolutely without question that I was not speeding. Didn't you, Betty?'' Quill turned in her seat. Betty gave her a thumbs up.

"Quill, keep quiet," Howie said, between his teeth.

"Let the record show that the defendant has admitted passing the school bus and that the driver Betty Hall can identify her," Al Santini said loudly. "Judge Bristol, I believe you were going to continue with the charges?''

"Um . . . ya. The state of New York provides a minimum fine of seven hundred dollars and seven days in jail and a maximum fine of eight hundred dollars and one hundred and eighty days in jail for this offense,'' Bernie read aloud. "How do you plead, Miss Quilliam? Not guilty? Guilty? Or guilty with an explanation?''

Quill said weakly, "Well, guilty with an explanation, sir. I—''

"QUILL!" Howie shouted. "Be quiet! Your Honor, I demand a recess. I demand an examination of the judicial process involved in these proceedings."

"I believe my colleague is in contempt, Your Honor," Al Santini said smoothly.

"What?" asked Bernie.

"Contempt. He's in contempt," Al muttered.

"Stuff it, Santini," Howie said.

"That's no way to talk," Bernie Bristol said reprovingly.

"Your Honor, there is a motion to dismiss before this court." Howie, Quill noticed, turned dark red when he was angry. "My client has not been notified of this most serious misdemeanor."

"She open her mail?" asked Al Santini. He waved a certified mail receipt under Howie's nose. "These electronic tickets get sent by certified mail." He turned back to the bench. "Your Honor? I'm going to ask for the maximum penalty here. To keep this kind of menace off the roads and pathways of our fair state."

"Menace?" said Quill.

"And to keep the money rolling in, too," Bernie added in a helpful aside to the steadily whirring camera. "Lot of financial opportunities being missed with these kinds of cases."

Howie ran his hands through his graying hair, which didn't much affect his hairstyle but added to the appearance of frenzy. "On what *possible* grounds could you ask for a maximum penalty here, Santini?! God knows why I'm even participating in this dog and pony show. Your Honor, if a ruling is not made on my motion to dismiss, I am going to file a protest with the O.C.A."

"I told you we should have repainted," Judge Bristol said to Dwight Riorden. "Now we'll have OSHA on our necks."

"Let me explain, Your Honor." Howie gave an exasperated laugh. "The Office of Court Administration is a disciplinary body—"

"Shall we get back to the case at hand, Counselor?" Santini laid a thick file in front of the judge. "I have here in evidence the defendant's MV104, dating back fifteen years to a multitude of V&T charges in the city of Manhattan, Your Honor."

"Um . . . ya," said Judge Bristol.

"Oh, dear," said Quill. "Oh, dear, oh, dear, oh, dear."

Howie cast an accusing glance at Quill, and said loudly, "I object!"

"A perusal of this document will demonstrate without question that Ms. Quilliam is one of the many, many reckless drivers at liberty in the state of New York—"

"I object! Objection!"

"—endangering the lives and physical well-being of our citizens."

"Your Honor!" Howie roared. Quill, impressed, hadn't realized he was so excitable.

Santini raised his hand for silence. "Your Honor, at the least, the very least, I request that you commit this woman to the county jail. She is a virtual felon—"

"Your Honor!" Howie, suddenly cold (and, Quill saw, very, very angry), folded his arms and lowered his head, like a bull about to charge. She put a hand on his arm. His voice was tight. "Go on, Santini. Hang yourself."

"She has been identified by the bus driver, and has a driving record which clearly places her in the ranks of the reckless. All the conditions for the severest penalty have been met, and I request the maximum sentence."

As if recognizing a cue, Bernie Bristol thwacked his

gavel. "Seven days . . ." he said directly into the rolling camcorder.

Howie clenched both hands. "Your Honor! I must warn you that I will immediately contact the Office of Court Administration to file a complaint!"

". . . and seven hundred dollars for the much-needed budget of the state of New York. Bailiff? Escort the prisoner to the jail house, please." He adjusted the collar of his judge's robe and smiled at Nora Cahill. "You get all that? You want me to do it again?"

CHAPTER 5

The drive from the Tompkins County Courthouse near Ithaca had taken about twenty-five minutes, which meant, Quill thought, that it must be about eleven-thirty, although she wasn't certain. Deputy Dave had taken her watch.

The Municipal Building at the end of Main Street housed the Sheriff's Department and Town offices. The jail was on the west end of the building facing Main, so that Quill could see most of Hemlock Falls through the barred window. The sun was pale gold through a light snow, creating a veiled and misty landscape worthy of attention by Turner. If Turner'd ever gotten to America to paint, which he hadn't. And if he weren't dead. Which he was.

Most of the stores lining Main Street were cobblestone. Marge Schmidt's diner, Esther West's dress shop, and a few others were of white clapboard with black trim. The contrast was pleasing, even, Quill thought gloomily, from this vantage point. Four inches of new snow covered rooftops and bushes and made feathery cones on the wrought-iron standards of the streetlights. The snowplows had left the curbs knee-high with pillowy drifts. Through the heavy gauge wire screen, Quill could see Esther West in a bright red ski jacket, mounting a pine wreath on the front door of her shop. Esther finished hanging the wreath and walked the three storefronts down to Marge's diner and went in. A few cars drove by. Quill started to count the squares to the inch in the screen. Some minutes after Esther disappeared into Marge's diner, Mayor Henry, portly in a black and green ski suit, ran out of his office, crossed the street to the diner, and charged inside. Then the street was quiet.

Quill sighed, coughed, wound her hair around her finger, and sat on the bare mattress of the fold-out cot. She debated her chances of getting a cup of coffee. She'd been in the cell before, having interviewed incarcerated suspects in several murder cases in years past, and it was as utilitarian and boring as ever. Caffeine might keep her awake.

Open bars on the cell's fourth side faced the solid door to the sheriff's office. This door was half open, and she could see Davy Kiddermeister's feet propped up on his desk. His socks were sagging. Quill's own feet were cold and bare except for her panty hose, since Davy'd taken her boots and then had been unable to find a pair of prison slippers. Quill loved her boots. They were crushed leather with a fleecy top. They'd been soaked with snow and mud on the outside, but the inside always kept her feet warm, no matter how poor the weather was. Quill sighed again, chewed on her hair, and stared at the ceiling. Perhaps she should have called Meg, although Howie had assured her she'd be out before lunch. A flash of red in the street caught her eye and she went back to the window.

Like two fireplugs on either side of a skinny poplar, Mayor Henry, Esther, and Marge stood in the middle of Main Street staring at the Municipal Building. Quill untied her silk scarf, a bright teal and gold, and wagged it

back and forth. Esther clutched Elmer. Elmer pointed at
the jail window, his mouth moving soundlessly. Marge
socked Elmer in the arm, then all three waved together,
tentatively. Quill waved the scarf in response. Esther
semaphored back, knocking the mayor's knitted hat sideways and poking him in the eye. There was an excited
colloquy, then Marge stumped to her Lexus, the mayor
and Esther on her heels. They piled in. Marge peeled
out from the curb, slush spraying from beneath the
wheels.

"Coffee!" Quill shouted futilely through the barred
window. "Bring coffee."

"You need anything, Ms. Quilliam?" Davy Kiddermeister stood outside the cell, his thumbs hitched in his
belt loops. Davy was blond and fair-skinned. In winter,
the tips of his ears were perpetually chapped.

"No, thanks, Davy," said Quill. She sighed and twid-
dled her thumbs. "Has Howie had any luck finding that
judge? The real one, I mean?"

"Mr. Murchison's down to the courthouse right this
minute, paying your fine. I told you that, twice. Not that
I mind saying it more than once," he added hastily.
"No, ma'am."

"Seven hundred dollars," Quill murmured darkly.

Davy shuffled. He was able to shuffle, Quill noted,
because he had boots. She, on the other hand, didn't.

"I really hated to lock you up like this, Ms. Quilliam,
but the law's the law."

"Then how's about my boots? Honestly, Davy, why
can't I just have my boots? They aren't exactly lethal
weapons."

"Sheriff Dorset'd have my guts for garters if I hadn't
processed you in right, and prisoners can't have shoes
or belts or anything like that. Says so in the manual."

"Where is Sheriff Dorset, anyway?"

"Out," Davy said vaguely, "with that senator."

"Al Santini is not a senator." Quill explained with restraint, "He lost the election. He's an ex-senator. Which, if I'm not mistaken, is why I'm here at this very moment."

Davy, who clearly had something on his chest, ignored this and said earnestly, "I just hope that you won't, you know"—Davy's ears turned an even brighter pink—"tell Kathleen that I treated you bad or anything like that. You want something, I'll get it for you. Just lemme know. Unless it's your boots. Can't give you your boots."

Quill felt an attack of tartness coming on. "Kathleen is perfectly capable of deciding that her brother is a Nazi all on her own. She's not only our best waitress, she's the one with the most sense." She sat on the cot and sank her chin in her hands. She wondered if she'd be in here if Myles had been reelected sheriff. Nobody knew much about Frank Dorset, except that he lived at the very edge of Tompkins County and farmed pigs. Myles, she thought, wouldn't have let things get to this point.

"I've been thinking maybe of getting out of law enforcement, like Sheriff McHale did," Davy said with remarkable prescience. "Stuff like throwing you in jail just isn't right, to my way of thinking."

"If you think at all, David Emerson Kiddermeister," said Marge Schmidt, entering the cell area with a great stamping of feet and a rush of snowy air, "which I doubt. The men in this town have all gone crazy. Look, Esther. It's true. Every word of it. There she is!"

Esther, Marge, and the mayor crowded next to Davy and stared at Quill like owls on a fence. Esther patted a stiffly lacquered curl over one ear and chirped in distress.

"I don't know as how you all are allowed in here,"

said Davy. "Prisoner's only allowed one visitor at a time."

"Stuff it." Marge planted a thick palm in Davy's chest and shoved him aside. "You all right, Quill? Getcha anything?"

"Coffee," said Quill, "I'd love some coffee. And something to do. A book, maybe?"

"How long they send you up for?" asked the mayor. "Are you going to need a lot of books? I could set up a fund-raiser, maybe."

"She isn't going to be here that long," Esther said stoutly. Esther, whose taste in clothes seemed to have been formed by watching old movies starring the McGuire sisters, adjusted her patent leather belt and added, "Are you?"

"Seven days," said Davy. "Judge says she's supposed to serve the whole time."

"He can't do that," said Marge. "I knew that little squirt Bristol never shoulda been elected. And it's your fault, Mayor. You and your nekkid friends running all through the woods like a bunch of assholes."

"Maybe the judge *can* do that," Esther gasped. "I mean—if she did what she did, she could be in here for years. Did you do it, Quill? I mean, we heard that you ran over a little child, but which little child? And the child couldn't have died, because we would have heard about it."

"I ran over a little child?" said Quill. "What? What?"

"You got it wrong, Esther. You always do. She didn't run over a little kid." Elmer sighed, regret all over his round face. "She *almost* ran over a little kid. Came this close." He held a pudgy thumb and forefinger minimally apart.

"I passed a school bus," said Quill. "A parked empty

school bus. There weren't any little kids within forty blocks of that school bus.''

"Well, there had to have been little kids within forty blocks," said the mayor reasonably. "The whole of Hemlock Falls isn't forty blocks, so there must have been little kids around somewhere. But you—"

"I did NOT run over a little kid!"

"You heard it wrong, Elmer, you hopeless little shit." Marge put her hands on her considerable hips and surveyed the cell and the shoeless Quill with a suspicious touch of satisfaction. "Just look at this. Cold, hungry, and practically bare nekkid. I'm going to go down to the library and check out a couple of books for Quill, here. Esther, you find some slippers in that shop of yours, and then give Betty a call. She can run over here with some hamburg and a thermos of coffee." She fixed a malevolent eye on Davy. "And don't you touch a drop of my coffee, David Emerson Kiddermeister. I ain't subsidizing any damn fool that had a part in this. And speaking of damn fools, where's that useless son of bitch sheriff?''

"You talking to me?"

To her fierce annoyance, Quill jumped and her breath came short. Franklin Douglas Dorset, newly elected sheriff of Tompkins County, didn't look at all like Travis Bickle, he only sounded like him. He looked, as Meg had stigmatized him at the start of his election campaign, like a canned asparagus. He unzipped his quilted winter jacket and regarded the group crushed in front of the cell with speculation. Dorset was tall; his skin, hair, eyes, and clothes a uniformly nondescript pale brown. His hair was thick, standing almost upright, and his shoulders, chest, and hips were of similar circumference, so that if you had an imagination as food-oriented as Meg's it was possible to imagine Dorset as one of the more cylinderlike vegetables. Quill thought he looked more like a bleached-out Elvis Presley than an asparagus.

Meg also claimed Dorset had the brains of a boiled onion. Quill, after one look at his flat brown eyes, wasn't sure about that.

"Deputy?" said Dorset. "There some good reason why all these people are in here?"

Marge drew breath. Quill waited confidently for the explosion. Blessed with the psychic drive of a Patton tank, Marge could flatten sumo wrestlers with a single glance from her turretlike eye.

"Guess we better be getting along," Marge said meekly. "I'm bringing her coffee and a book, Sheriff," she added. "And somethin' to put on her feet. If you don't mind."

"What I mind," said Sheriff Dorset, lifting a corner of his lip, "is you taking that intersection at Route 15 and 96 at seventy miles an hour last Sunday at 4:32 p.m., Marge Schmidt. That's a three-hundred-dollar, three-point V&T violation."

"Route 15 and 96?" Elmer asked alertly.

"Maybe it's there," Dorset said with relish, "and maybe it isn't. I'll see you folks sometime, right?" He held an imaginary camera to one eye and pretended to click it.

Quill watched Marge leave, followed by a studiedly careless mayor and a nervous Esther. She said to Dorset, "You mean you can move the darn thing?"

"The hidden camera? Bet your cute little ass. No use in a town this size if you can't."

Dorset unclipped the keys to the cell from his belt with a flourish and opened the cell door. His gaze flicked over her carelessly, avoiding her eyes, and concentrating on her breasts. He stood slouched, one hip thrust out.

"Deputy here says you want to go home. Says you're a little scared. Can't say as I blame you."

Quill thought carefully about her response to this. She probably wouldn't get much more than seven years jail time if she punched Franklin Douglas Dorset right in the nose. On the other hand, her feet were cold and she was going to die if she didn't get a cup of coffee. "Ahem," she said, in a noncommittal way.

"Tell you what. Senator out there wants to have a little talk with you, then he figures you pay the fine, you've served a little time, it's all settled, you can go back up to the Inn." Dorset smiled ingratiatingly.

Quill didn't say anything.

"Well, ma'am?"

"What kind of talk?" she asked suspiciously.

Dorset jiggled the keys. "Whyn't you come right out here and see?"

Dorset behind her like an ugly sheepdog, Quill marched into the sheriff's office and into a glare of lights, cables, and Nora Cahill's camera crew.

"Sarah Quilliam was released at 12:22, having spent all of two hours and forty-seven minutes of her seven-day sentence in jail," said Nora Cahill in her professional anchor voice. "Senator? Do you have a comment?"

Quill's stockinged toe caught on a piece of curling linoleum. She pitched forward. Al Santini grabbed her elbow and pulled her upright. Howie Murchison draped her down coat over her shoulders, grabbed Quill's other elbow, and pulled her toward the door.

"Sarah Quilliam is a wealthy businesswoman and Hemlock Falls' third largest employer," Santini said into the camcorder's little red light. "The level of this fine is a joke."

Ex-Senator Al Santini and Sheriff Dorset smiled for

the camera. Howie looked pained.

"Here're your boots, Ms. Quilliam," Davy whispered apologetically. Quill grabbed them and pulled the left one on, hopping around the linoleum on one leg. They were still soggy with snow and mud.

Nora Cahill shoved the microphone in Quill's face. "Do you have a comment, Ms. Quilliam? Do you think this criminal charge will affect business at your upper-crust Inn? And how do you feel about Senator Santini's efforts to reform small-town America?"

Quill, who thought of herself as a generally equable person, felt the last shreds of her temper fray and snap. She grabbed the right boot by its wet, muddy top and swung.

"And he's going to press charges?!" Meg said indignantly some twenty minutes later. "That lunatic! That creep! I would have whacked him right in the balls."

Quill, wanting nothing more than to sit quietly for two minutes and warm her feet, looked at the kitchen with the nostalgic affection common, she supposed, to the recently paroled. She never wanted to see Al Santini or Bernie Bristol or Frank Dorset again in this life. She wanted to stay in the kitchen forever. The cobblestone fireplace was hung with dried bay leaf, braids of pearly garlic, and sheaves of lemon thyme. A fire burned briskly in the grate. Meg's collection of copper pots gleamed reassuringly from one of the oak beams running overhead. The air was filled with the scents of baking bread, orange sauce for the game hens, and freshly ground coffee. Admittedly, the view from the mullioned windows at the kitchen's west end was not quite as picturesque as that from the county jail; the herb gardens out back were still producing parsley and brussels sprouts. Sometime yesterday Mike the grounds keeper

must have cleared them of snow. The mulched beds
were consequently muddy with well-manured straw, but
they looked beautiful to Quill. "Free," mused Quill,
feeling warmly toward the mulch, "I'm free."

"The son of a bitch," Meg continued.

"Do you kiss your mother with that mouth, Miss
Margaret Quilliam?" demanded Doreen, who had insisted that Quill completely change her clothes. "Lice,"
she'd said. "And I ain't sayin' a word more."

She tapped Quill on the shoulder. "The senator got a
powerful lot of mud up his nose, or so I hear. But that
don't make it right for Meg here to cuss him out. Jail!
The good Lord give me a stummick to hear this. Jail!"

"Actually, I was aiming at Nora Cahill. I didn't mean
to get Al Santini, although I'm glad I did. And why are
you mad at me, Doreen?"

Doreen darted a beady, somewhat proprietary eye
around the kitchen. Six of the kitchen staff scrubbed
vegetables, stirred sauces, and washed pots with unconcern for Doreen's cool reception of the fact that Quill
had spent two hours and forty-seven minutes in the
county jail. In her middle fifties, Doreen had been head
housekeeper at the Inn for almost six years and regarded
both Meg and Quill as sometimes satisfactory but fre-
quently recalcitrant daughters, and everybody knew it.

"I'm ashamed of you," Doreen said severely. "The
whole town's talking about it."

"It's not that big a deal! It was a setup! A mistake!"
Quill sank her head in her hands. "I suppose Axminster's going to run a story in the *Gazette*."

"Huh," said Doreen. She scratched her nose vigorously.

"Isn't anyone glad to see me?" Quill asked somewhat
plaintively.

The kitchen got very quiet, although, thought Quill,

the kitchen was never really quiet. Even at two o'clock in the morning, the Zero King refrigerators filled the air with a gentle hum. And at one o'clock in the afternoon, four days before Christmas, with the rest of the McIntosh family due that evening and a wedding due at the end of the week, the Inn's kitchen was filled with the clank and clatter of *sous*-chefs at the Aga, the oceanlike hum of the lunch crowd in the dining room, and the slam-whack of doors opening and closing.

Quill thought about the sound of doors closing: storeroom doors, cupboard doors, oven doors—all of it far preferable to the unique sound of a cell door being shut and locked. But at the moment, the kitchen was quiet only in relation to the usual people noise: Usually Meg alternately shrieked at and sang to the Cornell interns; Doreen recited the latest depredations of departed guests on the Inn towel supply; Frank, the assistant chef, called out food orders to the hapless Bjarne; the other workers whistled, gossiped, or hummed. At the moment, everyone in the kitchen was dead silent, out of sympathy, Quill had assumed, for her recent incarceration. Now she wasn't so sure.

"Oh, for Pete's sake." Meg, shaping meringues into swans, paused and waved the palette knife in an accusing fashion. "Anyone would think you'd spent three days in solitary instead of three hours chitchatting with Davy Kiddermeister."

"I was not chitchatting with Davy Kiddermeister. I was in jail. A prisoner. And I was cold. I told you. They took away my boots."

Doreen made a surreptitious note on a pad she kept handy in her apron. Quill had seen the pad. It had a little logo of a mouse with a reporter's hat and five large capital *W*'s running down one edge for Who, What, Where, When and Why. Doreen had ordered it from the

Lillian Vernon catalog soon after she married Axminster and they bought the *Gazette*. Axminster had proved surprisingly good at publishing the weekly, although Quill suspected that Doreen's nose for gossip had a lot to do with it. That, and her savings from her wages as the Inn's housekeeper. Doreen was notoriously thrifty. Doreen caught Quill's eye and shoved the pad back in her pocket. Doreen's gray hair frizzed around her high forehead like a ruff on a grouse and her nose was beaky. Spurious attempts at innocence increased her resemblance to a startled rooster.

"Axminster's going to run a story about this, isn't he?"

"It's publicity," Doreen offered placatingly. "Publicity's good for business."

Meg snorted, "Publicity! If you'd just told Howie Murchison about those priors, none of this would have happened. What I want to know is, how come when the Inn gets publicity, it's always bad publicity? At least this time it isn't a corpse. I hate it when the headlines involve a corpse."

"They better not, missy," Doreen said darkly.

"Better not what?" asked Quill.

"Involve no corpse."

Meg grinned to herself and added a wing to the swan's body with meticulous care.

"What are you talking about? I didn't kill anybody!"

"Passin' a school bus, you might of, is all," said Doreen.

The silence intensified.

"I didn't pass a school bus!" said Quill. "I mean I did, but it was a parked school bus."

"That's when you're supposed to stop," Doreen said tartly. "When the school bus is."

"It was a parked, *empty* school bus!"

"Empty?" said Frank, the assistant chef. "You mean you didn't almost run over a little kid?"

"No!"

"That's what we heard," Bjarne said apologetically.

"I told you guys," said Meg.

"Told them what?" said Quill.

"I told them you didn't almost run over a little kid. You would have confessed to me." She winked.

"There is," Quill said stiffly, "evidence that I didn't run over anybody."

"Evidence?" asked Doreen.

"A videotape. From that damn hidden camera that started this whole mess. They showed it in court. All it showed was my car passing that school bus!"

"They show the whole thing?" Doreen asked alertly. "Stuff like that can be faked, ya know."

"All right, all right." Meg gestured widely with the palette knife, spattering egg white. "Doreen, you know gossip in a town this size. Quill didn't run anybody over with anything." She shook her head at Quill. "You're right, I should have stayed with you this morning. Next time you get arrested, I will. Sisters forever!" She began to hum an Irving Berlin tune so old Quill didn't even know where she'd picked it up. "Sis—ters. Sis—ters. Dah-dah-dah-sisters . . ."

"Thing is," Frank said earnestly, "if you didn't almost run over a little kid, what else would bring someone like Senator Alphonse Santini all the way to Hemlock Falls to prosecute a little traffic case?"

Quill rose from her seat behind the counter. "He's here for the wedding! He is not a senator. He's an ex-senator. Clearly he's turning even his wedding into a media circus! And he's running so hard for reelection he's going to need oxygen infusions before New Year's. As to why he picked on Hemlock Falls first, beats the heck out of me. Maybe because he's getting married here. You heard what Nora Cahill said—this is part of a whole campaign to reform small-town America. And he's started here. If anyone's a hit-and-run driver, it's him. I mean it's he. Whatever. I'll bet you a week's pay that right now he's off to the next town and the next victim, trailing his pet little media person and her camcorders behind him. He'll be jailing innocent people over in Covert next. Or maybe Trumansburg. And he'll come back here to get married, and I'll kill him."

"The guy's a jerk," Meg said loyally. "If the McIntoshes weren't spending all this money on his wedding, I'd do more than shove a few handfuls of mud up his nose."

"Gee, thanks, Meg," said Quill. "Food first, sisters second." She paused, cleared her throat, and said huskily, "I can't believe you guys thought I did something as terrible as almost hitting a little kid."

"Somebody circulating that rumor again?" John came through the swinging doors from the dining room, a sheaf of lunch orders in his hand. At his seemingly casual comment, everyone busily resumed work. Quill had always thought his chief asset as business manager was his unflappability. She decided now that it was his easy air of authority. He smiled at her. "Glad to see Howie sprang you from the slam. I was about to call out the cavalry."

Quill gave him an unwilling smile.

"Mr. Raintree? This rumor that's been going around about Quill's jail time . . ." Frank began.

"You're too smart to believe that one, Frank. And even smarter enough to stop anyone who spreads it. Quill? You have a few minutes to spare? Mrs. McIntosh would like to go over some of the wedding plans."

"Sure." Quill latched on to the proffered diversion

with relief. "Where is she?"

"Office. I'll meet you there in a second. Kathleen's busy with customers out there. The RV conventioneers from the Marriott snowmobiled over here in a huge group. I told her I'd turn these lunch orders over to Frank for her."

Quill hesitated, waiting for him.

"You go on ahead, Quill. I just need a few minutes with these guys."

Quill pushed her way through the swinging doors slowly enough to hear John say, "Everyone in this kitchen is going to listen to this once, and only once . . ."

The doors whispered closed. Behind her, John's admonitions rose and fell. Phrases like "innocent until proven guilty" would be hurled next. Not to mention, "going through a tough time at the moment." Quill folded her arms and glowered, startling a guy in an unzipped snowmobile suit at table fourteen into spilling Meg's pumpkin soufflé onto his T-shirt. Mindful of a public television special on psychic well-being she'd seen recently, Quill took deep breaths, strove for inner calm, and exhaled noisily, further alarming the gentleman seated at fourteen.

Quill concentrated fiercely on the McIntosh wedding, clearing her thoughts of a persistent sense of injustice. Mrs. McIntosh would want to know if they could accommodate the extra eighty people who'd somehow sprung up at the last minute.

She still wasn't sure how they were going to handle the entire McIntosh reception without opening the terrace, and there was no way to open the terrace because it was December and too cold for anyone except the S.O.A.P. diehards. She mentally rearranged the mahogany sideboards, the breakfront, and the tables. She waved absentmindedly at Kathleen, who was moving gracefully among the tables like a skater on a pond, and thought about taking out just one more wall. The sturdy building was used to it, and she'd been convinced they needed the extra space for a long time anyway.

When they had purchased the Inn seven years before, Meg and Quill had decided on twenty-seven guest rooms, a Tavern Lounge to seat a hundred, and an equivalent number of seatings in the dining room. They'd remodeled with that in mind. John had added a conference center for possible corporate business when he'd signed on with them two years after they had opened, over Quill's protests. The past summer John had encouraged them to open a small, boutique style restaurant in the Sakura mall which almost ran itself.

Neither Meg nor Quill had anticipated the sudden spurt of success of the last year or so resulting from John's management. Not only had the number of business parties increased—but so had the private. The McIntosh wedding would be the largest Meg and Quill had ever planned, and it would be the first of many, if the current trends held.

She felt John come into the room behind her and said, "If we could just take out the wall between here and the foyer, I know we could seat those extra eighty people."

"I think we should stick with the buffet."

"I hate to stand up when I eat. And so does everyone else."

"Well, by all means. Let's call Mike and get that wall down, the place recarpeted, and the walls repainted by Friday."

"Oh, ha." She paused. "I don't know, you're probably right about the spacing." She scanned the room. Mauve carpeting covered the floor. The tables were covered with deep dusty rose cloths in winter, to make the room seem warmer. The east wall gave a view of the snow-filled gorge. Sunlight sparkled off the icicles formed on the granite by the waterfall, a welcome change from the gloom of the day before. The contrast between the blue-white iridescence of the winter outside and the warmth of the room had a lot to do with the animation of the people eating Meg's food, she thought. *They're happy, they're full. This is a business that gives people a little peace of mind. And I like it.* She pushed the thought of Myles, and a home and children a little further into her subconscious.

A plump blond woman at the foyer entrance waved agitatedly in Quill's direction. "I almost forgot about Mrs. McIntosh," she said suddenly. "Poor thing!" She tucked her hand into John's arm. "Let's go relieve her agitation."

"That," murmured John, "will be quite a trick without Prozac."

On the way through the foyer to the office, Elaine McIntosh circled them like a retriever asked to herd sheep—plucky but easily distracted. She was a pretty, plump, beautifully shaped woman who wore well-tailored trousers and plain blouses trimmed with a bit of lace on the collar or the cuffs, high-necked and long-sleeved.

Quill had discovered that Elaine's physical appearance, combined with a more or less permanent state of soft-spoken distress, brought out odd impulses in men. Even John, who was as reserved around women as the Pope, fussed over her. He settled her on the couch in Quill's office, buzzed the kitchen for tea, and pulled the McIntosh wedding file from the drawer in Quill's cabinet with a minimum of words and a maximum of composure. With a cup of hot Red Zinger in her hand and John's solid height next to her on the couch, Elaine exhibited all the aplomb of a woman who owned a large amount of property over the San Andreas Fault. This was an improvement over her usual state of mind, which was that of a periodontophobe waiting for a root canal.

"There's two things," she said breathlessly. "The first is, I just wanted to thank you again for the use of this lovely, lovely building. It's so antique! It's so historic! You know, Claire—I mean, her father—well, our money is plumbing fixture money and Alphonse is so . . ." She waved helplessly.

"Fatheaded?" Quill ventured under her breath.

Mrs. McIntosh twisted her rings in agitation. "Ritzy," she finally managed. "The Santinis are bigwigs. My husband Vittorio gets so mad when I say that. He says money made in plumbing fixtures is as good as anybody's, but you know, it's not!"

"Of course it is," Quill said indignantly. "My goodness."

A brass plaque set near the fireplace in the Inn's foyer read "Est. 1693," the implication being that the Inn building with its copper roof and weathered shakes had been there for three hundred years. And most people, Quill knew, thought that antiquity conferred prestige. Quill never passed the plaque without a mild sense of guilt over the aristocratic implications; three hundred years ago, the Inn overlooking the Falls of Hemlock Gorge had been a one-room log cabin owned and operated by a lady of dubious virtue called Turkey Lil. From the War of 1812 on, the Inn had been added to, until it reached a sprawling twenty thousand square feet mid-century. Subsequent owners had adapted the Inn to fit various purposes, and it had been a girls' school, a rest home, and even, briefly, the home of the deservedly unknown Civil War General C. C. Hemlock. The Inn was a lot of things, but it wasn't, in Mrs. McIntosh's parlance, ritzy, aristocratic or even prestigious. Merely old.

"And the second thing?" Quill prompted.

"It's Vittorio, my husband." Mrs. McIntosh apologized and Quill got the impression she was apologizing for the marital relationship as well as the existence of the man himself. "Actually it's Vittorio's mother, Tutti."

"Tutti?" asked Quill, leaning forward so she could hear better. Elaine McIntosh became almost inaudible when stressed, and since Elaine seemed to be stressed all the time, no one at the Inn had been entirely certain whether the McIntosh celebration was a wedding or an anniversary until Mrs. McIntosh confirmed the plans in writing last August. A secondary frustration was that no one knew why the McIntoshes—who were clearly Italian—had a Scottish cognomen; Meg had given up altogether on being able to figure that one out. "Has she decided not to come after all?"

Elaine gestured. Her eyes filled with tears. Quill, who'd been seriously alarmed the first, second, and third time Elaine's eyes had filled with tears over a crisis reached automatically for the box of Kleenex on her desk and handed it over. John, rarely demonstrative, put a sympathetic hand on her shoulder.

Elaine, hand stuffed against her nose, shook her head and wailed, "No! No!"

"She *is* coming," guessed Quill.

Elaine nodded, gulped, and folded the Kleenex into a neat oblong. "She's coming. And she had a vision. Tutti's famous for her visions. She's always right."

"A vision? You mean, as in a psychic vision."

"Yes! About . . . you know."

Quill, who'd been experiencing some mild concern about her level of tolerance—an essential trait of any innkeeper—for some hours since she'd allowed Alphonse Santini to provoke her into battery, made a conscious effort to be calm. "Your mother-in-law had a vision about the wedding?"

Elaine picked up a fistful of Kleenex. "She said . . . she said . . . he was going to leave Claire. At the altar. That the wedding's not going to come off. That I've been pushing. That it's my fault. That he really doesn't want to marry Claire."

"Of course he does," soothed Quill. "I mean, all grooms are supposed to be a little anxious before the wedding."

"The thing is, I just know everyone thinks that Claire's marrying him because . . . you know . . . plumbing fixture money. Not the same!"

"Oh, Elaine, Al loves Claire. I'm sure he'll make a good and reliable . . ." She tried to think of a polite substitute for demagogue and gave up. There were limits to her policy of honesty. "You've spoken with him, John, about the bachelor party. He seemed . . . you know, didn't he?"

"Al Santini?" said John. "Oh, yeah, Quill. Very you know."

"But you don't understand!" wailed Elaine. "Tutti wants to call the whole wedding off!"

"With all due respect for your mother-in-law, how can she?" Quill asked gently.

"You don't know her," Elaine said tragically. "You just—what's that?"

A soft tap came on the office door.

"Our receptionist, I think." Quill called, "Come in, please," with a guilty sense of relief. Dina poked her head around the edge of the door, her eyes large. A low-pitched wailing from outside accompanied her. "Excuse me. Quill? You'd better come."

"What's that noise?"

Dina glanced nervously over her shoulder. "It's Mrs. McIntosh. The mother-in-law. Claire's grandmother. She says to call her Tutti. She's standing in the middle of the foyer. Prophesying."

CHAPTER 6

"There will be three knocks!" cried Tutti McIntosh. "Three knocks on the door! And then . . . blood, *blood*, BLOOD!" The hairy little dog in her arms yapped twice. Tutti rather absentmindedly set the dog down on the Oriental rug. With a pugnacious scowl he squatted and piddled on the celadon and ivory rose medallion in the center.

"Oh, Tutti, dear!" Elaine McIntosh burst into tears.

Quill, nonplussed, stood for a moment to assess the situation. Claire's grandmother was plump and wide, with the frilly softness of a crocheted doll over a telephone. She had dimples, soft white hair, and very pink cheeks. The dog was some sort of pug. Tutti was wearing a fur coat the same color and texture as her little dog—a burnished red that was close to Quill's own hair color. Her prophecy wail was low, windy, and dirgelike, which made it easy to hear Dina's perplexed explanation.

"She came in. Saw the plaque that says 'Established 1693.' Closed her eyes. Spun around for a second saying 'prophecy' a couple of times and then started hollering about three knocks on the door and blood, blood, blood, blood, *blood* . . ."

"Stop," said Quill.

Dina gazed consideringly at the little old lady for a moment, then said indignantly, "I didn't do a thing to her."

"Of course you didn't," Elaine McIntosh said in a helpless way. "She does this all the time!" She grabbed her mother-in-law's wrist and shook it gently. "Tutti. Tutti! TUTTI!"

"What!" Mrs. McIntosh demanded in a suddenly pragmatic tone of voice.

"Are you all right?"

"I'm fine, dear. Thank you." Mrs. McIntosh regarded Quill, John, Dina, and Doreen—who had appeared at the dining room entrance rolling her mop-bucket—with cheerful equanimity. "How do you all do?"

"Lot better since that caterwauling stopped," said Doreen. "What'n the hell was that all about? You woulda thought . . ." Her suspicious gaze fell on the carpet. "Dog pee!" she murmured. "Dog pee. On my carpet."

"Tatiana didn't do it," Mrs. McIntosh said immediately. She bent to pick up the pug, who backed away, snarling ferociously. She sang, "Good doggie, good doggie, good—OW!" Then she dropped it.

"Outta the way," Doreen snarled. She jerked the bucket forward, the water sloshing. Tatiana stood defiantly over the small pool on the rug and yapped.

"G'wan," said Doreen, brandishing the mop. "You little bastard."

"Doreen," John said mildly.

Tatiana's yaps ascended the scale and increased in pitch. Dina clapped her hands over her ears. Doreen bent over, pushed her nose into Tatiana's and roared, "SHUT UP!"

Tatiana's little pink mouth closed. Her button eyes

bulged. She panted, yipped once, rolled her eyes up into her head, and spasmed. She rolled on her back and lay upside down, all four legs in the air, motionless.

"My God," breathed Dina. "It's dead!"

"Huh," Doreen said, pleased.

Quill clapped her hands over her mouth.

"She's not dead," Tutti said briskly, "she's fainted. Actually, she just wants us to think she's fainted. She's faking. Does it all the time." She nudged Tatiana with her toe. "Up, darling. Up. Up. Up."

Tatiana, still upside down, opened her eyes and gave Doreen an evil look.

"Come to Mummy!"

Tatiana rolled to her feet, gave a standing jump, and landed in Tutti's arms.

"Wow!" said Dina. "That's a valuable dog, Mrs. McIntosh. I mean, jecz. Did you see that, Quill? John? How did you train her to do that, Mrs. McIntosh?"

Doreen, on her knees scrubbing at the damp spot on the rug, looked up at Tatiana with a steady considering stare. Tatiana stared steadily back.

"Um, Doreen," said Quill. "Maybe we could all just kind of forget this. Mrs. McIntosh, I'm Sarah Quill—"

"Sarah Quilliam," she said with a gracious air. Her voice was high and sweet. "The *noted* painter. I am very, very pleased to meet you. I've seen your work in the galleries in New York. Such an eye for color, my dear! Such sensitivity! *You* of all people should understand the aura here. You feel it, too, don't you?"

"Well, actually," said Quill, "I don't . . . feel what, Mrs. McIntosh?"

Her voice dropped an octave. "The Coming Disaster. I felt the vibrations as soon as I walked in that door. This marriage must *not* take place!"

"Tutti!" Elaine wailed.

"Where's Claire?" Tutti demanded briskly.

"Claire?" asked Quill. "Um. Yes. Claire."

"The bride," John said helpfully.

"Oh! Of course! Come to think of it, I haven't seen her today. Have you, Dina?"

"Nope."

Mrs. McIntosh gestured, her bracelets clanking. "I must see her. As soon as she arrives. There is danger here, I tell you. Three knocks at the door, and then blood, blo—"

"Mrs. McIntosh!" Quill said firmly.

"Claire took the Caddy to pick up her father at the train station, Tutti," said Elaine. "They should have been here by now, but with the snow coming on so fast, they must have been delayed."

"I told Vic to take the train," said Mrs. McIntosh. "It's more comfortable. It's safe. And a lot cheaper." She adjusted the large diamond brooch on her scarf with a virtuous air. "I just hope he doesn't get into an accident coming from Ithaca. Norton almost ditched my limo twice on the way up from Boston."

"They'll be fine. Vic's a wonderful driver." Elaine looked a question at Quill. "Now, Tutti, why don't I take you up to your room?"

"What a good idea! We've put you in the Provençal suite, Mrs. McIntosh. I'm sure you'll be very comfortable up there. And would you like a tea? We've got fresh scones and Devonshire cream. And our hot chocolate is very good."

The little dog in her arms barked.

"And I'm sure we can find a biscuit for, um . . ."

"Tatiana," Mrs. McIntosh supplied.

"Of course, um . . . good doggie," Quill said inadequately.

"We don't hold with dog pee here," Doreen said in an ominous way. "I don't do dog pee. Windows. Terlits. Refrigerators. I do all that. I don't do dog pee."

"Of course you don't!" Mrs. McIntosh said sunnily. "Now, if this very good-looking young man could escort me upstairs, I think I could use a little rest. It's Mr. Raintree, isn't it?"

John inclined his head gravely.

"Are you married, Mr. Raintree?"

"No, Mrs. McIntosh. Not yet."

Mrs. McIntosh took his arm and twinkled at him. "Call me Tutti! Everyone does. And I'd adore it if you could meet my granddaughter. She's single, too."

Quill watched them proceed up the winding stairs to the upper floors. Tatiana, flopped over Tutti's furry arm, regarded Doreen unblinkingly with her shoe button eyes.

"I didn't know you had two daughters, Mrs. McIntosh," said Dina.

Elaine took a deep breath. "I don't. She doesn't either. Have another granddaughter, I mean. Oh, Quill, what am I going to do? You see what I mean?"

"Well, I think your mother-in-law is *cool*," Dina said in a reverent tone. "I mean, is she really, like, psychic and all? Did you see how she knew John's *name* before anybody, like, introduced him?"

Quill tapped the nameplate under the "Reception" sign, which read, *Your Hosts: Sarah Quilliam/Margaret Quilliam/John Raintree*.

"Honest, Quill, she walked right in here and started prophesying right away. She didn't have a chance to read a thing! Besides, John could have been anybody. Like, another guest or something."

"I don't think so," Quill said repressively. "Elaine, why don't we go back to my office and rework the plans for the reception? We're essentially doubling the number of guests, is that right? It's going to put a bit of strain on the kit—''

The knocker on the Inn's oak door sounded once, twice, and a third time, echoing impressively in the foyer. Dina screamed. Doreen raised her mop like a club, grasping the handle firmly in both hands.

''My God,'' said Elaine. ''Oh, my God.'' She backed against the newel post to the stairway, quivering.

The knocks on the door were succeeded by a series of thumps and bangs. Quill marched across the foyer and flung the door wide. A gust of cold air blew snow across the Oriental rug. An extremely cross male voice ordered Quill to get the goddamned luggage.

''Vic!'' cried Elaine. ''You made it! I was so worried!''

''Roads were a goddamned pain,'' he snarled. ''Claire? Will you get your ass in here, for Chrissakes?''

''Quill, this is my husband, Vittorio,'' Elaine fluttered.

Vic grunted. This was the first she'd seen of Vittorio McIntosh. And there was blood all over his hands.

''I hadn't even heard of him before, other than the name on his gold card,'' Quill said to Meg and John in the kitchen a few hours later.

''Well, I have,'' said John. ''The fortune is privately held, but a conservative estimate would be in the area of fifty million. And Nora Cahill's information was sound. There have been rumors about his links to organized crime for years.''

''He was bleeding?'' asked Meg.

''Of course he was bleeding!'' Quill, exasperated, bit into a leftover pâté puff. It was soggy. ''That's why I had to give Dina an aspirin. He'd barked his knuckles on the door knocker trying to get in out of the snow. He said it was locked.''

"The door's never locked until lights-out," said Meg.

"If you ask me, Mrs. McIntosh—I mean, Tutti—locked it when she came in," Quill said gloomily. "That old lady's a corker. And she sure doesn't like our Alphonse. Did John tell you what she did to him at dinner?''

"No!"

"Hot coffee," said John.

"All over his trousers," said Quill.

Meg grinned. She was sharpening her kitchen knives. She tested the blade of her favorite paring knife with her thumb, then asked, "What's Vittorio like?"

"Well, I'll tell you," Quill said crossly. "He could be Alphonse Santini's older uglier brother."

"That bad, huh? Dang." She counted through the knives laid out on the counter. "I'm one short."

"Check the dishwasher," John suggested.

"They know better than to put my good knives in the dishwasher.''

"He called me dolly twice," Quill said loudly, feeling ignored. "Why is it, Meg, that women are just nicer than men?''

"Nicer? You think Nora Cahill's nicer? I mean, here Santini's her sworn enemy and she ends up in cahoots with him just like that. All for a good story."

"It's a lousy story," Quill said firmly. "Back to my point. Women are nicer than men. If you put one hundred women in a room with one hundred men, eighty percent of the women would be nice versus . . . versus . . ."—she waved her hands in the air—"twenty percent of the men. Would be nice."

Meg and John exchanged looks. "So!" Meg said brightly. "The Santinis and the McIntoshes will all be gone and it'll all be over in three days. Unless it keeps on snowing. You mind if I switch the television on? I want to get the weather report.''

''No you don't,'' Quill said indignantly. ''You just want to see if Nora Cahill's plastered my face and my boots and my ugly coat all over the eleven o'clock news.''

''I do not!'' Meg made a deprecatory face. ''Well, maybe a little. But I also want to be sure that the weather's not going to interfere with the food order getting here from New York in time. I grabbed Elaine after dinner and we finally reworked the buffet menu.''

''Are we going to hire extra help?''

Meg, clicking though the channels of the small television set built over the Zero King refrigerator, nodded in an abstracted way. ''Yeah, but I can't do much cooking—so it's a lot of fresh stuff: caviar, crab, shrimp. Dull, dull, *dull!*''

''And expensive,'' Quill said.

John agreed, then said, ''There it is. The Syracuse channel.''

Meg shrieked. ''You're on! You're on!''

Quill stuck her fingers in her ears and hummed loudly, but try as she might, she couldn't keep her eyes shut. So she saw, although she didn't hear, a full color videotape of herself in her ugly down coat, hair every which way, a scowl on her face, sock Nora Cahill in the nose with her boot.

The station cut to a commercial.

''I need a haircut,'' said Quill.

''You need a new coat,'' said Meg. ''Don't turn it off! Her commentary's next.''

''That's not Nora Cahill,'' said Quill.

''It sure isn't,'' said Meg. ''It's some guy.''

''She told me she was on vacation,'' said Quill, with

hope. "Maybe she just forgot about the story. What kind of story is a small-town traffic ticket, anyhow?"

". . . that news flash repeated," the male anchor said soberly into the camera. "The body of Syracuse television newswoman Nora Cahill was found under the traffic light of an intersection in the central New York village of Hemlock Falls. Sheriff Frank Dorset has refused to release details of the death pending investigation. No further details other than the report of the death are available at this time. KSGY-TV will be the first to bring you periodic updates on this tragic event. And now, for a look at the weather. The word is snow . . ."

"She was killed? Here?!" shrieked Meg. "Right here?!"

John reached up and switched the television off.

"You don't suppose . . ." said Quill. Her mind leaped to the last time she saw Nora, in angry conversation with Alphonse Santini. Except that it wasn't the last time she'd seen Nora. The last time, the very last time, struck her with the force of a fall on thick ice; she'd been wiping her cheeks free of the muddy spray from Quill's boots.

"Car accident," said John. "Had to be, in this weather."

"They would have *said* car accident," Meg insisted. "And that bozo Dorset refusing to release details? It doesn't sound good at all. Poor Nora! Maybe we should poke around a little bit, Quillie. You know, a lot of people must have had it in for that poor thing."

"No," said Quill. "No investigation. No murder inquiry. We are out of that business and into the Inn business. Full-time. This time I really mean it."

"Things have been so quiet lately," Meg complained.

"Quiet for you, maybe. I don't need to remind you that while you were peacefully chopping away in your

kitchen I spent practically the entire morning in jail.''
Except, she thought, *for the part where I tried to whack Nora with my boots.*

"Three hours," Meg muttered. "Big deal."

"You try it! God, I feel awful. I mean, the last time I saw her, I tried to break her nose.''

"Oh, Quill. You were really provoked. Anyone would have tried to—um . . .''

"Um, what? I feel like a jerk. I'm a swine. I don't know why I ever agreed to run this place. All I've seemed to do is create one huge mess after the other. It's not worth it.''

"Of course it's worth it,'' Meg said stoutly. "We have a terrific business, great guests . . .''

"Oh, *right*, Claire the cranky bride, Elaine the water faucet, Vittorio the mysterious Scottish-Italian, *and* let's not forget his psychic mother. And who has to deal with all this craziness while you retreat to this chrome and stainless steel haven? Me, that's who! And poor John has to run around cleaning up after all the messes I create.''

"Quill, you are hardly responsible for Alphonse Santini and his choice of prospective in-laws,'' said John. There was a faint grin behind his eyes.

"She's hysterical,'' said Meg. "And about time, too. I was wondering when all of this would hit her.''

" 'Three knocks,' '' Quill repeated with what she felt to be justifiable bitterness. " 'Three knocks and then, blood, blood . . . ' ''

Three knocks sounded at the back door. They tolled through the kitchen like the bell announcing the arrival of the Ghost of Christmas Yet to Come. Like Scrooge, Quill felt like flinging the covers over her head, but the only thing at hand was a dish towel. She clutched Meg. "Sassafras,'' Meg said, patting her arm, "or comfrey.

Herbal teas'll help you get right to sleep."

"I'll get it." John walked unhurriedly to the back door and snapped on the outside light. There was a murmur of male voices, John's voice louder than the others, an argumentative note to it. The door slammed and he stepped back into the kitchen. His dark hair was sprinkled with snowflakes.

"Quill," he said, so quietly that she had to strain to hear him, "get upstairs and lock yourself in your room. No questions. Just do it. Meg, get Howie Murchison on the line as fast as you can."

The back door rattled. A cold eddy of outside air curled around Quill's feet.

"Move, Quill!"

"But, John, what in heaven's name is going on? Why should I lock myself in my room?"

"Sarah Quilliam?" Frank Dorset pulled the hood of his dark blue parka away from his face. Davy Kiddermeister shuffled behind. Their snow boots left muddy tracks on the floor.

"You know very well who she is," Meg said tartly. "Have you come to apologize? It's about bloody time."

"You're under arrest, Ms. Quilliam, as a material witness to the murder of Nora Cahill. You have the right to representation by an attorney for your defense. If you do not have an attorney, the court will appoint one for you. You have the right to remain silent." He grinned, his teeth sharp and yellow. "And I sure as hell hope you do. Nothing worse than a yapping female behind bars."

The drive to the Tompkins County Sheriff's Department had taken about five minutes, Quill figured, which meant it must be about eleven-thirty. She wasn't sure. Deputy Dave had taken her watch. She was sitting under the halogen lights in the sheriff's office huddled in

John's parka. She'd been too dazed to find her own coat, and she missed its comforting warmth. The room felt too small. The linoleum—which had been installed at some point in the dim and faraway sixties—was as cracked and peeling as it had been that morning, although there was a fresh smell of disinfectant. Metal filing cabinets lined one wall. There were two metal desks, of the type found in every state and federal office Quill had ever seen: battleship-gray, incredibly heavy, with tarnished strips of chrome along the desk top edge. She sat behind the larger one, in the black Naugahyde chair that still, she thought, held a faint scent of Myles McHale. Frank Dorset balanced one buttock on the edge of this desk and leaned into her face. She pushed her feet along the floor and edged back, hitting the green-painted wall. Dave Kiddermeister sat at the adjacent desk, holding a small tape recorder.

"You want to go over this again?" Dorset asked. His voice was calm. Silky.

Davy cleared his throat. "She might better wait for Mr. Murchison, Sheriff."

Dorset twisted his head over his shoulder, so that Quill couldn't see his face. "Your shift about up, Deputy?"

"Nossir." Quill could hear both embarrassment and determination in his tones. "I mean, yessir, it is, but I should prob'ly stay here. You might need a wit—"

Dorset interrupted like a knife shaving beef. "That wasn't a question."

"Sir?"

"I said get your ass out of here."

Quill, who recognized that she was too mad to be scared, said, "I'll be fine, Davy. Don't worry about a thing."

"Thing," Dorset repeated softly. "Not a thing." He said loudly, "Deputy!"

Quill jumped.

Davy shuffled reluctantly to his feet.

"Leave the recorder, son."

Davy put the tape recorder near Quill's left hand, then shrugged himself into his anorak. "I'll be around, Sheriff. Just down the street at the Croh Bar."

Dorset grunted. The clock on the wall filled the silence with a soft and steady tick-tick-tick. She heard Davy close the outside door, then the crunch of his feet in the snow in the parking lot. His car door slammed. The engine turned over. He drove out of the lot and out of hearing.

Dorset leaned close. He smelled like peppermint toothpaste, sour sweat, and damp wool. "Ms. Quilliam? One more time. When did you last see Nora Cahill?"

"Right here. About twelve-fifteen this afternoon."

"She got back to the Inn around five-thirty this evening."

"Well, I didn't see her," said Quill.

"I can spit from one end of that place to the other. And you didn't see her? Not once? All evening?"

"It was a busy night, Sheriff. In case you hadn't noticed, we've got a full house."

"Huh."

He was so close she could see flecks of red on his canine teeth.

"Did you have pizza for dinner?"

His right hand came up, palm out. He shoved it into her left shoulder so hard that she spun and smacked her cheek against the wall. He grabbed the teal scarf at her throat, twisted it, and pulled her forward. "You listen," he hissed, "to me. You get that? You *listen*"—he whipped the scarf back and forth, pulling her from side to side—"to *me!* Are you listening?"

"Yes," Quill said calmly. "I'm listening."

He released the scarf with a swift, upward movement that jerked her chin backward. "I want you to sit there. Sit right there." He swung himself off the desk and turned his back. He whipped around so suddenly that she jumped. "You sitting? You sitting just nice and quiet, like?"

Quill nodded. It was an effort to keep her face still. She wanted to gasp for air. She took slow, shallow breaths through her nose. She felt as if she were suffocating.

"Good."

The tall metal cabinet was padlocked. Dorset pulled his ring of keys from his belt and opened it, and took out a small, hand-held videocassette viewer from the top shelf. He began to hum in a high nasal whine, an insinuating, minor-keyed tune that Quill had never heard before. He set the viewer on the desk, then scrabbled inside the cabinet for a tape. He turned, shoved the cassette into the viewer, and plugged the cord into an outlet on the wall. He swayed a little as he moved, humming.

Quill took a long, quiet breath.

He whipped his head around. "You sitting? Nice and calm, like? You little, little thing." He leaned across the desk, shoving his face against her cheek. He whispered, "Watch. This." Holding his head against her, he reached out and turned the viewer on.

The tape was black-and-white. Flickering. Grainy. The tape from the hidden camera. The LED flashed the date and 09:15, 09:16, 09:17. P.M. P.M. P.M.

The remote switched on, triggered by the approach of a car headed west on main. The car slowed, stopped, the headlights casting a dim field across the snowy street.

Someone opened the driver's door and got out. Nora Cahill, her sharp nose prominent for a moment, bent down in front of the headlights to knock the snow from her boots.

A second figure emerged from the darkness. Tall. Slender. Wearing a long down coat and a round fur hat.

My God, thought Quill. She knew that coat. And that hat. And she hadn't been able to find them half an hour ago.

There was a pause in the tape. Quill strained her eyes. The other person, the one who was not Nora—*the one*, thought Quill, *who is not me! Not me!*—pulled an envelope from the depths of the coat and handed it to Nora. She thumbed through the contents.

"Money," Quill said involuntarily. "Money."

"Yowser," Dorset said in his soft silky voice.

The tape jumped, flickered, and resumed its steady whirr. Nora stuffed the money in her purse, tossed the envelope to the ground, and turned.

The dark figure stirred. Swung. And struck.

Nora fell, faceup, the headlights illuminating her face. Her lips moved. Silently. Quill shuddered and closed her eyes. She heard a click. The tape stopped. She opened her eyes to see Nora, frozen in time, her hand lifted in a last gesture, the fingers splayed out like claws, mouth open, eyes open.

"Dead," said Dorset.

"How?" asked Quill.

"You should know."

Quill shook her head.

Dorset pulled at her coat. John's coat. "When did you last see Nora Cahill?"

"This is ridiculous," said Quill. "Look. The time on the monitor. 9:23 p.m. I was at the Inn this evening."

"You got somebody besides your sister's gonna

swear where you were between five after nine and nine-thirty? 'Cause that's all the time it'd take to hop down the road and off that broad. Maybe less. Haven't found a witness yet could swear to a time frame that tight in court. We blow this tape up, we're gonna see your cute little face right there.''

"You will not," snapped Quill. "And somebody stole my coat. They must have."

He leaned close again, and blew out once, twice, against her cheek. Quill felt her stomach roil. "Just. Tell. Me," he coaxed. "Just me." He sat up suddenly, like a dog that hears the approach of an intruder. He laid his hand on her shoulder and squeezed it painfully tight. Quill heard a car door slam, then the sound of two—no, three people outside. There was a banging on the door, and then Howie, Meg, and John came in, the three of them abreast, like the cavalry in the kind of movies they didn't make anymore.

"Hi, guys," said Quill, dismayed to hear the quiver in her voice.

Howie glanced briefly at her, then turned his attention to Dorset. Meg, for once completely silent, came to the chair and stood to her right; John took up a position on the left. Meg reached down and squeezed Quill's hand hard.

"What's the meaning of this, Dorset?" Howie asked mildly.

"Should be obvious. I have a warrant for the little lady's arrest as a material witness to the murder of Nora Cahill this evening at 9:23. The good news is that she won't be charged with murder until the coroner's report comes in. Should be some time tomorrow. The deceased was taken to the county morgue not forty-five minutes ago."

"Can I see the warrant, please?"

Dorset pulled it from his shirt pocket. Howie unfolded it and read intently.

"This is absolutely ridiculous, Sheriff," Meg snapped. "Quill was at the Inn all evening. She was never out of my sight."

"Never?" said Dorset. "Never's a long time. I may as well tell you now, I've got affidavits coming from a couple of people up to the Inn."

"Who?" Meg tightened her hand on Quill's shoulder. "What kind of—Quill, *what's the matter with your shoulder!?*"

"Gave me a bit of trouble," said Dorset.

Meg's face turned white. John took an involuntary step forward.

"You watch it, Raintree," said Dorset. "I've read your record."

Quill stood up and grabbed John. Meg regained her breath and shrieked, "You hit my sister!"

"Meg, I'm fine. Let's not get too excited here, okay?"

"QUILL, for God's *sake*. What the *hell* do you mean, gave you a bit of trouble? Who the hell do you think you are?"

"Deputy'll bear me out on that."

"The hell he will," stormed Meg, who'd apparently lost the variety of curses usually at her disposal. "Get out of my way, you son of a bitch. I'm taking my sister home! Howie?!"

Howie folded up the warrant and tossed it on the desk. "I'd like to see this videotape."

"File a request with the judge."

"And this physical evidence found at the scene?"

"Envelope from the Inn. Says so right at the top. Decedent's name written in the accused's handwriting on the front."

"Who identified the handwriting?"

"File a request with the judge."

"Did the medical examiner give a preliminary cause of death?"

Dorset grinned. "Nope."

"He must have had some idea."

"Didn't say a word to me."

"You didn't ask him?"

"Didn't have to. Pretty much could see for myself."

"She was stabbed," Quill said tiredly. "With what seemed to be one of the knives from our kitchen."

Meg's hand jumped. Quill didn't think it was possible for her to get any more pale, but she did. "Oh, no, Meg! I saw the videotape. He showed me. It's right there."

John's right hand shot out like a snake. He pulled the cassette from the viewer and turned toward the door, seemingly all in one motion.

"Hold it," snarled Dorset. He snapped open his holster and drew his pistol. Meg screamed in furious indignation.

Howie said, "Put it away, Sheriff. John?"

"No," John said.

"You have to. Give it back."

"You're going to leave it with this bastard? There's no telling what he'll do with it."

"It's the law," said Howie. "I'm sorry."

"Is Quill coming back with us?"

Howie looked at the sheriff questioningly.

Dorset shook his head.

"Don't be a fool, Dorset. I'll get in front of a real judge tomorrow and she'll be out by nightfall."

"File a request with a judge."

John set the videotape on the desk. "This is some kind of setup, Howie."

"That's clear. The question is, why? Dorset, I'd like a few minutes alone with my client."

"Sorry."

"What the—" Howie calmed himself with a visible effort. "You can't deny her counsel."

"When she's accused of something, I can't, you're right about that. But she's being held as a witness. I got thirty-six hours before I have to let you talk to her at all. Now, tomorrow? Tomorrow after she's been accused of this murder, you can have all the time you want with her." His eyes flicked over Quill's breasts. John made a fierce noise.

"Wait for me in the car, will you, John?" said Howie.

"Murchison. This is bullshit. Absolute bullshit."

"I know. It's better if you wait for me in the car. Trust me. Please."

John shook his head and buttoned his coat. "I'll walk back to the Inn."

"You sure? It's cold out there."

"I need it." John paused in the doorway and looked back. Dorset shifted from one foot to the other under the stare. John opened the door, slid out noiselessly, and was gone.

Quill cleared her throat. "There's nothing we can do, is there, Howie?"

Meg's face was fierce. "What do you mean?! Of course there is! You're not going to leave her here!"

"I don't have much choice, Meg."

"Choice? What do you mean, choice? She's got to stay in here? Overnight?!"

Quill tried a laugh. A little weak, but a laugh nonetheless. "You didn't think a day in jail was so awful this morning, Meg."

"That was different. I thought it might teach you something about traffic tickets."

"Oh, you did, did you?"

"Well, yeah! You can't just go around thinking

you're above the law. You can't—'' She bit her words off in mid-sentence. ''So she has to stay here? Then I'm staying, too.''

''No, you're not,'' said Dorset.

''I am *not* leaving my sister in the Tompkins County jail overnight and that's that.''

''There's only one cot in the cell,'' said Quill.

''So one of us can sleep on the floor.''

''Which one? It's concrete. And cold.''

''Concrete.'' Meg set her chin. ''So what? I don't trust this creep.''

''Meg, I'll be fine. Come by in the morning with some hot coffee, will you? And a toothbrush and stuff like that. I'll be better off if you're on the outside.'' She forced herself to smile. ''Honest. You can nag Howie into getting bail set for me as early as possible. Okay?''

Meg scowled.

''Please, Meg. We'll get this all straightened out in the morning.''

''What do you think, Howie?''

The lawyer's steady gaze had never really left Dorset. ''I think,'' he said easily, ''that Frank here ought to remember the number of friends I have on the State Supreme Court.''

''Sure thing, Counselor.''

''I want to see where she's going to be for the night.''

''Suit yourself.''

Dorset slouched through the metal door labeled LOCK UP. Meg put her arm around Quill's waist and, with Howie leading the way, they followed Dorset into the cell. The overhead light was harsh, the cell as bare as it had been that morning.

''She'll need another blanket,'' said Meg.

Dorset grunted and returned to the office.

Meg glared after him and turned to Quill. "And a nightgown. You can't sleep in that skirt and sweater."

"I'll be fine," said Quill, who had no intention of taking off her clothes within thirty blocks of Frank Dorset. She gave Meg a warning pinch.

Meg stared back at her, reached over, hugged her, and whispered, "Use it. If you have to. Even if you don't." She slipped the paring knife she'd been sharpening in the kitchen into Quill's hand. Quill slid it into her skirt pocket, then sat on the cot.

Dorset returned and tossed a thin wool blanket through the open door, then gestured Meg and Howie out of the cell. He clanged the door shut and locked it. Despite herself, Quill shivered.

"I'll take the key," said Howie.

"The hell you will."

"The hell I won't. Is there a duplicate?"

"Deputy carries one."

"I'm just down the street, Dorset. If you need to get her out before I'm back in the morning, call me."

"Fuck you, Murchison."

Howie's voice never rose above its mild tone of inquiry. "I don't know what the hell you're planning, Dorset. You know as well as I do that, at the very least, I can have this arrest tossed out because you prevented me from seeing my client privately. I'll tell you this. No matter where you are in the next few days, I'll prosecute you to the fullest extent the law allows—and maybe a little more than that. This woman has friends. She and her sister have a national reputation. You step an inch over the line, and it'll be safer for you in jail than out."

"You don't scare me, Murchison."

"Then you're a fool. Give me that key."

"Howie," said Quill, "don't. For one thing, what if there's a fire? For another, he'd be a real idiot to assault

my, um—virtue—after you and John and Meg have witnessed all of this. You guys go and do what you have
to do to get me out of here—okay?''

"You're sure, Quillie?'' Meg, pale, rubbed her face
with both hands. "I really think I ought to stay with
you.''

"I'm sure. I'll be all right. Just go away and do what
you have to do to get me out of here.''

"We'll be back in the morning,'' said Howie. "I'll
drive to Ithaca tonight, get Judge Anderson out of bed,
and be back about six. Try and get some sleep.'' He
frowned. "Dorset? Watch yourself.''

At first Quill was grateful for the overhead light. The
cell block was very quiet. Outside it had started to snow
again, and the whisper/slide of a heavy fall brushed
against the barred window. She lay back on the thin
mattress, pulling the blanket over her shoulders, wrig-
gling her stockinged feet through the folds at the bottom,
trying to warm them. Meg's paring knife made a lump
in her pocket, and she ended up sticking it under the
pillow.

She fell into a broken doze, jerked awake every now
and then by the relentless overhead light when her eyelids blinked half open. Eventually, she slid into heavy
sleep.

She woke to whispered voices.

Confused, she sat up, swung her feet to the floor, and
encountered cold concrete.

"... in there right now,'' came a murmur, "trust
me ...''

A response, derisive.

"... show ya ...''

The metal door swung open. Dorset's lanky figure

shambled through the flood of light from the office.
Quill blinked, blinded by the overhead light. Dorset
whistled as you whistle for a dog. There was someone
behind him. Shorter than Dorset, about Quill's own
height. Shapeless in her down coat. Face concealed by
her fur hat.

Suddenly, the overhead light went out.

She flung her hand up, shading her eyes against the
glare from the office door. The man? woman? behind
the sheriff stepped back, arm upraised. Light flashed
against steel. The arm came down, once.

Dorset screamed.

And again.

Dorset twisted, hands scrabbling for the unknown
face. Quill willed her eyes open, strained against the
dark.

The knife came down a third time, hard. Blood came
from Dorset's mouth and nose. He cried, "Uh! Uh!"
and fell in a clatter of boots and keys, arms outstretched.

The door to the office slammed shut. The cell was
totally dark. There was a fumbling in the dark. The cell
door clicked open. Quill shoved herself against the cold
wall and grabbed the paring knife from beneath the pillow. She held it steady, blade out. There was the sound
of dragging, then a shove and a grunt. Dorset's body
rolled against her feet. She gasped and flung herself
away, bruising her hands and knees on the iron bed
frame.

A clatter and rattle of something dropped. The cell
door clanged shut, and the lock clicked. The door to
outside opened; the down-coated figure slipped through.
Quill went to her knees and fumbled along the floor.
She felt the knife, the butcher knife.

"Sheriff? Sheriff?"

"No," said Dorset. "No. Help. Help."

There was a horrible gurgle, like waste bubbling from a clogged pipe.

It didn't take him long to die.

CHAPTER 7

"Drink that tea right up," Doreen said with rough affection. "It's a mercy that bozo didn't come after you, too."

Quill, freshly showered and in a white terry cloth robe, drank half a cup of the Red Zinger and sat on her couch. Meg moved restlessly around the room, successively picking up a small ceramic vase, a replica of a Chinese horse, then a crystal swan, and putting each one down again. "You can't pin down the time of the murder any more exactly than about dawn?" asked Meg.

"John said he didn't stop to look at the time when he heard me scream, and Davy didn't give me my watch back until you and Howie came with the order for release." Quill looked at it. "But it's eight-thirty now, in case you were wondering."

"Oh, ha."

"Howie must have gotten that judge up in the middle of the night. I can't believe you guys came back for me before the sun was up."

"Anderson was pretty annoyed at Howie."

"You went with Howie to Ithaca?"

"What did you expect me to do? Go to sleep?! Be-

135

sides, the roads were awful and I didn't think he should
go alone.''

''Well, thanks.''

''I didn't do a darn thing, except ride shotgun.'' Meg
sat next to Quill with a thump. ''Are you sure you're
okay?''

''Yes. The worst was not being able to help him. And
not being able to see.''

''And he didn't say a word about who did it?''

''He couldn't,'' Quill said dryly. ''Not once the blood
started to . . . never mind.''

''I don't know why you're wasting perfectly good
sympathy on that bozo. It's a mercy whoever killed Dorset didn't kill you, too,'' Doreen reiterated.

The snow had stopped and sunlight streamed in
through the window. She looked old. Quill sighed. Myles had told her once that each murder had more than
one victim, that every violent death resulted in little murders of the living.

''Quill survived because the murderer wanted Dorset's
killing to be pinned on her,'' said Meg. ''If John hadn't
been sitting outside her cell window and seen him take
off, there wouldn't have been a thing Howie could have
done to get Quill out of jail. The knife that killed him was
from our kitchen, her fingerprints were on it, and a spare
key was found inside the cell under the mattress, proving
that Quill could have locked herself in and tried to blame
the murder on person or persons unknown.''

''Somebody did some good thinking ahead.'' Doreen
scowled. ''John didn't see who it was, either?''

Meg shook her head. ''Too dark. And he couldn't
exactly walk in and ask Dorset what the heck he was up
to, could he? He wasn't after any visitors to the sheriff's
office. John was worried about Quill and was planning
on standing guard outside the cell window all night. And

a good thing, too. Otherwise . . . otherwise . . ." Meg trailed off.

"Otherwise," Quill said cheerfully, "I would still be locked up, although without a corpse in my bed. I just wish the killer hadn't taken off with the key to the cell door, or that I'd know the other key was under the pillow. It seemed to take hours before John located Dave and let me out."

Meg drummed her fingers on her knee. "Wait until we find that creep."

"When are we going to have time to find that creep, Meg? We've got Santini's bachelor party tonight, not to mention the terrace party for S.O.A.P."

"And who is going to catch this killer?"

"They're sending the state troopers to investigate. Until we find another sheriff, they'll be in charge of it."

"We gotta do somethin'," muttered Doreen.

Quill set her teacup on the oak chest and got to her feet. "What we've got to do is keep the Inn running smoothly. I'm going to get dressed and meet you guys in the kitchen."

"It is a full day," Meg admitted. "The rest of the Santini wedding party is checking in this morning, and that nutty Evan Blight is checking in this afternoon."

"You don't know that he's nutty," Quill said.

"That's true. I don't know that he's nutty. But he's written a nutty book. Do you know what state of mind you have to be in to write a book?"

"No," said Quill, "and neither do you."

"I know that I have to be in a custard frame of mind to make custard. And dough is my world when I bake brioche. I," Meg continued, jumping up and waving her hands, "am one with the *pig* when I am in a roasting sort of mood."

"I see things are back to normal," John said, tapping

at the door and walking in. There were dark circles under his eyes. Andy Bishop, the local internist, was right behind him, black bag in hand.

"Therefore," Meg shouted triumphantly, "Evan Blight is a fruitcake because it's a fruitcake sort of book he's written. Andy! My love!"

Andy Bishop skied in winter and played tennis in the summer and was always faintly tanned. He was slender, well-knit, and a mere head taller than Meg, who stood five foot two with shoes. He gave her a sunny, intimate smile, and then looked with concern at Quill.

"How are you feeling?"

"A little stiff and a lot sleepy. Otherwise, fine."

"Let me just do a few physicianly things, then I'll let you alone."

"Andy, I'm fine. Who called you, anyway?"

"Let's just say I was in the neighborhood. Hey!" Meg wound her arms tightly around his neck and gave him a noisy kiss on the cheek. "Thanks, sweetheart, but you have to let me do my medical thing, here." He looked down at her. "Are you okay? I'm not going to have two patients on my hands, am I?"

"You are going to have no patients," said Meg. "I'm giddy with relief, I think. And Quill's okay, at least physically. And who did call you? Not that *I* wouldn't have, sooner or later. Probably sooner."

"Doreen. Due to a little case of frostbite."

"John!" Quill leaped to her feet, penitent. "Are you okay? I didn't even think! And I had your parka!"

John made a slight movement in protest, and Andy went on smoothly, "As I said, I was in the neighborhood. Sit right there, Quill, and let me take your blood pressure and your temperature."

"Do it," said Doreen, forestalling protest. "You might check her for nits, while you're at it, Doc."

"DoREEN!" shrieked Meg.

Quill held her arm out while Andy wrapped the blood pressure cuff around it and made an inquiring face at John.

"I'm fine," he said.

"Everybody's fine," Andy said absently. "Ninety-three over sixty, Quill. I wish I had your metabolism. You're looking a little thin, though. Lost any weight recently?"

"Mmm," said Quill.

"At least five pounds," said Meg. "Courtesy of that rat, the ex-sheriff McHale."

"Meg," said Quill, "don't."

"Well, he is a rat, If he'd stuck around the way he was supposed to, you never would have ended up in the clink. It's all," Meg said obscurely, "his fault."

Myles, who was lousy at entrance lines, cleared his throat in a perfunctory way. He stood at the open door, his khaki raincoat rumpled, his battered leather bag in hand, a day's worth of stubble on his cheeks.

The silence was profound.

"Quill," said Andy, "I don't like this pulse rate at all."

"Well," said Doreen, "*I* can get back to work, I guess." She punched Myles on the shoulder as she passed. "Don't tell anyone it's good to see ya." John grinned, slapped him on the back and shook his hand, and followed Doreen out the door. Meg snapped Andy's doctor's bag shut, handed him the blood pressure cuff, and pulled him toward the hall.

"I haven't finished the physical," he protested.

"Is she anywhere near sick?"

"Well, no. A little shocky, maybe, but . . ."

"Then you're being persistent." She eyed Myles with enormous goodwill. "Not that I have any objections to persistent men. On the contrary. See you for breakfast, Sis.''

"Don't call me Sis," Quill said automatically.

The door closed to a second, uncomfortable silence.

Quill sat down on the couch and covered her face with her hands. She held herself very still, then said between them, "Did Howie call you? Or John?"

"No." She heard him set his suitcase on the floor, then the rustle of his raincoat as he tossed it over a chair.

"There's coffee in the kitchen."

"Would you like some?"

She nodded. He crossed the carpet with his quiet, measured step. The coffee gurgled into the cups. He set it down and she felt the heat of the cup next to her knee, which was wedged against the oak chest she used for a coffee table. Myles settled next to her. He smelled of foreign places, of cigarette smoke, and—faintly—of fatigue.

"Were you on a smoking flight?"

He laughed. "Are you going to take your hands away from your face?"

Quill shook her head no.

"Why not?"

"If I do, I'll cry. If I start to cry, I won't stop. And I've got a busy day ahead. My hands," she explained, "are sort of holding my face on."

"I see."

"Did you . . ." Her throat was clogged and she stopped to swallow. "Did you hear what happened?"

"Just now. Downstairs. From Dina. Of course, having had experience with Dina's reportage before, I'm taking a lot of it under advertisement. I take it you didn't run over a little kid."

Quill shook her head.

There was a different note to his voice, a note she'd

only heard once before, the day she'd been shot. "And you weren't raped by Frank Dorset."

"Good heavens, no." Quill took her hands away from her face.

"And the séance this afternoon isn't your method of determining who killed Nora Cahill and Dorset."

"The what?" Quill sat up straight and took a healthy swig of coffee. "Séance. Tutti," she said darkly. "Oh, *swell*." She looked directly at him for the first time since he'd come back. "I suppose you heard all about Nora Cahill and the videotape and my missing coat and hat."

"Your coat? You mean that ratty—er—cherished sort of down thing you wear in the winter?"

Quill nodded, then gave a coherent account of the last two days.

Myles asked a few questions, then said, "I think I have the gist of it." He got up and put on his raincoat.

"Where are you going?"

"I'm going to have a little talk with the mayor. To inquire about the availability of the sheriff's job."

"Myles!" She set her cup down and rose to follow him.

"Later, dear heart. After this mess is cleared up."

The door clicked shut behind him. Quill slipped off her robe and began to dress.

"Wow, you look fabulous." Dina made a credible attempt at a wolf whistle as Quill came down the stairs into the foyer. "Where'd that sweater come from? And I love the lace at the throat. Medieval. You look medieval." She wriggled her eyebrows. "And happy. Sheriff McHale came down the stairs about ten minutes ago and he looked happy, too." She sighed. "I sure feel better. Sheriff McHale said that of course you didn't stab that creep Dorset when he tried to—you know—that somebody else did it. Stabbed Dorset, I mean.''

"Nobody tried to you-know. Especially Dorset."

"But Davy told Kathleen who told me that Dorset tried to . . . and *somebody* stabbed him."

"Somebody sure did. But it wasn't me. I. Whatever."

"Well, Sheriff McHale will find out who did it. And who killed Nora Cahill, too. Unless you and Meg find out first, like you've done before. Although, really, all either one of you has to do is ask Tutti. She's going to find out this afternoon, you know."

Quill, who was absolutely famished, stopped on her way to the dining room and turned around. "Which reminds me. What's this about a séance?"

"At one-thirty. Just after lunch."

"I didn't ask when it was. I asked what about it?"

"What about it?"

"Is it Claire's grandmother? Mrs. McIntosh?"

"You mean Tutti? Yep. And Tatiana."

"Tutti and her dog? The dog's psychic, too?"

Dina looked uncertain.

"Who's attending?"

"You mean who's going to be at the . . ." She quailed at Quill's expression.

Quill reminded herself that Dina was one of the brightest Ph.D. candidates at the limnology department at Cornell University. The fact that she knew far more about freshwater ponds and copepods than real life had stopped astonishing Quill, but it didn't keep her from occasional irritation.

Dina said (meekly enough to make Quill feel badly about her momentary ill temper), "Tutti invited Tatiana, Claire, Mrs. McIntosh—the one that's Claire's mom, that is—Mayor Henry, and that Mr. Blight."

"Evan Blight? I didn't have him listed for check in until this afternoon."

"Well, he showed up this morning. Said he'd been out all night under the hunter's moon and wanted the amenities of a civilized existence before he returned to the primitive glory of the woods . . . that's what he *said*, Quill, honest to God."

"It's not what he said, it's about where he was. Out all night? Where?"

"In the Gorge. Mayor Henry picked him up at the Ithaca airport, I guess, and they went off for one of those S.O.A.P. meetings. Anyhow, when the mayor brought him in this morning, I told him that you were in jail for murder and that's why you couldn't meet him yourself." She smiled sunnily. "I remembered what you told all us employees about being meticulously courteous to guests, and being in jail was a pretty darn good reason you couldn't meet him."

"I suppose it was," said Quill. She reflected briefly on the fact that she'd spent the best part of the previous night in the cold embrace of a corpse, survived with seeming equanimity the unexpected (and emotionally cataclysmic) return of her lover, and that it was twenty-four-year-old Dina Muir who was going to drive her to hysterics. "And after you'd welcomed a best-selling writer with the news that his host was in the slam for murder one, what did he do? I mean other than ask about the availability of rooms at the Marriott?"

"He had a reservation here. John made it himself. Well, he walked in with Mayor Henry and, Quill, you know me, I'm not one to gossip, because gossip is *tacky*, but my goodness, they smelled!"

"They smelled? Like what?"

"Like . . . like . . . I don't . . . dirt."

"They smelled like dirt?"

"Yep. And the mayor looked like he hadn't shaved since the elections, and of course Mr. Blight has that

ratty—sorry—that long beard, and there were all kinds
of twigs in it.''

"Dina. I'm starving. I want my breakfast.''

"You want me to hurry up,'' Dina said wisely. "So
they came in smelling like—you know—and Tutti was
bombing around waiting for that icky Claire to come
downstairs for breakfast, and Tutti started prophesying
the minute she saw Evan Blight. He said she—Tutti, I
mean—had the spirit of the ancient wise women, and
like that. *He* was very impressed.'' She added with a
slight tone of injury, "I mean, you and Meg dismiss
things you can't hear or touch or see awfully easily,
Quill, if you don't mind my saying so. So she got him
to come to the séance.''

"What did she proph—never mind. I don't think I
want to know. Where is this séance going to be held?''

"The Provençal suite. Where Tutti's staying. Quill?''

"What.''

"Could I? I mean, I definitely, absolutely did NOT
ask Tutti to invite me, but I did say that I was pretty
good at taking care of little dogs.''

"You mean you want to go to the séance?'' Quill
thought about this. Prone to breathless exaggeration as
she was, there was always a strong foundation of truth
to Dina's stories. And if Evan Blight and the men of
S.O.A.P. had been rattling around the woods last night,
she wanted details. Even details from Beyond.

"Sure. I don't mind if you take the time. Ask Kathleen if she'll cover the desk for you.''

"Great. Look. You have a good breakfast.''

"Thanks.''

Quill walked through the foyer and into the dining
room.

At nine o'clock on a Thursday morning in December,
the Inn had very few breakfast guests. She hadn't been

expecting Claire McIntosh (who normally rose around eleven), or Elaine (who never seemed to sleep at all, but roamed the halls in agitated fits), or Al Santini, but she wasn't surprised to see them at the table overlooking the Gorge. Vittorio sat with them, looking ill-tempered.

She *was* surprised to see Marge Schmidt and Betty Hall. Their Hemlock Hometown Diner did a brisk business in the mornings, beginning with the dairy farmers who came in after milking at six a.m., and ending with the early coffee breaks at ten-thirty of the business people on Main Street. Quill wondered who was covering the shop for them, then figured Marge had probably left out the coffee urn, cups, some of Betty's fry cakes, and a coffee can for cash.

Marge waved her over. Quill, whose stomach was now positively demanding breakfast, gave a cheerful wave in response and kept on going toward the kitchen. Marge placed two fingers between her lips and whistled, then pointed to the empty chair at their table.

Senator Santini jumped and looked nervously over his shoulder. Claire sent a sullen glare in Marge and Betty's direction. Elaine twisted her napkin into a tortured shape then dropped it on the floor. Vittorio shoveled Gruyère scrambled eggs into his mouth and didn't react at all.

Kathleen came bounding through the swinging doors from the kitchen, and Quill stopped her with a gesture. "Could you bring me some breakfast? I'll be at table five with Marge and Betty."

"Sure thing. Meg's whipped up a bunch of stuff. Raspberry crepes, eggs Florentine, some of that Breton sausage. And fresh grapefruit juice."

"Great."

"Uh—Quill? Could I talk to you a second before you talk to Ms. Schmidt?" Kathleen gazed at the carpet and rubbed at a spot with one toe. "Hmm. I thought Doreen got that out. She sure hates that little dog.''

"What is it, Kath? If I don't get some breakfast I'm going to fall over dead.''

"Yeah. Sure. Look, Quill. About David.''

"Your brother?''

"He was just following that jerk's orders. Dorset, I mean. And now that Myles is back . . .''

Quill checked her watch. As far as she could tell, Myles had been back in Hemlock Falls for approximately forty-five minutes. And apparently the whole town knew it.

Kathleen took a deep breath. "Could you maybe put in a good word for him? For Davy, I mean?'' She made a face in the direction of Marge and Betty's table. "There's a lot of folks around here that are pretty upset with him. That hidden camera wasn't his idea, you know. It was Dorset and that judge.''

"Justice, not judge,'' said Quill. "There's a big difference. You mean Bernie Bristol.''

"Davy,'' Kathleen said desperately, "didn't have a thing to do with it. And when the camera caught people speeding, well, what's he supposed to do? Just ignore it? He was only doing his job.'' She darted a look at Marge and away again.

"Marge got a ticket?'' Quill guessed.

Kathleen nodded miserably. "Yesterday afternoon. And, of course, everyone's furious with what Dorset tried to do to you—''

"They are?'' said Quill, pleased.

"And since you ki—I mean, since Dorset's dead, it's Davy that everyone's blaming, and if you sort of, you know, were publicly nice to him, maybe at the bank this Friday when everyone's in cashing their paychecks, or at the diner on Sunday mornings when everyone's in for brunch—''

"Kath. Wait a second. I didn't kill Dorset."

"Nobody cares if you did," Kathleen said warmly. "People are *glad* that you did. The guy was a sicko."

"*I* care if people think I killed him. Davy knows. I didn't even have a weapon. I mean, he searched me, the jerk, before I went into that cell."

"Bjarne said there was a paring knife *and* a butcher knife missing from the kitchen. And you were arrested in the kitchen last night. And Davy says Meg and Howie and John went to see you *after* he searched you. He took a statement from Howie, and Howie admitted that all of you went into the cell together and that Meg found an excuse to send Dorset out of the cell. Davy says any one of those three could have slipped you the weapon and be an accessory."

"Howie admitted what? Excuse me? Meg asked Dorset to find a blanket for me. That was no excuse. It was cold in there."

"Yeah, yeah. So. Anything you can do for Davy. Without getting yourself into more trouble, of course."

"Kathleen, I am not a murderess. Murderer. Whatever."

"Yes, ma'am. Would you like your breakfast now?"

"I would. And why are you calling me ma'am? The only person who calls me ma'am is Meg, and that's when she's so mad at me she wants to throw me in a snowbank."

"Nobody liked him, ma'am. Dorset, I mean. People are glad you took care of it. You're *due* some respect, Esther West says."

"Aaagh," said Quill. "Bring me a *lot* of sausage, okay?" She crossed to Marge and Betty's table and sat down.

"You look okay," Marge said after a short, sharp scrutiny.

"I feel fine. A little tired, though." Quill reached for the carafe of coffee and poured herself a cup. "I hope you two aren't going to congratulate me on killing Frank Dorset."

Marge chuckled. "That's what everyone's saying down at the diner," she agreed. "You didn't get a look at the fella who did it?"

"Hey," said Meg. She set a platter of food in front of Quill, then sat down at the last empty place setting at the table. "Marge, Betty. Mind if I join you?"

"Not if you quit using frozen spinach in the Florentine dishes," said Betty Hall. Her thin face split in a grin.

Meg flushed. "Dang. I didn't think this crowd would notice. I didn't have time to set up the sourdough pancakes last night, which is what I'd scheduled for the special this morning, and the only thing I had on hand was frozen spinach. Let me get you some oatmeal. I got a delivery from Ireland earlier this week, and it's wonderful stuff. I created a brown-sugar sour cream seasoning for it I think you'll like." There was a brief, professional discussion between the two chefs, involving the length of time needed to really scramble eggs. Twenty minutes under slow heat seemed to be the consensus. Quill ate her breakfast. Marge watched Quill tackle the eggs Florentine and waited a bit before asking again if Quill had seen the murderer's face.

"No. I'm not even sure what gender the murderer is." Quill, who had a number of reasons for believing the murderer was male, had decided to keep those facts, and the problem of her furry hat, to herself, at Myles's request. Everyone, he'd said, should know about the coat. The more people the better.

"Male," said Betty. "Fact."

"I'm not so sure." Quill thought of the videotape from the hidden camera, with the killer dressed in her coat and hat. Dave and John had both searched the sheriff's office for it with no luck. It'd been tossed into a fire by now, she was certain. "Whoever it was, man or woman, was about my height." Quill had a sudden afterthought. "Unless he, she, it wore heels."

"He," said Betty. "Ninety-nine percent of serial killers are white males between the ages of twenty-five and forty-nine. Fact."

"What about that woman in Florida?" asked Meg. "The one who murdered six guys in a row."

"She had an extra Y chromosome. Fact."

"But this guy . . . woman . . . person . . . isn't a serial killer," said Meg.

"There's been more than one murder, ain't there?" demanded Marge.

"I suppose so," Meg said hesitantly. "But—"

Marge burped. "There you are. Betty's right. Adela Henry gave a whole report on this serial killer business to the committee just last week."

"What committee?" Meg asked.

"S.T.S. The H.O.W. committee for Stop the Slaps. Wimmin united against domestic violence."

"I'm all for that," said Quill. "But this wasn't a case of domestic violence, you know. It was a case of murder for gain."

Meg cocked her head alertly. "How'd you find that out?"

Quill explained about the exchange of money on the videotape, a fact both she and Myles wanted public.

"And the tape is missing, of course," said Betty. "Dumb male bastards."

Quill pointed out that if a woman was the murderer, a woman could have swiped the tape as easily as a man, then shut up when all three of her tablemates glared at her. Betty pointed out that of course with a guy like

Sheriff McHale around, it just went to show you. Quill got so indignant over the implied slur on her feminism that she shut up altogether.

"So what happened, exactly?" Marge demanded.

"I'd fallen asleep on that cot, and I think it must have been the voices that woke me up."

Marge's eyes narrowed in a calculating way, which for some reason irritated Quill profoundly. "You heard their voices?"

"Uh-huh. One was Dorset. But as soon as they came in the cell block, the lights went out. The killer stabbed him, then shoved him through the door to my cell and rolled him in next to me. Then the killer relocked the cell door and took off, taking the key with him."

"Dorset musta weighed all of a hunnert and seventy pounds," said Marge. "Musta been a man, to wrestle all that deadweight."

The Breton sausage, one of Quill's favorites, stuck halfway down her throat. She swallowed carefully, then said, "He didn't die right away."

"Hung on awhile, did he? He musta said somethin' about who killed him, then."

"He whispered for help." Quill set her fork carefully on her plate and folded her hands in her lap. "His throat was cut. I don't think . . . he couldn't get anything else out."

Marge pursed her lips. "Hmm." Then, "Lemme pour you a little more coffee." She did so, then pulled a small notebook from the pocket of her bowling jacket. "You got times on this? And did you get any impression at all of the murderer's weight?"

"Marge!" Meg said suddenly. "Are *you* investigating this case?"

Marge shifted her large shoulders and scratched her neck with an abstracted air.

So that's why I was irritated, Quill thought with guilty surprise. *Petty old me. I don't like the competition.* She sat back, frowning. This feeling had something to do with Myles. And she didn't like what it said about her own motives for failing him in their relationship. If she had. Marge nudged her, and she blinked, startled.

"Thing is," said Marge, "Adela dropped to the diner this morning, early, with the milk crowd, and said she'd about had it up to here with town guv'mint. I mean, she'd just heard on that police scanner she carries around in her purse about you offing Dorset—"

"I did NOT—" Quill began hotly.

"Well, I see that now, don't I," Marge said equably. "Anyways, she's all hot for me to run for mayor."

"You, Marge?" said Meg. "But Elmer's mayor. I mean, to tell you the truth, you'd be an absolutely super mayor, and I wish we'd thought of it before the November elections, but there you are. Elmer's mayor. Duly elected and sworn in."

"That's as may be," Betty said mysteriously, "that's as may be. Anyways, let Marge go on. Go on, Marge."

"Right. What H.O.W. needs is some good P.R. Public relations, like. So, I figger we find out who killed Nora Cahill and Frank Dorset, this'd be just about the best P.R. we could get."

"So all of H.O.W. is investigating this?" asked Meg.

"Thought maybe you two'd give us and Adela a hand," said Betty, "seein' as how you have so much experience in the detective line."

"But," said Quill, "Myles—I mean, Sheriff McHale is back."

"Don't we know it!" said Betty. "And a damn good thing, too. Marge was thinking maybe now you'd put some of that weight back on."

Marge, whose nineteenth-century German forebears

seemed to have passed on a genetic predisposition for substantial poundage, nodded judiciously, her three chins folding and unfolding.

"Thing is, Adela didn't know the sheriff'd be back when she laid out the campaign this morning." Betty hitched forward and hissed conspiratorially, "See, what we have here is Marge for mayor and Adela for justice. What d'ya think?"

"Marge would make a terrific mayor," Quill said promptly. "I'll go door-to-door for Marge anytime."

"Me, too," said Meg. "But Adela for town justice?" She rolled her eyes. "Sheeesh. Remember the year she was judge at the geranium competition and she brought in those Dutch imports and said they were hers and she tried to arrange a boycott of Esther's shop when Esther blew her in?"

"Yeah," said Betty. "I'd forgot about that."

"And don't forget what happened after the Jell-O Architecture Contest."

"Um . . . yeah," said Marge.

Meg swallowed most of Quill's grapefruit juice, burped, and added, "That lady is mean."

"Well, Bernie Bristol's crooked," Quill said flatly. She gazed with a ruminative air at Alphonse Santini, who was saying goodbye to his bride at table seven with a remarkable degree of indifference. Of course, practically anyone contemplating marriage with the whiny Claire the day after tomorrow was going to have to be equipped with indifference to whining. "But why do we have to choose between mean and crooked? Why can't we find a town justice who's fair and honest? Like Howie Murchison."

Marge snorted, leaned over her eggs, and rumbled, "The point of H.O.W. is, see, that it's the wimmin who are going to run this town."

"Oh," said Quill.

"And Adela's right. If the wimmin find this killer and make the streets safe again, then it's the wimmin the voters are goin' to put in government."

"By and large, I agree with you," said Quill. "Except that Adela Henry's a witch."

"She's right, Marge," Betty said without officiousness. "We'll have to think about this. In the meantime, are you with us, Quill?"

"Well, sure," said Quill. "I guess so. Except that I really think Howie'd make a great—"

"Lame, girl, lame." Marge patted her shoulder with one elephantine hand. "Now, what's the next step in this investigation?"

"Me?" asked Quill. "You're asking me?"

"You solved three murders before this," said Betty.

"Who better?" asked Marge.

Meg went, "Whoop!" and finished the last of Quill's sausage. Quill, both flattered (at the tribute to her investigative skills) and annoyed (Meg had eaten most of her breakfast—and who was it that had spent a sleepless night with a corpse, anyway?), looked over her shoulder. The McIntoshes had gone. More important, Alphonse Santini had gone.

"Okay, guys, I'll tell you my theory. I had a lot of time to think about it last night, while John was looking for Davy to get me out of that cell. In the videotape of Nora's murder, a figure dressed in my coat waited for her by the intersection. The figure was tall for a woman, short for a man. That coat was down and really huge. I don't know if you remember seeing me wear it."

Betty hooted. "Everybody in town knows that coat. That's the ugliest winter coat I've ever seen in this life. I dunno how many times I seen you walking into the bank in that coat and wonder why the heck—oof!"

Marge, who'd given Betty a substantial poke in the midriff with her elbow, rumbled, "Go on, Quill."

"So if you had a little potbelly, it wouldn't show when it was zipped up."

"A nine-months pregnancy wouldn't have shown with that coat," Meg remarked. "I know you loved that coat, Quillie, but, honestly, it was an *ugly* coat. I'm glad it's at the bottom of the Gorge, or wherever it is that the murderer put it. Same for the hat." Meg yawned.

"Shut *up*, Meg. Now this is mere supposition at this point, because that tape has disappeared, but I think the only person it could have been was Alphonse Santini."

"The senator?" gasped Betty.

"Of course," said Meg. "You said the person dressed in your coat gave Nora a fistful of money."

"And took it back," Quill reminded them. "And I'll get to what happened to the money in a minute. Nora Cahill told me the day before she was murdered that she had 'more dirt on that guy,' meaning Santini, and that she'd love to publish it, but she didn't yet have enough proof. *And* she told me she was close to finding out something that would really nail him. Finally, I know for a fact that Santini hated her anyway. He blamed that whole H.O.W. fund-raiser debacle on her. I saw him reading her the riot act right after H.O.W. stopped throwing forks and spoons at him. I think what happened is this: Nora was blackmailing Santini, and he'd been paying her off right along. She said herself she was the only media person to get invited to his wedding—and she was just a Syracuse anchor. I mean, if he's going to invite anyone, why not Sam Donaldson? Or Barbara Walters? He could have cried all over Barbara Walters and it would have given him an enormous advantage in the next election. He's a national figure. One of them would have come."

"But Nora showed up at the courthouse when you were arrested for running over that little kid," Marge objected. "Why should she do that?"

"I didn't run over a little kid," said Quill.

"But it was the start of his 'national' campaign to rescue small towns." Meg said. "Nora wouldn't want to miss that. Although it was so clearly *phony*."

Quill smiled gratefully at her. "Just so."

"I get it," said Marge. "There's no reason why Nora'd pass up a good news story, even if she was blackmailing Santini."

"We probably," Quill said a little stiffly, "will always disagree about whether my little traffic ticket was a good news story. Anyway, I think that Frank Dorset recognized Santini in that tape and wanted that money for himself. He went right along with that trumped-up disguise that Santini meant to look like me, and put me in jail on bogus charges."

"That makes sense," said Meg. "I mean, Howie was raving all the way to Ithaca about the high-handed way Dorset was handling due process. He didn't see why or how Dorset was planning to get away with it. But, of course, he was trying to blackmail Santini, too. He was probably planning on taking that blackmail money and hightailing it out of town."

"And Santini showed up at the sheriff's office . . ." said Quill.

"Pretended to give Dorset the cash . . ." added Meg.

"And whammo! Cut his throat. Shoved him into my cell. Wiped the knife and tossed it in after Dorset's body . . ."

"And tried to pin the second murder on you."

"Holy crow," said Betty.

"You two are damn good," grunted Marge. "So how do we go around proving this?"

"We need hard evidence," said Quill. "Something factual, like DNA or hair samples that will link Santini to the scene of the crime. We have to find my coat and that videotape. And, we have to get an eyewitness to place Santini at or near the sheriff's office around five o'clock this morning."

"If the fella's smart enough to stay in the Senate for three terms, he's smart enough to burn that stuff," said Marge. "Or bury it."

"It's a lot harder than you think to dispose of things like that," said Quill. "Where is he going to burn it? Our fireplaces? We can sift through the ashes and find fibers, bits of plastic from the tape—whatever."

"I'll do that," said Betty. "He don't know me from a hole in the ground, and I worked cleaning house in high school before I learned to cook. I'll walk around here with a bucket and look like I'm cleaning fireplaces. I'll get a sample from each one in the place."

"Label them and put them in Baggies," Meg advised. "And as soon as you find something suspicious, call Sheriff McHale. Otherwise, we'll contaminate the chain of evidence."

"I'll tell Doreen what you're doing," Quill offered. "And, although Meg and I have a strict rule about invading the privacy of our guests, this is an emergency. Santini's in the Adams suite, room 224. And his bachelor party's tonight in the dining room, so he's going to be occupied with that from eight o'clock on. If there's anything hidden in his room, tonight's the best time to search for it. What I'm afraid of is that he's buried the stuff, or thrown it into the Gorge."

"It stopped snowing late last night," said Meg. "Andy could ski the parts of the park that lead from here to the Municipal Building and look for turned up dirt."

"Likeliest spot's the Gorge," said Marge. "I could take Miriam and Esther and we could hike down there."

"Why don't you three look in the park instead of Andy," said Betty. "We want this to be a victory for wimmin."

"It counts if *we* tell the men what to do," said Marge. "My goodness, partner, what would we do without Mark Anthony Jefferson at the bank buyin' and sellin' every time I tell him to? I'd be worth squat if I didn't work with male bankers."

"Good point," Meg said seriously. "So it's all right if I ask Andy to go ahead and search?"

"Long as Doc Bishop reports back to you," Marge said generously. "Be my guest."

"There's one last thing," said Quill. "The witness to Santini's presence near the sheriff's office."

"He sharin' a room with that lemon-faced fiancée?" asked Marge. "Course, she'd probably alibi him, anyhow."

"No," said Meg. "Claire's in the Pilgrim suite on the ground floor. Santini's in the Adams suite on two. Claire's father didn't think Tutti would approve if the two of them shared a room, so they aren't."

"So he's by himself. That helps some." Marge sniffed. "Witnesses, huh? Who'd likely be out in a gol-danged blizzard in the middle of central New York in December that might have seen him?"

Quill made a diffident noise and offered, "S.O.A.P."

"Hot damn," said Betty.

Marge swung her head like a turret on a tank. Her eyes gleamed. "Speak of the devil, here comes one a them now."

Mayor Elmer Henry bustled into the dining room, accompanied by the swish-swish-swish of his Gore-Tex ski pants. He caught sight of the four women as soon as he entered, waved weakly, and veered toward the table like a boat in a low wind.

" 'Lo, ladies," he said stiffly.

"You look a little pooped, Elmer," said Marge. "Little frostbit, too. Have a good time in the woods last night?"

"I have no idea what you are talking about. Quill? I'd like to speak to you about our meeting this evening."

"Of course, Mayor. Would you like to go to my office?"

"Sure. Ladies? Good to . . . um, 'bye."

Quill let him go ahead. She turned and nodded violently to Meg, who mouthed "Find out about last night," waved to Marge, and had to trot to get ahead of the mayor before he stamped into her office.

"No, I won't sit down. This won't take but a minute or so." He took a couple of deep breaths, whether because he was hot in his snowsuit or out of breath from racing away from the twin terror of Marge and Betty, Quill wasn't sure.

"John told you we've set you up on the terrace?"

"What? Oh. Yeah."

"We're bringing in some of the heating pots from Richardson's apple farm. Your members should be a lot warmer than they were, um, last night."

Elmer had soft brown eyes, rather like a cow's, Quill thought, or the more amiable breed of dog. He fixed them on her and asked earnestly if she was all right.

"Oh. You mean about this business with Dorset. Yes, Mayor. I'm fine."

"Talked to McHale just now. Seemed to think I . . ." Elmer flushed. "Quill, you gotta believe me when I tell you I had no idea what these fellas were up to."

"You mean Frank Dorset and Bernie Bristol?"

"And that scum Santini." He shook his head. "And to think that a United States senator . . . well, by God, I never would have thought it, or I wouldn't have done it."

"Done it? Done what?"

"Authorized the purchase of that dang hidden camera. Cost the town plenty."

"How much is plenty?"

"Pretty near fifty thousand dollars—"

"Fifty *thousand*!" gasped Quill. "Good grief. Where'd the money come from?"

"Discretionary budget," he said gloomily. "Pret' near emptied it for the next year. Means no town celebration this summer, that's for certain. And here," he said indignantly, "and here this Santini is tellin' me how much money the village is going to make from this and how we'll have money comin' out our ears and look-it. The traffic fines all come from the townspeople anyhow. I did some figuring and it comes out even worse. I'd be a sight more popular if I'd just gone ahead and raised property taxes. And now, after this—ah—unfortunate incident last night . . . Well. I'm sorry, Quill. If I'd ever thought this would happen in a million years, I never would have done it. You can," he said hopefully, "yell at me if you like. I cert'nly deserve it."

"The town's going to do a lot more yelling when they find out how much you paid for that camera," said Quill, who was, in fact, awed at the amount. "Wow."

Elmer nodded miserably. "They're talking special election anyways, you know. The women. On account of what happened to you. If they find out I spent that money, I'll be out on my ass—sorry, but you know. Just like what's her name from England. Thatcher, that's it."

"Oh?" asked Quill, not sure if the mayor was allying himself with Labor or the Conservatives in that debate.

"Word of this gets out, I ain't going to have a friend left in this world."

"I won't tell anyone, Mayor. I mean, the episode's over, as far as I'm concerned."

"Myles thought as you might not need to mention any more than you had to, if I came and told you I was sorry," he said ingenuously.

Quill, who had been experiencing warmer than charitable feelings about the six-foot-tall, baritone-voiced sheriff since his sudden reappearance in her life that morning, set her teeth. "He did, did he?"

"Knows you pretty well, I expect."

Quill reflected on this and had to laugh a little. Myles certainly seemed to know her better than she knew herself. She realized she didn't mind that as much as she used to. "I suppose he does."

"You glad he's back?"

She smiled.

"My," he said. "I can see that you are. I am, too. I'd sure like things to be the way they were before the November election. Myles back in office and Howie, too."

"A lot of people would have preferred a different result from the general election, Elmer. If there's nothing else, I'd better talk to Meg about any preparations for your meeting. You're sure you don't want Meg to cook anything?"

"The guys are cooking a whole steer in the woods," Elmer said proudly. "On a huge spit. Mr. Blight himself had the idea. You met him yet?"

"Not yet."

"He's amazing. Just amazing. He's gonna join us at the sayance this afternoon with Mrs. McIntosh. There's going to be a whole pile of us there. All the McIntoshes, Santini, and, of course, Mr. Blight. I thought maybe I'd get a chance to ask about the special election, you know, in case these spirits of Tutti's really know anything. I'd be happy to ask anything you want to know on your behalf.''

''The senator will be there? Then you sure can,'' Quill said flippantly. ''Ask them who was in the woods last night. Ask them who murdered Nora Cahill and Frank Dorset. Tell them,'' she said, inspired, ''that you know for a fact the murderer was seen.''

''You're kiddin','' said the mayor. ''Who seen 'im?''

''Just tell them that several of us in town know,'' said Quill. ''Tell them the word is getting around.''

''You're up to something.''

Quill reached over and patted his hand. For the first time in three days she was the pattor instead of the pattee and she was glad of it. ''What we both know, Mayor, won't hurt either one of us. As long as it reaches—or in your case—doesn't reach, the right people.''

The mayor sighed. ''Or the wrong ones. You watch it, Quill. You don't want this person comin' after you.''

CHAPTER 8

"What do you mean you can't tell me what the mayor wanted?" Meg stood in the middle of her full team of *sous*-chefs, looking like a pony among Percherons. "And you're going *where*?"

"Don't yell, Meg."

The Finns found this funny. The Canadian and the kid from Texas smiled at the Finns. The Frenchwoman—Lisette—frowned and went, "Pssstah!"

"If Meg doesn't yell, it's a day without sunshine," Bjarne explained.

"Orange juice. A day without orange juice is a day without sunshine," Lisette said. "They are confused in their English. Plus, they are watching too much television."

"That's what's confusing me, Quill, your English. I mean, I'm not hearing this. You're off to Syracuse *again*, when we have two huge parties—no, three, counting H.O.W. tonight. A rehearsal dinner tomorrow and a wedding on Saturday? And it's because of what the mayor said that you can't tell me?" Meg picked up a wooden spoon and threw it across the room. It bounced off a copper sauté pot and clattered to the floor.

"In-di-GEST-tion," sang the Texan, which sent the Finns off again.

Meg glowered at them and jerked her chin at Quill. "Check into my storeroom. I've got to get some sherry to braise the shallots."

Quill followed her meekly. She liked the storeroom, which was cool and quiet. It was a large room, slightly smaller than the kitchen, lined with shelves of root vegetables, flours, sugars, vinegars, oils, the raw ingredients from which Meg created the foods that had made them famous. The wine cellar was directly below the storeroom and had been the single most costly item in their extensive renovations of the Inn seven years ago. Meg took the key to the cellar from its hook on the wall, unlocked the cellar trapdoor, and stepped backward down the ladder to the wine vault.

"Any bodies down there?" Quill asked.

"Yours will be if you bug out on me during the busiest week of the year." She snapped the light on, and Quill could see her shadow moving along the bins. Meg muttered, "Damn it, I don't want the sauternes. If Doreen's dusted these bottles again I'll have her guts for garters. So," she hollered up, "tell me."

"The sherries are along the north wall. Next to the burgundies."

Meg's head reemerged. She looked both dusty and cross. "Tell me what Elmer said." She set two bottles of pale dry sherry on the storeroom floor, climbed out, and slammed the trapdoor shut. "Was it a clue?"

"I think so. Nora intimated that she was onto a hot story involving Santini. And now that I think back on it, she was trying to warn me about this small town campaign of Santini's. You know, persecuting innocent citizens with bogus tickets."

"Ya-ta-ta, ya-ta-ta. So?"

"So I think we may be looking at kickbacks. I can't tell you any more than that."

"Kickbacks?" Her eyes widened. "You don't think the mayor is involved in anything illegal?"

"Of course not. I think he's a dupe."

"Adela'd agree with you there."

"My guess is that Nora was on track with the story, and I want to go to Syracuse to talk to her editors at the news station."

"Won't it keep?" Meg wailed.

"If I don't go now, when would be a better time? Tomorrow, with Claire and Elaine and Tutti getting more and more frantic about the wedding? At least tonight they'll all be at the shower Meredith is holding for Claire in the lounge. Saturday, the day of the wedding, not to mention Christmas Eve when all those editors at the station will want to go home? Sunday, which is Christmas Day? Besides, if I wait much longer, the station will have cleared out her desk, and unless they've reassigned the story, what evidence there is may be destroyed or sent home to her parents or whatever."

"Look." Meg set the sherry bottles down with care, primarily, Quill thought, so that she could gesticulate without disturbing the sediment. She thrust her hands through her hair, tugged at it, and said with exaggerated patience, "Tell Myles. Have him go to Syracuse."

"I can't." Quill bit her lip. "I would really like to, but I can't."

"Why?!"

"Because I told the mayor I'd keep his secret."

Meg went, "Tuh!"

"Meg, I gave my word!"

"Then take Myles with you. Just don't tell him what the mayor told you."

"That's hairsplitting, Meg."

"You're right." Meg picked the bottles up and carried them tenderly out of the storeroom into the kitchen. "Myles swallowed his pride and came back here for you. Not because he heard you were in trouble. Not because he thought you'd welcome him with open arms. But because he loves you. Can't you at least call him and tell him where you're going?"

"It's not even noon. It's an hour round-trip to Syracuse and back. And it won't take me too long to talk to the editors. I'll be back before four."

"You are driving? In this weather?" Bjarne walked to the windows overlooking the herb garden. "You see this sky?"

"Blue," Quill said promptly.

"Those wispy clouds at the edges? Like mushy potatoes with too much cream? Very bad. Very, very bad. In a few hours, perhaps, there will be snow."

"Perhaps? Or for sure?" Quill hated driving in snowstorms.

Bjarne shrugged.

"I'll be back in less than four hours, Bjarne. Will it hold off until then?"

"It may not or it may."

"Great," said Meg. "I just hope the heck we get those food deliveries." She gave Quill a fierce hug. "Go do your thing. If Myles calls, do you have a message?"

"We're meeting for dinner at six. He won't call."

"Take my ski parka. And my hiking boots. And my hat."

"And make sure the gas tank's filled, ya-ta-ta, ya-ta-ta."

She went upstairs to her room and dressed for the drive, in a long sweater, ski pants, and long underwear. She rummaged through her bureau drawer for her "Investigations" notebook, unused since her last foray into murder, and slipped it into her shoulder bag.

She went back downstairs, and walked through the busy kitchen to the coatrack. The sleeves of Meg's parka were too short, but otherwise it was a comfortable fit. Quill added her own scarf and pulled out a pair of snow boots from the wooden box piled with odds and ends. She left by the back door to get her Olds from the garage.

The air outside was very cool and humid. A thin stream of water ran from the eaves, where the direct rays of the sun had melted the snow built up in the gutters. Mike the groundskeeper had shoveled the paths free, and she could see the Inn pickup truck, plow blade glinting in the sunlight, clearing the driveway to the road below their hill. The Olds would start easily in this weather. It always did. It was past time to get a new car, thought Quill, just like it was past time to get a new coat, but she was reluctant to give the Olds up. It was heavy, with front-wheel drive that gave her a lot of confidence in icy weather. It had also had its transmission replaced three times in its seventy-five-thousand-mile life, but the mechanic had assured her that this last install would last the life of the car. Quill skidded down the walkway to the outbuilding where they garaged their cars and maintenance equipment. She tugged on the latch of the overhead door, and it slid open, the bright day outside flooding the inside so that, for a moment, she saw the figure standing by the Oldsmobile as a blur of scarlet and tangled hair.

Despite herself, she gasped and jumped back, her heels skidding in the slush. Her voice was unexpectedly harsh. "Get out of there!"

Robertson Davies? Wearing my coat?

She raised her hand to her forehead, shielding her eyes from the sun. "Mr. Blight?"

"Yes?" The voice was unexpectedly gentle. Somehow, Quill had expected a gravelly rumble or a stentorian shout.

"Um. How do you do? I'm Sarah Quilliam."

"You are."

This was a statement. Not a question. Quill wasn't certain whether this was acknowledgment of her existence or mere inattention to the requirements of the spoken word.

"Mr. Blight? I'm sorry. I don't mean to be rude, but . . . where did you get that coat?"

Evan Blight stepped vigorously into the sunlight. The picture on the book jacket had smoothed out the wrinkles in his sun-beaten face and not really done justice to the impressive beard. There were bits of things in it—small sticks, a clot of scrambled egg, and possibly bird droppings, although Quill wasn't certain. Her down coat concealed the rest of him, but Quill had the impression he was thin and wiry. He could have been anywhere from sixty to ninety.

"Ms. Quilliam! Delighted. Delighted!" He grabbed her hand and shook it. His own was hard, muscular, and calloused, the fingernails blunt and dirty. "The irony implicit in the heart of the Flower series. The sardonic comment on the state of humankind! I saw the 'Chrysler Rose' in a traveling exhibit in New Jersey. Wonderful. Wonderful! There is a strong streak of the primordial male in you, Ms. Quilliam. The thrust of brush strokes! The intensity—if I may say so, the *masculinity* of the color—wonderful! Wonderful!"

Quill felt an immediate (and cowardly) impulse to tell Evan Blight she was proud of her breasts and really missed sleeping with Myles McHale. She suppressed these politically incorrect (and socially inappropriate) responses and thanked him, in as hearty a voice as she could manage.

"You have read my Book," he asserted. "There could be no other explanation for the quality of your work. How pleasing to see the effects of my own small efforts to stem the tide of corruption of our basic, most natural drives."

Quill, who had recently read a most interesting book on the way that men verbally dominate social and business conversations, interrupted firmly, loudly, and with a terrific feeling of guilt. "Mr. Blight?"

"Call me Evan. Not Urban, if you please, which was the highly charged response to a review of my Book by the female reviewer of the *San Francisco Chronicle*. I was not offended. No, not offended. Was Hannibal offended by the piteous mewings of the Romans when he swept down on Trebia? I think not. Was the Khan himself dismayed by the pleas of the reindeer people as he led the mighty charge against their tents?"

He paused, either for breath or agreement, and Quill said hastily, "That coat, Mr. Blight. Have you had it long?"

He looked down at himself. "This coat? A gift of the forest, my dear." He shrugged himself out of it with a decisive movement. "But your softer flesh clearly is more in need of it than I. The garment you yourself are wearing must have clothed you as a child."

"It's my sister's," said Quill. "She's shorter than I." She took the coat, holding it by thumb and forefinger. He was wearing a baggy, hole-at-the-elbows gray cardigan, a knitted vest underneath that the color of a bird's nest, tweed trousers, and a pair of sensible boots. He shivered in the cold air. "Oh, dear, Mr. Blight. Don't you have a coat of your own?"

"Nature's embrace is all that I need."

Any forensic evidence that might be in the folds of the down was already tainted, and Quill handed it back

to him with a resigned sigh. "Here. Take the coat back
and get into the car. I'll turn the heater on."

Blight accepted the down coat with an intolerant air,
although what he was intolerant of, Quill couldn't imagine, since he'd been wearing the coat only moments before. He lowered himself into the passenger seat of the
Olds with the tenderness of the arthritic.

"Why don't I drive you around to the front of the Inn
so you can go inside?" Quill suggested. "Then I'm
afraid that I will need my coat back, Mr. Blight."

"I am moving toward a profound Change," he announced, "an experience of a unique and perhaps Life
Enhancing Kind. The Inn's My Destination."

"You Bester," said Quill, who occasionally read sci-
ence fiction. She curbed her irreverence (but he *would*
speak in capitals!) started the Olds, and backed carefully
out of the garage. She pulled into the circular drive leading to the Inn's front door.

"Ah," said Mr. Blight. "They await."

"They sure do," said Quill, eyeing the crowd outside.
"My gosh. It's all of S.O.A.P. and Alphonse Santini.
And Vittorio McIntosh."

"They are waiting for Me. I am scheduled for an Address. Stop here, please."

Quill braked. "An address? You mean a speech?"

"On the link between the generosity of Nature and
the generosity of the human spirit."

Quill thought this through. The crowd of men, seeing
Mr. Blight in the passenger seat, began to murmur and
shift, like crows in a cornfield. "Is this a fund-raiser for
Alphonse Santini?"

Evan Blight's eyes were deep-set, gray, and, Quill
realized, very, very sharp. "That is *very* acute of you,
my dear. Not what one would expect of the softer sex.
Not what one would expect at all." He maneuvered

himself out of the down coat and opened the passenger door. "I leave you now for whatever may be your Destination."

"Syracuse," Quill said absently. "Channel Seven. My coat, Mr. Blight. Where did—um—nature present this to you?"

"At the base of the Root," said Blight. "Near the seed of the tree."

"Beg pardon?"

He clasped her wrist with strength. "Each Conclave of Men has a Center. A Totem. A Signal which—er—signifies the heart and thrust of male power. There is one such Totem here. Perhaps more. I will discover *that* in future."

There was only one even remotely totemic item in Hemlock Falls, which also happened to be five minutes swift walk from the sheriffs office. "The statue of General Hemlock? That's where you found my coat?"

He patted her cheek. Quill hated anybody patting her cheek. "Let no man gainsay the occasional wisdom of women." He pulled himself out of the car, slammed the door shut, shouting, "Farewell! And on to Syracuse." And turned to meet his fans.

"Aagh!" Quill muttered. "And aaagh again." Alphonse Santini must have heard Blight shouting out that she was headed to Syracuse. Most of the village must have heard Blight. She returned the wave and drove down the road to the turnoff for Route 96. She turned south instead of north, toward Buffalo, on the off chance that this would confuse Santini and discourage anyone from following her.

The only problem with this particular diversionary tactic was that it took her twenty minutes to get to an exit to turn around to head south, and she lost nearly an hour before she was on Interstate 81 to Syracuse.

She lost another half hour trying to find the proper exit to Genesee Street, where the television station was located. For some years in the late eighties Syracuse had been a dying city, its major employers having fled the punishing New York State taxation system for the better business climate in the South. But lately there'd been a resurgence, and a great many streets were undergoing repair. Quill passed work crews red-faced with cold, flagmen who seemed to have been recruited for the amount of ill temper they vented on drivers, and innumerable, irritating, annoying orange cones, which blocked each shortcut to Genesee with fiendish regularity.

By the time she reached the KSGY parking lot, the wind had risen and Bjarne's mashed potato clouds were thickening the blue sky. Quill parked in a space marked KSGY EMPLOYEES ONLY. ALL OTHERS WILL BE TOWED!

She'd worked out a cover story. It was risky, but, as she'd told Meg, time was running short. What she hadn't told Meg—or John—or anyone—except Myles—was that Howie wasn't all that certain she was in the clear. The way in which she spent the next twenty years, he'd suggested, was dependent on how believable John's testimony would be to a jury. Nothing would be gained at the moment, Howie had added, by ruminating on the fact that the new governor had promised to reinstate the death penalty once in office.

Quill took a deep breath, got out of the Olds, and sloshed through the inadequately plowed lot to the lobby. A middle-aged security guard sat behind a glass-walled kiosk. Quill pulled off her knitted cap, smiled, and rapped on the sliding glass window.

The guard raised her eyebrows and slid the panel open. "Can I help you?"

"Hi. I'm Sarah Cahill. Nora's sister." She bit her lip and thought about twenty years in jail.

The guard looked at her face sympathetically.

"I'm not too certain about whom I should see regarding Nora's personal effects. Has—um—any of the family arrived yet to take them? I've been out of the country and haven't had a chance to talk to any of our relatives."

"I thought your folks had passed on," said the guard. Her name tag read: "Rite-Watch Security, Rita."

"You must be Rita," Quill said warmly. "Nora's told me so much about you."

"She did? I on'y met her the two times."

"She said that the one who'd been here before . . ."

"Paula?" The guard looked smug. "I guess so!" She shook her head briefly. "You know how many jobs Paula's gone through on account of that mouth? I told her. We all told her. But there you are. So Miss Cahill remembered me, huh? Well, I remember her. Poor thing. Poor, poor thing. And you're her sister, huh?"

"We were quite close," said Quill. "I'm sure she's told you all about me, too."

"Yeah. Yeah. Look. I doan want to hurt your feelings or nuthin', but she never did say much about any of the family."

"Given her schedule," said Quill, "I can understand." She sighed, "All the same, it hurts."

"Poor thing," said Rita, "poor, poor thing. Well. I'll tell you. Mr. Ciscerone packed up all her stuff and said to wait sixty days and if nobody showed up, to ditch it."

Quill, who was beginning to feel genuinely sympathetic on Nora Cahill's behalf, said, "And no one's come yet? No one except me?"

"Nope. You hang on. I'll get her stuff for you." Rita reached through the open panel and patted Quill's hand, then disappeared through a door at the back of her kiosk.

Quill shifted nervously from foot to foot. Nero Wolfe always told Archie Goodwin to conduct his investigation based on his intelligence guided by experience. There was never any indication that either detective felt terrible about pulling the wool over various people's eyes. Quill tried hard to feel she wasn't taking advantage of Rita's warm heart and didn't succeed.

Rita reemerged from the back with a large cardboard box and set it on the ledge of the kiosk. It was stuffed with papers, disk files, a Rolodex, a flower vase with four dead daisies, a photograph of Nora with two other women on a beach, and a stack of magazines. Quill made a cursory examination. The computer disks were parts of software packages; the papers mainly office memos, clippings from magazines, and letters from fans and critics of Nora's show.

"Nora was really proud of an investigation she was conducting just before she—you know . . ." said Quill. "Did Mr. Ciscerone mention that? Nora would have been so happy to know that it had been reassigned."

Rita shrugged. Quill, under pretext of neatening up the box, lifted the magazine pile out. Bingo. A set of keys, marked "spares."

Quill reached over the box, hand extended. Rita got out of her chair and shook it. "Thank you so much! I feel a little closer to Nora, now that I've talked to you. I'll just take these, shall I?"

"Gotta sign for 'em," said Rita. "Hang on." She produced a manifest, marked an empty line with a large X, and handed it to Quill. She signed the first name in an illegible scrawl and the last, Cahill, in readable but sloppy script.

"Thanks, Rita. I'll be off."

"Poor thing," said Rita. "Poor, poor thing."

Back in the Olds, Quill turned the engine on and

turned up the heat. There was no address book—presumably the police had taken it—and the Rolodex was almost empty. It wasn't going to do a bit of good if she had the keys to Nora's apartment and car without her home address; no celebrity—especially an investigative reporter—was going to risk an open listing in the city phone book.

Quill turned to the papers; there, under a calendar for the coming year marked "compliments of Mac's Garage," she found a letter from Nora's HMO, addressed to 559 Westcott St. Quill hesitated a moment; it was getting late. She didn't want to risk returning to Rita to ask directions to Westcott. But it couldn't be too far; Nora had mentioned being able to walk to work.

Nora hadn't mentioned the fact that Syracuse was an old city, by American standards, and the streets a bewildering labyrinth, twisting around buildings that didn't exist anymore, truncated due to the building of newer roads, blocked by renovations to entire city blocks. She found Westcott after a series of frustrating dead ends.

This whole area, Quill realized, was oriented to nearby Syracuse University. Most of the students had gone home for the holidays, and the parking was relatively easy. She pulled up at the curb next to a row of storefronts that gave her a pang of nostalgia for her days in SoHo in New York: a pizza parlor with the phone number painted on the window in screaming red letters; a small gallery, filled with student work; a boutique clothing store; a business sign for a company called Oddly Enough. She scanned the store numbers and found a door marked 559. She fumbled at the entrance, going through three of the four keys on the ring before she found the right one. Inside, scanning a row of metal mailboxes she found N. CAHILL #3.

The single door at her right was marked 1. Quill

mounted the steep stairs. At the top of the landing, #3 was on the left.

The interior of the apartment belied the student atmosphere. Nora had corner rooms, with windows on two sides overlooking Westcott and Argyle. The style was Euro-Tech: Berber carpeting, a black leather couch, plain wrought-iron shelving, and a display of hand thrown pottery. A very nice copy of a de Kooning hung on the wall over the couch. The kitchen was through an open archway on the east wall; the two closed doors on the south wall probably led to bedrooms. The first Quill opened was to a room with a sofa bed and a desk. A window looked out over the back of the building, letting in dim gray light. Quill glanced out; light snow was falling, like spume from a breaking wave. She hesitated, a hand on the overhead light switch, and decided to work in the dimness as best she could.

There was a place on her desk where Nora's PC had been, marked by cables and an extra battery. Quill flipped through the file case of computer disks. They were all pre-formatted and, as far as she could tell, unused. Were they really empty? Quill wasn't sure. If she were an investigative reporter, she wouldn't label files. She slipped the disks into her shoulder bag.

The desk drawers were filled with stationery, envelopes, a folder of bills neatly marked "paid" with the date of payment, used check registers, and a few bank statements. Nothing unusual, except for the fact that Nora's affairs were so orderly. That was suspicious itself.

The front door opened into the living room, and someone walked in.

Quill swallowed so hard she choked. She stepped to the office door. A man in a suit stood in the center of the living room, behaving much as she had done, casting swift, appraising glances around the room.

Quill's visual memory was good; where Meg could separate flavors into component parts of recipes, Quill's artist's eye, like a good cop's, could categorize age, background, and dress. The man in the living room was from somewhere around the Mediterranean; her guess would be Northern Italy. He was wearing a medium-priced suit with a cut at the edge of this year's fashions. Like his haircut. There were a lot of guys like this one on the streets of New York, lawyers on their first job, mid-level bankers, entry-level stockbrokers.

Quill stepped into the living room. "Excuse me." She kept her voice as well under control as she could, but thought she could hear a nervous quaver. She scowled to cover it.

The guy in the living room didn't jump. This made Quill uneasy. Any friend of Nora's would have assumed the apartment was empty.

"Hi. You're Nora's sister, Sarah?" He stuck out his hand. "Joseph Greenwald."

Well, south of Northern Italy, Quill thought. Very south.

"Rita at the station thought you might be here."

Quill looked at him.

"Nora told me quite a bit about you two as kids." He grinned. Like a shark. "You don't know who I am?"

Quill cleared her throat. "I can't . . . that is, Nora never mentioned you."

"No? We've been dating almost a year. But she was pretty goosey about letting anyone know about us. Even you. Her favorite. Sister."

"Why?"

His eyelids fluttered. "She thought the single-minded career woman bit would keep the station focused on her performance. Was she as determined to make it big-time when you two were kids?" He shook his head, clicked his tongue against his teeth, and said admiringly, "That Nora. God. She was one focused lady. I miss her, you know? What a shame. What a rotten shame." He took a step toward her. Quill dodged and moved left, out into the living room, toward the front door.

"Rita said she'd given you the box of Nora's things from the office. If you don't mind, I'd like to take a look. Have you been through it yet? There was a picture of the two of us that I'd like to have, as well." He glanced around the living room. "It's why I came here. To pick it up. She used to keep it on the shelf right here. But it's gone. Was it with her stuff from the office?"

"I haven't had a chance to go through it." Quill added cleverly, "If you leave me your address, Joseph, I'd be happy to mail it to you."

"I'll see you at the funeral, won't I? Could I get it from you there?" He frowned at her expression. "You have been making the arrangements, haven't you? The police wouldn't tell me a damn thing. Just told me anyone could walk off the street and claim they'd known her and I had no proof that we'd been dating." His voice sounded bitter. "She was right on her way to being famous, you know. So anyone could take advantage. People are scum. Just like whoever killed her is scum."

Did Nora have a sister? Suddenly, Quill felt like the worst kind of liar, the most offensive kind of intruder. She was exploiting a tragedy.

Joseph Greenwald sat down on the couch. He looked sad. He also looked as if he had been there before. "The police must have told you if they have a lead on who did it. They'd let family members know."

"I haven't really heard anything," Quill said cautiously.

"You want to sit down? I'll make us some coffee." His expression was wistful. "I haven't been able to talk about her to anyone yet. She didn't want anyone to know about us.''

''Was there a reason she didn't? I mean, other than the fact that she thought it'd be better for the station not to know she had a personal life?''

''God, I don't know. I teach ninth grade math at the University High School. Nora knew a lot more about the real world than I did.''

''You never went to law school?'' Quill asked. ''Or banking? You were never interested in banking?''

''Me? Heck, no. I like kids. I've always liked kids. That was the one area Nora and I never did agree on. I wanted to get married and she—Say, are you sure you wouldn't like me to make you a pot of coffee?''

''No. Thanks.'' Quill, feeling more traitorous every minute, was positive that her cheeks were red. ''I've got to get back to the, um, hotel.''

''Where're you staying?''

''The Hyatt,'' said Quill. There had to be a Hyatt in Syracuse. Every large town in America had a Hyatt.

''I didn't know we had a Hyatt,'' said Joseph.

''Could you give me your phone number?'' Quill said desperately. ''I'll be sure to call you about the . . . you know.''

''The funeral. Yeah. You have a piece of paper?''

Quill drew her Investigations notebook out of her purse and took out a pen.

''It's a local area code, 315. And it's 624-9123.''

Quill wrote this down. After this was all over, she could call and explain and apologize. He might forgive her. By the next millennium. ''I'll let you know as soon as everything's been completed.'' She shoved the note-book back in her purse, dislodging the computer disks she'd stolen from Nora's desk. She laughed, ''Ha-ha!'' stuffed them clumsily into the depths of the purse, and held out her hand. ''Goodbye, Joe. I'm so sorry.''

''Yeah. Can I drop you off at the Hyatt? It must be new. Of course, you know us teachers. Never pay much attention to anything outside of test scores.''

''It's really more toward Rochester.'' She shook his hand. ''We'll keep in touch.''

She clattered down the stairs, her purse banging against the wall, warm with embarrassment. No detective she'd ever read in any of her favorite fiction, from Philip Marlowe to Dave Robicheaux, ever got embarrassed in the middle of an investigation. And they were sensitive guys. She'd have to work at being tougher.

She pushed outside to the sidewalk. The snow was falling faster now, and the temperature had dropped. She slid on the sidewalk. The Olds' windshield was covered with a thin coat of icy mush. She scraped it free with her bare hand, and removed the flyer some enterprising entrepreneur had stuck under the wipers with a click of irritation. She balled it up and wiped futilely at the glass, then turned and opened the driver's door. She glanced up. Joseph Greenwald stared at her through the living room window. She forced a smile, waved, and caught herself just before she tossed the flyer in the street. *''Red-haired, early thirties,''* Greenwald would tell the cops. *''Said she was Nora's sister. No, we've never met. But Nora told me a lot about their life together as kids. And I tell you this, Officer, Nora's sister was no litterer.''*

The Olds started, as always, with a cough and reliable roar. Quill buckled herself in and took a right off Westcott onto Argyle, from Argyle to Genesee and from Genesee to the entrance ramp of 81 north without really seeing anything at all.

She became aware of the intensity of the snow when she almost hit the car in front of her.

Its taillights flashed. Quill braked automatically, and the Olds skidded on the rutted slush, narrowly missing the car on her left. There was a blare of horns, a shout, and the Toyota next to her swung wide. She swerved into the skid and came to rest against the ramp curb. Behind her, a line of cars slowed, and inched by her stopped vehicle, an occasional hollered curse adding to her misery.

She pounded the wheel and yelled, "Ugh. Ugh *ugh*, UGH!"

It snowed harder as she watched, moving from a veil to a heavy curtain in minutes. She waited until her heart slowed and her breath was even, then inched out into the traffic. She made it to the expressway. The snow was thick, gluey, and treacherous. Her windshield wipers were on full speed, but the snow fell faster than the blades were moving. Quill hunched forward in the classic posture of the snow-blind driver and followed the taillights ahead of her.

She switched the radio on, punching the buttons until she hit the Traffic Watch.

"Seven to eight inches expected before nightfall," came the announcer's excited voice. "Most major thoroughfares have been closed to all but emergency traffic. High winds are expected to pick up as a front moves in from Canada. Our travel advisory has become a snow emergency. The sheriff's office has ordered no unnecessary travel, I repeat, no unnecessary travel."

Why, thought Quill, *do these weather guys always sound as though we're about to be bombed by Khaddafi?* Half of her anxiety about driving in snow came from the we-who-are-about-to-die-salute-you tone of this guy's voice.

She drove on, keeping her speed under thirty, and told herself that somewhere on the continent the sun was shining, the roads were dry, and the outside temperature wouldn't kill you if you fell asleep in it. She imagined a map of the United States, with the sun shining everywhere but this little stretch of Interstate 81 north. She pretended that all she had to do was drive a few miles more, and she would break into clear roads and blue skies.

The line of cars in front of her exited at the off ramp at 53. She looked in the rearview mirror. There were a few sets of headlights in back of her, not many. The snow whirled and spun like a immense bolt of cotton, now obscuring the road altogether, now whipping aside to reveal snow as high as her knees.

She switched the radio, found Pachelbel's *Canon*, which she'd come to loathe, then a mournful harpsichord version of Claude-Marie deCourcey's *Spring Fate*.

"Oh, humm," Quill sang. "Hummmm hummm." She shivered, despite the fact that the heater was going full blast.

She checked her watch. Three-thirty. At the rate she was traveling, she wouldn't be home before five. When it would be dark.

"This is stupid," she said aloud. She'd take the next exit, find a motel, and call Myles, then Meg, and tell them not to worry, she'd be back home in the morning.

The miles crawled by. On her left, headed south, two exits went by. The next one northbound would be 50. It was on the outskirts of the city, and her chances of finding a motel right off the ramp were not good, but at least she'd be close to the ground, near a gas station or a diner, where there would be light, and the warmth of human beings, and an end to the white that so ruthlessly wrapped the car.

She checked the rearview mirror. The traffic was gone, the road almost empty but for a pair of headlights traveling at speed in her lane. She slowed again, to under twenty-five, and signaled a move into the far right-hand lane. The headlights moved, too. They were high above the ground, shining eerily above the piled snow, plowing through the drifts like a fish through water. *Four-wheel drive*, Quill thought glumly. *I should have taken the Inn pickup.*

She turned her attention to the road in front. The Olds was lugging a little, the snow was halfway up the hubcaps. Her headlights were almost useless, bumping above the snow as often as they were obscured by drifts.

High beams flashed in her rearview mirror. She ducked, swerved, and cursed. She regained control and then the Olds jumped forward, like a frightened horse.

"No," said Quill.

The high beams filled the car, drenching the inside with light. Quill slowed to a crawl. The truck behind her was pushing now, its bumper locked into position. Quill leaned on the horn, the noise whipped away on the flying wind, driven on the snow. She blasted the horn once, twice.

The headlights behind her dimmed and flared in answer.

The truck backed off. Quill remembered to breathe. The headlights filled her mirror again, and she peered frantically out the windshield, looking for a place to stop, to let the bastard pass. The truck didn't hit her again, just hung there like a carrion bird, the headlights hovering.

The world was filled with snow.

The dark was coming.

She looked at her watch. A quarter to five. The exit to 96 had to be coming up next. She searched the side of the road. A green sign crawled by. Two miles. If she could just make it two miles.

The lights from behind filled her vision.

She squinted. She drove on. She rubbed her right hand down her thigh, pushing hard against the muscle to calm herself. Her gloved hand brushed the flyer she'd dropped in the seat beside her. "Pizza," she said, just to hear the sound of a voice. "Oh, I wish I had a pepperoni . . ."

She smoothed the paper out.

FREE DELIVERY!

"Lot of good that'll do me."

CALL 624-9123—ANYTIME!

"624-9123, 624-9123," Quill chanted, fighting a hopeless battle against the choking fear.

It's a local area code, 315. And it's 624-9123, Joseph Greenwald had said.

And then, from days ago, Nora Cahill's voice: *No offense, but if you tell me you've got your love life socked, too, I'm going to hit you with a stick. I haven't had a date for eight months.*

She got mad.

"You idiot!" she yelled. "You bonehead! You twink!"

I could pull over to the side, wait for him to come up to the car, and hit him with . . . what?

The tire iron was in the trunk. And she wasn't sure she could use it on flesh and bone no matter how mad and scared and stupid she was.

HEMLOCK FALLS, 10 mi., the green sign said.

Quill thought about the exit ramp. At this juncture of 81, the exit ramps were on a gentle upward slope to 96, which ran along a drumlin left by glaciers. So the snow wouldn't be any higher at the exit than it was now— more than likely less, since the wind would blow it downward. And the highway department always started plowing 96 here first, at the boundary of Tompkins County.

Unless the blizzard was too much for even the plows. "Nah," said Quill.

Then . . .

"It's just like the West End at rush hour," she said aloud, to reassure herself. "And you remember the West End at rush hour. Oh, yes, you do. In your short—and unlamented career as a taxi driver. . . ."

She gunned the motor. The Olds leaped forward. *Thank God*, she thought, *I never got a lighter car. Thank God . . .*

She signaled left and instead swerved into the center lane.

The truck behind her faltered, moved left, and spun briefly out of control. She had time. A little time.

She could barely see the signposts now, between the dark and the snow and the wind. The tiny mile reflectors flashed white-white-white as she hurtled by, the front-wheel drive giving the heavy car purchase in the drifts, her speed preventing a skid. She'd be all right until she had to make that turn.

The pickup behind her straightened out, barreled forward, and nudged her bumper with a thud.

The mile marker for the exit flashed.

Quill bit her lip, pulled a hard right, spun, drove into the skid, and gunned the accelerator. The Olds fishtailed. Quill let it ride, keeping her hands off the wheel, her foot off the brake.

She broke through the barrier of snow at the ramp's edge.

The upward incline slowed the Olds, steadied it.

She waited.

Behind her, the pickup roared and tried to turn to follow. The engine whined. The pickup bounced, the height and weight of the truck throwing it into a spin from which it couldn't recover—and she heard the squeal of the transmission. He'd thrown it into reverse. His engine screamed and died.

"Fool," Quill said, and slammed her foot on the accelerator again.

The tires bit into the powdered snow and held.

She drove up the ramp, the Olds' rear end slamming against the guardrail, now to the left, now to the right. She clenched her hands to keep them from the wheel and braked, gunned, braked, gunned, the car rocking back and forth until she broke through onto 96. . . .

"And thank you, *God*!" she shouted.

The road was plowed.

CHAPTER 9

Quill had approached the Inn at Hemlock Falls at least two thousand different times over the past seven years, in every season, at practically every time of the day and most of the night.

It had never looked more welcoming.

Warm golden lights shone through the mullioned windows as she drove carefully up the driveway. There was a pine wreath at each window—as they had every year at holiday time—wound round with small white lights. Mauve taffeta bows shot through with gold were wired to the wreaths. Hundreds of the small white lights sparkled in the bare branches of the trees clustered near the Gorge, casting jewel-like twinkles over the snow.

Mike the groundskeeper had been busy; white snow was piled in neat drifts on either side of the drive. The asphalt was powdered with at least a half an inch. He'd be out again with the plow later, when the snowstorm finally quit.

The Olds was lugging worse than ever. Quill took the left-hand path to the maintenance building out back in low gear, with a vague idea that this would save the engine. She hit the button for the overhead door opener, then pulled in and stopped. The engine died with a cough.

"Good *girl*," she said foolishly, patting the dash.

She was surprised to discover that her legs were weak. And she had trouble opening the driver's door. She got out, then turned back and opened the rear door to take the red down coat to Myles.

It was gone.

"Damn." She punched the light switch and the garage flooded with light. The coat hadn't fallen to the floor in that hairy ride down 81 and it wasn't under the seat. The box with the contents of Nora Cahill's desk at the office was gone, too.

"Damn and damn again." She slammed the rear door shut. Joseph Greenwald. She hoped he was up to his eyeteeth in snow. The computer disks from Nora's home office were still in her purse. Quill hoped her quota of luck for the week hadn't run out; she'd made quite a dent in it with Route 96 being plowed at just the right time. If her luck held, those disks would contain Nora's investigative files.

She marched to the Inn's back door, her adrenaline charged from annoyance, stripped off her winter clothing, and hung it on the coat pegs. She ditched her boots and walked into the kitchen in her socks. It was overly warm. There were six *sous*-chefs busy at the Aga, the grill, and the butcher block counters. To her surprise, Meg was seated in the rocking chair by the cobblestone fireplace, smoking a forbidden cigarette.

"Hey! I thought you'd be up to your ears in work. How come you're sitting down?"

Meg threw the cigarette into the open hearth with a guilty air and bounced out of the rocker. "Hey, yourself! I was just beginning to worry. You're more than an hour later than you said you'd be and that storm Bjarne predicted is a doozy.''

"In Helsinki, this is spring," Bjarne said. He whacked at a huge tenderloin with the butcher's knife, and whacked again.

"I thought you'd be run off your feet, Meg."

"You're kidding, right? Santini's closed the dining room so that he and his eleven pals can eat tenderloin in lofty seclusion. Ten pals actually. One of them got held up by the storm. Listen. I spent the day with Tutti McIntosh, and I've got something really interesting to tell you."

Quill interrupted, "Santini paid the table minimum? For all twenty tables?"

"Claire's doting dad did, I think. Anyhow, everyone's eating away and they're all taken care of. The mayor and his soapy friends ordered cold stuff, except for their roasted cow which they did somewhere in the woods themselves, and I made all that this afternoon. And the H.O.W. ladies each brought a dish to pass. That's where Tutti is now, surrounded by the entire protective brigade of—''

"John's not going to like that. Guests aren't supposed to bring their own stuff."

"I like it," Meg said firmly. "I've got enough to do with this rehearsal dinner for twenty tomorrow night. And then the wedding. Thank God the truck got here just before the snow. We got all that stuff unloaded. And then Tutti was with me in the kitchen all afternoon. I'll be glad when this is all over and we can put up our tree and close the place down for two days. By the way, Myles called and said he won't get here until midnight or after. The snow's caused the usual numbers of crises, including some damn fool wrecking his pickup truck at the 96 exit to 81 and you'll never guess what Tutti did—''

"At the moment," Quill said crossly. "I just don't give a hoot." She settled on a stool at the butcher block counter. Exhaustion overtook her like a dam bursting. She could just sit here and go to sleep. She yawned. "Can you tell me the fascinating news about Tutti later? I have to speak to Myles about that pickup." She glanced casually at Meg. "It sounds like the one that tried to run me off the road."

"Oh, yeah? Well, you can go pound on the driver personally tomorrow. The truck's been towed to Bernie's garage and the guy's at the hospital with a broken arm. Andy says he's not going anywhere soon. Let me tell you what happened *here* this afternoon."

"Oh, yeah? That's all you have to say when I tell you I was almost murdered right there on 81 by a crazed guy who very probably is involved in Nora Cahill's death, not to mention Frank Dorset's?"

"You're here all in one piece, aren't you?" Meg said callously. "Honestly Quill, sometimes you exaggerate as much as Dina does. It's either that or the other extreme—like failing to mention your absolutely awful driving record to Howie Murchison, which is when all this nutty stuff started. Try to be a little rational for once, will you?"

Pressure always upset Meg. In some remote part of her mind, Quill tried to remember this, and failed. "I am perfectly rational!" she shouted.

"Perfectly rational people don't shriek their heads off at a little mild criticism from a beloved relative. No, they don't. Wait until you hear about the séance this afternoon."

Quill slid off the stool. "I'm numb with cold. I'm sweaty with the aftermath of fear—"

"The what?!"

"And I'm going up to my room and call Myles and tell him about the evidence I just uncovered in this murder case, because it's practically solved, Meg, and then I'm going to take a hot, hot, hot shower, wash my hair, nap, and be gorgeous for poor Myles when he finally gets off road duty."

"Practically solved the murders, huh?" Meg shouted after her as she shoved open the swinging doors to the dining room. "Quill! Don't *go* that way!"

Quill took two steps into the dining room and encountered the affronted glares of Alphonse Santini, a well-known Supreme Court Justice, an equally well-known Democratic senator, and Vittorio McIntosh, among others.

They were all in black tie.

Quill was jerked out of her fatigue into the present. Sweat streaked her face. Her knitted cap had made a tangled mess of her hair. She'd been wearing black long johns under her snow pants, and she was suddenly aware that rather than resembling leggings—which they were not—they looked like long underwear. Which they were. And there was a hole in her argyle socks.

She retreated to the kitchen.

Meg looked smug. This, Quill reflected later, was the straw that broke the camel's back, the monkey wrench in the machinery, the penultimate push. Actually it wasn't the smugness as much as the pious comment that accompanied it:

"You *never* listen to me. You'd never get into half the trouble you do if you'd just listen to me."

Quill washed her hair in the shower, drained the tub, filled it with water as hot as she could stand it, and threw in four capfuls of Neutrogena Rain Bath Shower and

Bath Body Gel. She had, she realized, told Meg (and any interested person within forty feet of the kitchen) that in the past two days she'd a.) been thrown in jail for a bogus traffic ticket, b.) renounced her lover, c.) been humiliated on television, d.) been thrown in jail on a trumped-up murder charge, e.) been assaulted and sexually harassed by a human asparagus, f.) witnessed a murder, g.) spent the night with a corpse, and finally, been terrified almost to death by a high-speed chase in a snowstorm. Meg's tart rejoinder (''There's no need to get hysterical about it!'') made her so mad that she'd upended an entire canister of whole wheat flour on the kitchen floor. The Finns thought this was hilarious. ''Americans,'' Bjarne said with a pleased air, ''how I love this country.''

A knock on the bathroom door roused her from the gloomy contemplation of her soapy knees. ''Yes?'' Quill shouted.

There was a bout of furious yapping, a thump, and a muttered ''Gol-durn it.''

''Doreen?''

''Yap-yap-yap-yap,'' came Tatiana's voice, in a furious fusillade, ''yap-yap—''

Crash!

''YAP!!''

''You git, before I turn you into earmuffs!''

There was another crash, as of a mop hitting a hardwood floor, and a ferocious growl. Doreen wouldn't dare deep-six the dog. Would she? Quill waited for a canine gurgle. Maybe that growl had been Doreen. Maybe a short dog drowned in a tall mop bucket didn't have time to gurgle.

''Doreen?''

''It's me,'' came Doreen's familiar foghorn voice. ''You decent?—OW!''

Decent, she thought. *How decent is a person who yells at her sister?*

"I'll be right there." She sloshed out of the tub, pulled on her terry cloth robe, and opened the door.

"Doreen. You look really nice."

The housekeeper was dressed in a long velvet skirt, a metallic gold turtleneck with blouson sleeves, and sandals with rhinestones at the toes. This gave her a charmingly old-fashioned (if gaudy) appearance. She was carrying a mop. Quill smiled at her. "You ought to wear soft shapes more often. But why the mop?"

"You'll see," she said with a glower. " 'Bout this outfit, Stoke bought it for me. I think it makes me look like I'm plugged inta a outlet. Say, Quill. The girls, I mean the organ'zation members, sent me up to see if you're comin' to the meeting."

"The H.O.W. meeting?" Quill stepped barefoot into the room, the sash to her bathrobe trailing. "Boy, Doreen, I'm just so—OW!" Tatiana, who'd been hiding under the couch, retreated as soon as her needle teeth got Quill's ankle.

Crash! Doreen wielded the broom with prompt efficiency. "Durn thing," Doreen said glumly. "She'll do that. Ain't hit her yet."

"It doesn't seem to me that you try very hard." Quill nursed her ankle with one hand and hobbled to the couch. "Why is she up here?"

"She follers me around. Why it is, durn'd if I know."

"Is Tutti here?"

"Yeah."

"She's not at the shower for Claire, is she?"

"Heck, no. She's in the H.O.W. meeting. Where *you* bin, anyways?"

"To Syracuse. Why?"

"Big hoo-ha here this afternoon, I can tell you."

She remembered suddenly: séance. And Meg anxious to tell her about it just before Quill lobbed verbal fireballs at her over the tenderloin. "Did something happen at the séance?"

"You bet it did. That Tutti's amazin'. She ought to be on TV. You know how many serial killers that one'd catch if she went public?"

"What?! What serial killer?"

Doreen gave a patient sigh. "This one that killed that Dorset and that poor Nora Cahill. He spoke to us. Right there in the Provençal suite next to the fireplace. We don't have to worry about him. He's dead. Deader than a doornail. Which is how come he come back from Beyond to speak through Tutti. You shoulda heard him. You know how Tutti has that nice sweet voice? Well, it was like somethin' from that movie where the devil was in that Linda Blair and turnt her head right around like a screw cap. Ol' Tutti's head turnt around—"

"All the way?" Quill asked sarcastically.

"No, ma'am. Just partways. Then this here voice comes out. Low. Ugly-like. A man, of course." Doreen's voice, although hoarse, was generally clearly feminine. She pitched it several octaves lower than usual and growled, "I DONE FOR 'EM. I DONE FOR 'EM BOTH."

"Yap!" went Tatiana, "yap, yap!!"

"See, the dog's a familiar, like. Tutti don't do her sayance without her. Good girl," Doreen cooed suddenly. "Good girl. She got two mice in the storeroom today, too."

Tatiana made a noise like a Norelco shaver. Quill shifted back nervously. "Did Tutti say anything else?"

"You mean he, the murderer. Oh, yeah. RABBIT! RABBIT!"

Quill opened her mouth, then closed it. Nobody knew

about her rabbit hat. Except Dorset, and he was dead. Except herself, and she didn't do it. Except the murderer, who had worn it.

Tutti?

Impossible. She was too short. Too round. And the murderer was a male—Quill wasn't entirely sure how she knew that, except that she'd been no more than three feet away from him while he slashed Frank Dorset's throat. The sound of his breath, the way that he walked on the videotape. And the arms, she thought suddenly. The arms extended way past the sleeves of her coat. So the murderer was a man. She trusted her painter's eye that far. And Tutti, for reasons known only to herself, was letting the murderer know she knew.

But why? To stop Santini from marrying Claire? If she knew about the rabbit hat, she knew enough to turn Santini in to Myles. It didn't make any sense for Tutti to warn a man who had killed twice already.

"Alphonse Santini was at the séance, wasn't he, Doreen?"

"Yep. Shook him up some, I'll tell you that."

"I'll bet it did."

What did Tutti know? And how had she found out? More important, a man who had killed twice wouldn't shy away from killing again. Now that Tutti had revealed her hand, she was in danger.

Unless Tutti were protected, there'd be one less guest at that wedding, Quill thought, and it wouldn't be Alphonse Santini.

"Is the senator still in the dining room?"

"Yep."

"Doreen. You've got to get back to the H.O.W. meeting right away. I believe Tutti's in danger."

"Nah, Tutti said the murderer's dead. That no matter how long the sheriff—Myles, I mean—searches for him, he'll on'y find him in the next world.''

''Or at her daughter's side at the church.'' Quill shook her head to clear it. ''Doreen, you don't believe all this séance hooey.''

There was an all-too-recognizable glint in Doreen's beady black eyes. ''Tell you the truth, I was feelin' kinda psychic myself, the longer that there sayance went on. Anyhow, Tutti's holding another one for the wimmin of H.O.W., to help us find out ways we can get these men off our backs and into their proper role, she says.'' Doreen took a deep breath. ''You comin'?''

''Of course I'm coming! We don't want a third corpse in Hemlock Falls. What time is it?''

''Nine-thirty.''

Two and half hours until Myles came. ''You get down there right now. And stick to Tutti like glue, you hear me? Don't let Alphonse Santini come within a country mile of her.''

''If you say so,'' Doreen said doubtfully.

''Is everyone as dressed up as you are?''

''Not them boobs in the S.O.A.P. meeting. Members of the organ'zation have the sense to dress with respect. So you get dressed with respect. I'll see you down there.'' She turned and marched out the door, mop slung over her shoulder. Tatiana poked her blunt little nose out from under the couch and eyed Quill with suspicion.

''Go on,'' Quill said encouragingly. ''Go find Doreen.''

Tatiana rolled her upper lip over her teeth and advanced sideways, like a mongoose stalking a cobra. Quill jumped up on the oak chest. ''Beat it, Tatiana. Go hunt some ghosts. Better yet, go bite the senator.''

The prospect of senatorial flesh between her jaws apparently appealed to Tatiana. She cocked her head, trotted off, and Quill climbed down from the chest. She was so tired she felt as though she were swimming through mud.

She pulled on a stretchy ankle-length velvet dress over her head, swept her hair into a knot, and slid on a pair of black sandals. "The well-dressed host," she muttered, spraying herself with musk perfume, "goes to meet her fate."

She heard the drone of Tutti's voice halfway down the hall. The conference room was only three years old, and John had designed it for several purposes. Wood panels on the walls opened up to reveal whiteboards and film screens. The long credenza on the south wall opened up into a serving bar. And the long mahogany table in the center of the room could hold more than twenty people in a pinch.

Quill knocked on the door and opened it in a single motion. The room was dark, except for a single lamp at the head of the table. It was a lava lamp in the shape of a globe, the viscous red liquid churning like the contents of somebody's stomach. Tutti's round face hung over the lamp like a wrinkly white moon.

"Nnnnnnnnmmmmmmmm," she hummed.

"Nummmmmmmmmmm," responded the members of the Hemlock Organization of Women.

"Shut the damn *door*," somebody called out.

Quill flipped on the light. Doreen sat at Tutti's left, Marge Schmidt at her right. Tatiana barked from the safety of Tutti's lap. Tutti herself blinked owlishly and smiled. She was dressed in a fuzzy angora sweater, a long plaid taffeta skirt, and an emerald necklace that weighed more than her dog.

"Sorry," said Quill. "I hope I'm not interrupting anything."

"Of course you are," Miriam Doncaster said testily.

"What *is* it, Quill? We were just about to hear the truth about what goes on in that dratted men's group."

"I won't keep you. I have something to ask you guys. It's important, but short."

She walked to the head of the room. The women of Hemlock Falls looked back at her: Esther West, in a black chiffon cocktail dress with rhinestone earrings; Betty Hall in purple lamé, a red bow in her hair; Marge in a size twenty-two Diane Freis after-dinner suit that cost more than Quill's automobile when it was new. Even Adela Henry looked vulnerable in the sudden flare of the overhead lights.

Quill felt a wave of affection so strong she blinked back tears.

"You okay, honey?" Nadine Wertmuller (Hemlock Hall of Beauty) snapped her gum in concern.

"Yep," Quill said a little huskily, "I'm just tired, that's all."

"PMS," said somebody. "Gets me like that, too."

"I want to ask your help." Quill tugged at a tendril of hair. "Some of you were at the séance this afternoon. By now, most of you have heard what went on. And I believe that Tutti's been given a warning."

There was a swell of excited comment, like wheat rippling in the wind.

"Tutti was right—or rather, her—um—spirit guide was. The man who killed Nora Cahill and Frank Dorset is connected with rabbits."

"Those bums at S.O.A.P.," yelled Nadine. "Torturing animals in the woods!"

"Oh, no!" Quill flung her hands out. "The killings don't have anything to do with S.O.A.P. Sheriff McHale is very close to obtaining evidence that will convict this man."

"You find something in Syracuse?" asked Marge.

Quill made what she hoped was a noncommittal "hmm." Tutti regarded her with the set, unblinking gaze of her dog. "I found something that I think will be useful in bringing this person in. But until the case is wrapped up, I believe that Tutti is in real danger."

"Surely not!" Tutti protested.

Meg, dressed in jeans and a clean T-shirt (which meant that the kitchen was closed), appeared at the open door. She caught Quill's eye, wriggled her eyebrows, then folded her arms and leaned against the door frame. Quill straightened her shoulders and continued firmly, "I'm afraid so, Mrs. McIntosh. I *know*," Quill said, scanning the room, "that no one at this meeting is implicated in these murders. I saw the murderer myself."

Meg went, "Phuuut!"

Quill ignored her.

"Jeez," said Betty Hall. "You think you should announce it like that?"

"If we were weren't close to bringing him in, and if I didn't trust everyone in this room, I'd agree with you. As it is, I wonder if we could assign a guard for Tutti, just until Sheriff McHale gets back from this snow emergency. Would some of you volunteer to keep an eye on her at all times?"

"Of course we will," said Esther West. "My goodness, do you think she'll be attacked? Right here at the Inn?"

"It's possible."

Meg cleared her throat, rolled her eyes, and yawned.

"How long do we keep this watch?" asked Miriam.

"Midnight," said Quill, with a sangfroid unimpeded by Meg's giggle. "There's something else. Marge and Betty, how did the search go today?"

"Quill?" Adela Henry rose to her full thin, elegant height. "If there is to be a disclosure of the activities of the investigatory subcommittee, perhaps I should chair this meeting.''

''Well, sure,'' said Quill.

''What subcommittee?'' Miriam demanded.

''H.O.W. shall solve,'' Adela said grandly, ''the murders of Nora Cahill and that disgusting Frank Dorset.'' Her eyes flickered. ''And then we shall seek to replace the lamentable town government with a mayor of quality. A town justice of integrity, a sheriff of—''

''Be *quiet*, Adela,'' said Miriam. ''What's going on here, Marge?''

''Quill, Meg, Betty, and me have been looking for that down coat of Quill's. It's what the guy wore when he stabbed Nora and Frank Dorset.''

''And I've been looking for the videotape from that there hidden camera that shows him doin' it,'' said Betty. ''I checked each one of the fireplaces in the Inn today, Quill, and I didn't find a thing.''

''So that's why you dragged Esther and me all over the bottom of the Gorge today, Marge Schmidt,'' said Miriam. ''I'd like to have died from the cold, too. Why didn't you tell me?''

''I'm tellin' you now, or Quill is. What's next, Quill?''

''First, who wants to guard Tutti?''

''My goodness,'' said Tutti, her cheeks pink. ''And to think the spirit guides led us to this, Tatiana!''

''We want the big ones, like me,'' said Marge with satisfaction. ''That means you, Shirley Peterson, and you, Trish Pasquale. We'll stick to you like debentures in a bear market, Tutti.''

''And the rest of you have to turn this Inn inside out,'' said Quill, ''discreetly. And you should work in pairs, for protection.''

''What are we looking for?'' asked Betty.

"A videotape that's mini-sized, you know, about half the size of the ones you rent from the video store. It's the tape of Nora's murder. And a hat."

"A hat? What kind of hat?" said Esther.

"My rabbit hat."

"You mean that horrible old thing with the earflaps you wore all winter last year?" asked Esther.

"The murderer disguised himself in it," said Quill.

"Disguise?" somebody muttered. "Heck, you show up in that thing at a school picnic and half the little kids would fall over from fright."

"I always thought the hat was one of the reasons the sheriff dumped her," said somebody else.

Quill maintained her aplomb. "Just two caveats ladies. Don't be so obvious that the other guests suspect anything. And if you do find the hat or the videotape, don't pick either one up. One of you guard it, the other one should come and find me. Or the sheriff."

"Well, I'm ready," said Miriam. "Esther, you come with me. We'll start right away."

"What about the guest rooms?" asked Doreen. "You want I should get out the master key?"

"There's only one room I need to search," said Quill. "And I should be the one to take the risk."

Meg started to whistle the theme from *The Bridge Over the River Kwai*.

"Tutti," said Marge. "How'd you feel about a game of bridge?"

"Fifty cents a point? We'd love it. Wouldn't we, Tatiana?" The dog gave her a skeptical glance, hopped off her lap, and followed Doreen and the other H.O.W. members out the door. Tutti pulled a deck of cards from her capacious handbag and shuffled them expertly. Quill strode toward the hall. She felt great.

"Colonel!" Meg snapped to attention and saluted.

"Cut it out, Meg."

"You're right. I should be addressing you as Inspector Alleyn. He always gathered the suspects in the drawing room and exposed the murderer. Nope. Sorry. Wrong again. It's Holmes himself and the Baker Street Irregulars."

"Why are you bugging me, Meg? I've had a tough day. And you didn't tell me what went on at that séance."

"You didn't give me a *chance* to tell you about the séance!"

"Tutti's clearly in danger, and you didn't do a thing about it."

"I most certainly did," Meg said indignantly. "Why the heck do you think she was in the kitchen with me all day? I mean she's a sweetie, Quill, and I learned a great new recipe for homemade pasta, but this is one of the busiest days of the whole darn year!"

"Oh," Quill said.

"I mean, really. How irresponsible do you think I am? You never look at anybody the way they really are, Quill. You look at them the way you think they should be."

"I do?"

"Yes, you do. You make up your mind first and then you decide what's happening. Have you ever known me to boot an important clue like the one Tutti rolled out this afternoon?"

"No, Meg."

"And don't we usually solve these cases together?"

"Yes, Meg."

"So how come you came in all hissy this afternoon and picked a fight with me?"

"Because I was scared out of my mind!"

"Then why didn't you tell me? Honestly, Quill, it

does nobody any good if you keep your emotions buttoned up. It doesn't do any good with me, that's for sure. And look what happened with that lunch with Myles. You were so busy keeping a stiff upper lip that you didn't even talk to each other. And look what almost happened. If Miles hadn't taken the risk to come back . . . restraint is all very well, Quillie. But not when it screws up your emotional life."

Quill stared at her. "You really think so?"

"I really think . . . what the *devil* is that noise?"

"The bachelor party, I suppose. Meg, I was scared out of my mind, but only partly from being almost run off the road."

"Somebody really did? Quill!"

"Somebody really did. But that's not what's bothering me."

"My Lord, Quill. Did you report this man? Are you hurt? It's a good thing you have that big heavy car."

"I'm pretty sure that the truck's at Bernie's and Joseph Greenwald is in the hospital. Do you think you could call Andy and verify that he's going to be in overnight?"

"Joseph Greenwald?" said Meg.

"There's a funny look on your face."

"He showed up here right after you left for Syracuse. Good-looking guy? Looks like a Philadelphia lawyer?"

"He showed up here?"

"Tried to check in, but of course there wasn't any room. So I sent him on to the Marriott."

"Well, I'll be dipped, as Nora Cahill once said."

"That's not the reason you should be dipped. The reason you should be dipped is that he's an attorney. And he asked for Alphonse Santini at the desk."

"Wow. Meg, I think we should interrupt that bridge game."

"I think you're—Quill. If that's the bachelor party I hear, it's getting really out of hand. We'd better check that out first. It sounds like a riot."

Quill had heard sounds like that before: whoops, yells, screams of laughter, cheers, the thump of running feet. "Pamplona, Meg. The summer I spent in Madrid? With the foreign exchange group?"

The thrumming of running feet drew nearer and shook the walls of the solid old building. Marge burst from the conference room. Tutti, with a perplexed expression, trotted after her, her bridge cards in her hand. Her two other guards peered over Marge's shoulder.

"What'n the hell?" asked Marge.

The door at the end of the east end of the hall led to the Tavern Lounge. It shuddered, rattled, and for a moment seemed to bow outward from a massive weight on the other side. It burst open, to reveal Mayor Henry, naked but for a loincloth, with red stripes on his cheeks and his forehead painted stark white, dragging Claire's bridesmaid by the hand.

"Meredith!" called Quill. "Are you all right?"

"Let *go*, you geezer!" Meredith said irritably.

"Lances UP!" shouted the mayor.

"Lances UP!" came a male chorus in response.

"Lances UP, UP, UP!" yelled Evan Blight.

The members of S.O.A.P. stampeded through the hall like maddened buffalo. Most of them dragged a person of the opposite sex by the handiest protuberance: an arm here, a collar there, three or four by the hair, for those participants of H.O.W. and the bridal party whose hair was long enough for the S.O.A.P. snatch-and-grab technique. One of Harland Peterson's Norwegian cousins— a blacksmith notable for the breadth of his shoulders and the strength in his back—carried Esther West over his shoulder. She looked thoughtful. Her screams were perfunctory.

Evan Blight himself—womanless—cried, "On, men, on! Remember Romulus! Forward, in the name of Romulus. Lances UP! UP! UP!"

Meg and Quill shoved themselves against the wall. Marge and the rest of the bridge party beat a prudent retreat into the conference room, to reemerge as the sounds of the raid faded on the nighttime air.

"They left the back door open," Marge observed.

"I'll get it." Meg walked down the hall, turned around, walked back, and said crossly, "You didn't see Andy with those idiots?"

"They weren't carrying any lances," Tutti observed after a moment.

"Heck, no," said Marge. "The 'Lances UP!' part of this is pret' obvious. But who's this Romulus guy?"

"Um," said Quill. "The Sabines. He needed wives for his troops." She went to the west door, opened it, and peered out. "It's okay," she reported. "It's turned into a snowball fight." She paused. "And the women are winning."

Myles was late. Quill stood at the French doors to her balcony and watched the clearing sky. The storm left a swathe of tatterdemalion clouds. Stars emerged through the misty remnants like lilies floating up from the bottom of a pond. A chilly breeze sprang up. The moon came out. And Quill waited, a cup of coffee in her hand, until she heard him at the door.

CHAPTER 10

Sunlight crept across the lace coverlet Quill's grandmother had brought from England almost a century ago. The fabric lay in folds at the foot of the bed, and the sunshine threw the rose design into sharp relief. The years had aged the lace from white to cream. Quill, propped against the pillows, thought about how the lace had traveled for over ninety years, to end up here, covering her bed.

She was facing the large mullioned window that kept her bedroom light and airy, even in the depths of winter. The glass was old, perhaps even older than the lace, and her view of the snowy fields outside was distorted, wavy, as though she were underwater.

Myles walked in carrying a tray of coffee and fresh brioche. A pink rose nodded at her from a crystal vase, and the scent of the flower mingled with the odor of fresh yeast.

"Wow." She smiled at him. "You didn't go downstairs dressed like that?"

"Undressed like this?" He grinned. "The bread and the rose were outside the door. Doreen must have left it for you. Or Meg."

"How late is it?" asked Quill. She accepted a cup of

coffee and held it steady as he climbed back in beside her.

"Ten o'clock."

"Oh, dear. I should get downstairs. The florist from Ithaca is bringing the flowers in this morning and they're going to decorate for the wedding. Meg's going to be all wrapped up in the kitchen. And John hates doing that stuff."

She set her coffee on the nightstand and stretched, then turned and burrowed into Myles's shoulder. "Well. Here we are again."

His hand, large and warm, smoothed her hair. "I wouldn't have given odds that I would see you again, like this. Wrapped in lace. With your hair tumbled down your shoulders."

She didn't answer right away. "So what about this blonde?"

"What blonde?"

She drew back her hand to punch him, and he caught it, kissed it, and clasped it in his own.

"Meg said that you're wasted as sheriff here in the village. That if it hadn't been for me, you would have taken a job like this global thingy a long time ago."

"That's probably true."

Quill sat up, indignant.

"But it would have been a stopgap. Until I found a village like this again. With someone like you in it."

"That's a . . . a . . . perplexing sort of statement."

"Is it? It's what I want. You. A family. A town small enough to know. A town large enough to be comfortable in. I'm forty-seven, Quill. And I'm tired. Not of life. But of the kinds of ambition that drove me when I was younger. I want a certain . . . orderliness to my daily life. That might be the wrong word. I don't believe that I want to see much more of humanity in the raw than I have already. I've had enough.''

There was a puckered scar on his stomach from shrapnel, a dimpled hole in his right shoulder from a gunshot wound. Quill traced these marks with one forefinger. ''In a way,'' she said at last, ''I haven't seen enough.''

''Mmm.''

''Was that surprise?''

''I suppose it was. I think you're right.''

''I love you.'' Her voice was husky. She cleared her throat. ''I'm not whining, you understand. But why do women always have to choose? Between life outside and making a home?''

''If I were younger, you'd met me before I'd been satisfied I'd seen enough, maybe you wouldn't have to. We're at different stages, Quill. I don't want you to give anything up.''

''I don't want you to give anything up, either.'' She sighed. ''I wish I were a clone. Had a clone. Whatever.''

His arm tightened around her shoulder. ''Let's take it one day at a time. Now, I gather from what you said last night that Greenwald gave you quite a chase.''

''Green . . . oh! The jerk in the pickup truck. You're sure my coat wasn't in it?''

''Positive. I've sent a couple of troopers out to search 81, but it doesn't look good. He dumped it before the rescue trucks got there. But the coat wouldn't be enough, Quill. It's circumstantial at best, unless we find either Nora's or Dorset's blood on it, and even if we do, we'd need harder evidence to convict.''

''But you do think it's Santini?''

''I'm not willing to make that leap yet. What's his motive? Guesswork's hazardous in this business, Quill. So far, you're operating on mere surmise.''

''Surmise.'' Quill made a face.

''Intuition? Feeling? What do you want me to say?

You don't have any facts. You think that Nora Cahill was blackmailing Alphonse Santini, but you have no proof. And without that fundamental fact, Quill, the rest of the motive falls apart. Why would he kill Dorset? I admit that the videotape you said you saw—"

"I did see it."

"I know you did. But who is a jury going to believe? You can't convict a man of a capital crime on hearsay, Quill."

"But I have proof. Or at least I think I have proof. I didn't get a chance to tell you everything last night . . ."

He smiled.

She blushed, then went on, "But I took some disks from Nora's apartment."

"Quill." He stopped himself, then said with obvious patience, "I won't talk to you about breaking and entering. You know all about that already. But I have told you about the importance of the chain of evidence. And if you've entered the victim's apartment unlawfully and gathered it unlawfully . . ."

"Stop." Quill held up her hand. "I know all that. I told the H.O.W. members last night that if they found anything not to touch it, but to call you first."

Myles grabbed his forehead with both hands, in a gesture reminiscent of Meg. "You sent thirty women from a feminist organization careening through this Inn looking for evidence against Alphonse Santini?"

"The wedding is tomorrow. Then, he'll be gone. I feel awful about poor Claire. And I'm worried about Tutti."

Myles shut his eyes for a moment. "You don't have to worry about Tutti."

"Why not?"

"I'll let you know after I call New York this morning. I'd like to know something right now, though. Was it the H.O.W. search that kicked off the riot?"

"It wasn't exactly a riot," Quill said a little guiltily. "They didn't find anything, anyway. They all went home to nurse their bruises after that snowball fight. And besides, Myles, you're forgetting the hard drive."

"The hard drive?" He shook his head. "We're talking about you breaking into Nora's apartment again? You mean the hard drive for Nora's PC?"

"Yes! You have her laptop in custody, or whatever, don't you?"

"Yeah. It's been entered into evidence. We do."

"And her laptop was collected in a proper and legal way, wasn't it? Almost every newer PC backs up files automatically. There's bound to be a copy of whatever is on those disks in Nora's hard drive. So it doesn't matter if you can't submit the disks in evidence. You've got the hard drive. All the disks will do is give us the right kind of lead. I hope. They aren't labeled."

He rubbed his chin. "Hmm. You might be right. You still have the disks?"

"Right in my purse. And I can use John's PC to go through them. If you don't mind."

"I don't mind. I've got two murders to solve." He raised an eyebrow. "And I need all the help I can get. But first, I need a shave."

Quill kicked the covers off and jumped out of bed. "Last one in the shower's an unemployed sheriff."

"Eleven-thirty," said Meg. "I thought you two were never coming down."

"Don't be vulgar." Quill settled onto the stool at the butcher block counter and raised her cheek for Myles. He bent down and kissed her. Meg beamed.

"You two want some lunch?"

"He's off to apply a rubber hose to Joseph Greenwald," Quill said. "But I'd love some lunch."

"I'll get something at Marge's later," said Myles. He left, and the kitchen seemed suddenly empty.

"Crab cheese soup?" Meg asked.

"Sounds great. The dining room booked for lunch?"

Meg glanced at the agenda posted on the wall. "Most of the wedding party's out skiing."

"Not Tutti," said Quill, alarmed.

"No, not Tutti. She and Doreen and Elaine are in your office hassling the florist about the flower delivery. The senator and one of the aides—it's either Frank or Marlon or Ed—are still upstairs making phone calls. Which is a lot better," Meg said cheerfully, "than any of them hassling me about the reception. Claire and the brides-maids and the groomsmen are out skiing. There's a plot afoot to make Claire drunk, so she can actually go through with the wedding. Or maybe the plot's to make the senator drunk. Either way, nobody innocent's going to get hurt, if the nuptials do come off."

"Meg," Quill protested. "This is a tragedy shaping up. You're not being very kind."

"It's a tragedy all right," Meg said tartly, "but not the kind you think." She ladled a portion of the crab soup into a small crock and set it in front of Quill. "How sure are you that the senator's behind these murders?"

"Who else could it be?"

"Lots of people. Maybe this Joe Greenwald. Maybe . . ."

"Maybe who?"

"Maybe Tutti."

Quill put her spoon down. "That's ridiculous."

"Is it? Maybe she's setting Al up. Wouldn't you try to get him out of the way if he was going to marry your granddaughter?"

"I wouldn't commit two murders to do it. And if she's going to kill people, why doesn't she just go straight to the source of the problem and kill Al himself? You've been smoking funny cigarettes, Meg.''

"Okay. So Tutti as murderer is a ludicrous idea. I'd just like to point out—"

"That I'm engaging in wild surmise?"

"Well, yeah."

"I've already been informed of the dangers of engaging in wild surmise. So let's change the subject."

"You want to change the subject because you want to solve this case all by yourself."

"Well, I do," Quill admitted. "But not all by myself. I've got a partner."

"Sure you do. Me."

Quill swallowed a spoonful of soup. Then another.

Meg's face changed. "Not me. Myles."

"Do you mind?"

Meg's eyelids flickered. "No." Then, "Yes. Yes, I think I do. This is a real reversal, Quill. Normally it's you looking out for me."

"I'm looking out for you!"

"Then that's not what I mean. I mean normally it's been the two of us. Together. Now it's not." Meg ran her hands slowly through her hair.

"So you do mind."

"It's just . . . different."

Quill couldn't think of anything to say to this. Except that just when you seemed to have one relationship problem solved, another popped up in its place. Meg drummed her fingers on the butcher block, pulled the agenda from the wall, and started making notes with a dull pencil. Her face was flushed.

After a moment, Quill said, "This is terrific soup." Then, "How many for the rehearsal dinner tonight?"

"Twenty. And it's a fabulous menu, Quill. I'm having the best time. I've made a brandied fruit compote, a squash soufflé, and the pièce de résistance—potted rabbit." The flush on her face had faded to two bright red spots.

"Rabbit." Quill bit her lip and chuckled. "Is this an unsubtle signal to the senator?"

"Is what a signal? What?" Alphonse Santini banged through the swinging doors into the kitchen. Both women jumped. "So you heard already? I think it's a sign, too. Like, I shouldn't be getting married again. I mean, one ball and chain in a lifetime's enough, you get my drift. The old lady's loaded, but still. Shit."

"It's Tutti that's—er—loaded?" Quill asked casually. "I thought it was Vittorio, her son."

"In that family, where the money comes from isn't the issue. It's who's got the balls. And in that family, it's Tutti."

"Then how come . . ." Quill began. She stopped. She couldn't very well ask Santini to his face why Tutti—if she was the driving force in the McIntosh family—was permitting a marriage to go forward of which she clearly didn't approve.

"Then how come what?" Santini moved restlessly around the kitchen, snapping his fingers. He stuck a finger in the soup crock, licked it off, and moved to stick it in again.

Meg took two long strides forward and moved the crock out of reach. "Is there something specific we can help you with, Senator?"

"This dinner tonight. The rehearsal dinner, we got a problem."

Meg raised her eyebrows politely. "With what?"

"Can't have the rehearsal in the church. It's drifted in and the plows can't get to it until later today. So we'll want to push the dinner back, see, and have the rehearsal here, about nine o'clock."

"How far back?" There was an ominous note in Meg's voice.

Quill slid off the stool and said hastily, "It really isn't necessary, is it, Senator? There's been such a lot of disruption around here lately, it'd make life a lot easier for everyone if we just kept to the original schedule." She grabbed him by the arm, guided him back to the dining room, started to ask him how his dinner had been the night before, realized that the reenactment of the rape of the Sabines had probably altered his view of the hospitality offered by the Inn, and blurted out instead, "Why did you send Joseph Greenwald to burglarize Nora Cahill's apartment?"

"Huh?" His eyes narrowed to slits. "You out of your mind, throwing around crap like that? Joe Greenwald?" He grabbed her by her upper arms and thrust his face close to hers. "Joey doesn't even work for me," he hissed. "And if he did, which he doesn't, what the hell were you doing in that broad's apartment?!"

Quill regarded him as steadily as possible with her heart pounding and her hands damp. "I'm onto you, Senator Santini. So are a lot of other people. If I were you . . ."

His grip tightened. He was stronger than he looked. "Well, you aren't, you little bitch. And let me tell you something . . . Goddammit." He dropped his grip abruptly. "I never should have gotten into this. Married to a whining cow. For what? Money. Goddamned money."

"Alphonse!" Tutti's voice cut across the dining room like a sledgehammer. She stood in the doorway to the foyer, erect, her face stern. Quill had the sudden, eerie feeling that the genial, sweet-voiced grandmother who believed in spirits had been replaced by a refugee from a *Godfather* movie.

Santini dropped his hands and backed off. "Sorry, Gramma."

Sunlight flashed off the rhinestones in Tutti's spectacles, obscuring her eyes. There was an uneasy silence. She resumed, in tones approaching her normal voice, "I thought you were planning on skiing with Claire, Alphonse."

"Yeah, yeah."

"Don't yeah, yeah me." The whiplash was back.

"Tutti?" Elaine fluttered behind her, a moth against her mother-in-law's stolidity. "The flowers are here. Shall I tell them to bring them in? Quill?" Her voice trailed off into its usual inaudibility. She was wearing yet another long-sleeved blouse with lacy sleeves and high collar, and looked fragile, despite her substantial curves.

Quill stepped away from Santini. "I'm sorry, Elaine, I wasn't paying attention. Would you like me to talk to the delivery people? Are the Cornell students here to do the decorating? They are? Then it shouldn't take too long to have the whole dining room looking wonderful."

"The church," muttered Elaine. Her eyes teared up.

"We'll put the flowers for the church on the terrace. They won't freeze and they'll keep just fine until morning. Then we'll whip over to the church and get them up."

Tutti gave a discreet little cough. "We'll see you at dinner tonight, then, Alphonse." The benign grandmother was back. Alphonse snarled at the three of them and stamped off, presumably, Quill hoped, to cool off skiing down the slope of the Gorge.

"Well, dear," Tutti said briskly. "Let's get those roses up."

"You'll have to excuse me, Tutti, Elaine. But I have some pressing business in the office," said Quill. She badly wanted to go through the computer disks, if only to save Claire and her female relatives the embarrassment of having Alphonse Santini hauled off to jail at the church door.

Tutti fixed her with a gimlet eye. "My dear. I have no wish to be more direct than necessary. But my family and I have spent a great deal of time—and money—at your Inn. I would appreciate it if you would help in the arrangement of the flowers." Her rose-leaf cheeks crumpled in a smile. "It won't take very long at all."

The dining room was decorated in less than two hours. And it was because Tutti, Quill realized, had the instinct, if not the outright talents, of a second Napoleon. "Except there *were* two, weren't there? Or three?" she murmured aloud.

"Three what, dear? No! Redo that swag, young man. I want all the roses facing out. And the drape needs to be loosened just a little. That's it. That's too far. Put it back. Good." She clapped her hands. "I want this mess cleaned up and all of you gone. Five minutes." The crew went to work with a will.

Quill turned slowly in a circle. "It's not just good, Tutti. It's beautiful."

"It is, isn't it?" Her faded blue eyes sparkled. "I never had a formal wedding myself, my dear. I took a great many pains with this one."

"The rose swags were designed by . . ." Elaine leaned forward and whispered a name most of America knew into Quill's ear. "But he wouldn't come here to direct it himself, of course. So Tutti said she'd do it."

"Why wouldn't he come himself?" asked Quill. She caught the exchange of glances between the two older women.

Tutti said tactfully, "Well, it's the family, dear."

"Nonsense," said Quill. "Shaw was right, you know.

Good manners don't have anything to do with whether you treat a shop girl like a duchess, good manners have to do with whether you treat a duchess like a shop girl.''

"I'm afraid I don't quite understand, dear," said Tutti.

"Just that plumbing money is morally neutral. It's what you do with it that says whether or not you have taste. And this is wonderful.''

Quill looked around the dining room again and was delighted. It must have cost the earth, but the florist had delivered outdoor roses in the depths of December. The vibrant peach-orange of Sutter's Gold, the full glorious yellow of Faust, the paler yellow of Golden Fleece were all mixed in glorious confusion with the rich reds of Frenshman and Dickson's Flame. An ivy of a deep, pure green twined around the rose bouquets, interspersed here and there with full-leaved fern. The rose garlands hung from the long windows, swung gracefully from the center chandelier, and twined down freestanding vases in the corners.

"It smells like June," Quill said. "It's amazing.''

"Now," Tutti said briskly. "The crate's arrived with the table linens. Elaine, dear, if you'd go find that nice groundskeeper . . .''

"Mike," said Quill.

"Mike, and ask him to wheel it in here, we'll set out the tablecloths for this evening. Then tomorrow, Sarah, we'll use the white damask and the linen napkins. But tonight is a quiet, family celebration, so we don't need to be as formal.'' She smiled at Quill as Elaine left in search of Mike. "I had a chintz sent directly from England. It has a wonderful Chinese yellow background with aquamarine accents. It just makes these roses.''

"Tutti," Quill began. She hesitated. "I thought . . .

Forgive me, I don't mean to be rude. But do you want Claire to marry Alphonse Santini?''

"Of course I do. It's time we had a little political connection in the family. At least, one that we can count on." She twinkled at Quill's expression. "You can't count on money alone, my dear. Blood ties are everything."

"Oh," said Quill. "But, Tutti. What you said about the rabbit. At the séance. You know who killed Nora and Sheriff Dorset. I don't understand. I don't understand at all."

"You think Alphonse was responsible?" Tutti took a small muslin handkerchief from her purse and patted her cheeks. "That's warm work, decorating. Well. My little messages to Alphonse were more in the nature of letting him know who's the head of the family. Not, my dear, that that's any of your business. As far as I'm concerned, if Claire wants him, she can have him. As long as he treats her well. As long as he understands the rules."

"But murder, Tutti. If you know something, you really have to tell the police. Have you met Sheriff McHale? He's wonderful. A wonderful sheriff, I mean. And you won't find it difficult to talk to him at all."

Tutti began to laugh. It was a warm rich laugh, and it made Quill think of her father's mother, a round woman with a joy of life that was infectious. Quill touched her arm. "I don't want to upset you. But I'm almost sure that the senator is behind these murders. And since Sheriff McHale's been here, every single murder that's been committed in Hemlock Falls has been solved. All this beauty," Quill said. "I just hope it's not wasted."

"We'll be fine, my dear. Just fine." Her pink cheeks got a little pinker. "There's Dina. Yoo-hoo! Here we are, dear."

" 'Scuse me, Quill?" Dina, unusually tentative, crossed the dining room with a hesitant air.

"Now, Dina, did you call that young nephew of mine?" Tutti asked fondly. She pinched Dina's cheek. "He's first-year law, Cornell," she said to Quill. "The poor boy doesn't have time to find himself a nice girl, so when Dina came to the Welcoming—those of us with the Gift don't call it a séance—it's so—Fox sisters, if you know what I mean. We call it a Welcoming. So, you called him?"

"Your nephew Anthony, Mrs. Mc—I mean, Tutti. No. There's this botanist I've been dating—"

"Botanist!" said Tutti. "What kind of living does a botanist make? Now a young lawyer . . ."

"Well, there's one to see you," said Dina. "A Mr. Greenwald."

"Oh, really?" said Quill. "I certainly would like to see him, too, Tutti."

"Joey? Here? How nice!" Tutti beamed at them both. "He's engaged, though, to my brother's third daughter, Christina. A beautiful girl."

"Where is he, Dina?" Quill asked grimly.

"I put him in your office." She gave Tutti an apologetic glance, leaned forward, and whispered in Quill's ear, "Meg said that's the guy who tried to kill you!"

Quill nodded.

"Shall I get a gun or something? John's got that rifle he uses for rabid woodchucks and stuff."

Quill shook her head. "How does Greenwald look?"

"Pretty banged up. His arm's in a sling and his face is purple."

"Oh, dear."

Quill marched after Tutti and found her fussing over Joseph Greenwald, who was, to Quill's guilty satisfaction, looking very banged up. He rose to his feet as she came in. Quill folded her arms and glared at him.

"I see you've met," Tutti said comfortably. "Sit down, dear." She settled herself behind Quill's desk and waved at the couch.

Quill sat.

"I received a phone call from Joseph this morning, after your sheriff had a little interview with him down at the Municipal Building."

Quill blinked at her.

"Joseph is a young member of a law firm that has represented my family's interests for years," Tutti said.

"Then you absolutely need another law firm, Tutti. This man tried to run me off the road last night. In the storm."

"Why in the world would he want to do that?" Tutti cocked her head. One white curl fell charmingly over her left ear. She patted it back into place. "If Joseph was following you, and I say if, it was because perhaps you had something that belongs to me."

"Belongs to you?"

"What are those little things called, dear? You know, they stick them into those machines all the young people have these days."

"Computer disks?" Quill, perhaps because she'd had a late night, was feeling a little faint.

"That's it. Computer disks." She turned to Joseph, who had resumed his seat next to Quill on her couch. "Now, Joey. What's the number of that New York State statute you were telling me about?"

"The breaking and entering statute? Or the fraudulent impersonation statute?"

Tutti turned her blue gaze onto Quill. There was a scene in *Jaws* that had scared the dickens out of her as a little kid. The one where Bruce the shark pulls along the boat, and his flat black eye hypnotizes Robert Shaw.

"Either one," said Tutti, with a click of her white teeth. "Either one."

"I have no idea what you're talking about." Quill kept her hands still and her voice steady.

Tutti pulled out a jeweled compact, a lipstick, and frowned at herself in the mirror. Then she reapplied the lipstick, put the compact away, and said, "Rita the security guard does. The boy from the pizza parlor who stuck the flyer under the windshield of that battered Oldsmobile of yours does. On the other hand—if you said that you'd met Joseph on Interstate 81 headed north—there wouldn't be anyone who could gainsay that—or prove it, either. You see, dear." She leaned forward. "No witnesses." She sat back. "We'll wait here."

"It's not going to do you any good." Quill stood up. "You know about computers, Mr. Greenwald."

"Some."

"What type did Nora Cahill use?"

He shrugged.

"I can give you a hint. Those software disks you found in the box of her office equipment? It was the latest edition of Microsoft Word. Practically every PC with the power to run that software automatically backs up files. Even if Nora erased it, the likelihood of one of those disk doctors being able to recover it is pretty high. And you know who has her laptop?"

"Who?" Tutti demanded.

Joseph Greenwald rubbed his forehead. "Mrs. McIntosh, ah, McHale's got it."

"The local sheriff?" she asked sharply. "How much trouble can we get from a local sheriff?"

"He's not just any local sheriff."

Quill got up. "If you two will excuse me, I have some work to do."

Tutti jerked her chin at Greenwald.

"If you don't mind, Ms. Quilliam, we'd like to recover our property despite the—er—circumstances."

There was a long silence.

"They're in my room," Quill said finally.

"Go with her," snapped Tutti. She got to her feet
with a groan. "This arthritis is acting up again. I'm going to have a hot bath before the dinner." She patted
Quill's arm. "I hope we see you there, my dear. In one
of those lovely velvet gowns like the one you wore last
night." She patted Quill's cheek. Quill had to restrain
herself from biting her.

"And you gave them to her?" Meg asked, several
hours later. She was standing at the Aga, an egg whisk
in one hand and her copper sauté pan in the other. A
brown sauce was bubbling in the pan. It smelled rich,
earthy and winey. Quill, dressed for the evening in
bronze silk, nibbled at a piece of sourdough bread.

"What else could I do? I can just see poor Howie
trying to defend me on felony charges of breaking and
entering."

"It's a misdemeanor, I think. Depending on what you
swiped. Whatever. Tell me I was right. She *is* the murderer."

Quill cut a piece of Stilton from the wheel Meg had
set out for the rehearsal dinner. She added it to the bread.

"Will you stop?" Meg said testily. "You're wrecking
the display."

"Okay. You were right. But you were right for the
wrong reasons. I can't believe you care about the quality
of the food you're going to serve to a family whose
business is organized crime. And a sweet little old lady
who's capable of knocking off six people before breakfast."

"It's not whether you win or lose, it's how you play the game," Meg said obscurely. "And you don't know that they're members of organized crime."

"Ha!"

"Or that Tutti's the Godmother."

"Ha, again. It should be obvious to the meanest intelligence."

"What's obvious to the meanest intelligence is that you're still no further in discovering who killed Nora and Dorset and why."

"If we could just find some hard evidence," said Quill. "The videotape. Or my coat. Even my hat, which has got to have blood on it."

"Whoosh." Meg shuddered. She dropped the whisk, startled. "Darn it, do you hear that? You don't suppose it's those idiots from S.O.A.P. again?"

Quill listened: muffled barks and equally muffled curses, followed by the crash of a mop against the floor. "Tatiana," she said. "From the dining room. Maybe she caught another mouse. And that's Doreen whacking along behind her. She seems to have taken a liking to Doreen."

"That'll shorten her life." Meg dipped a spoon into the sauce, tasted it, scowled, and dumped it down the sink. She rinsed out her copper bowl and began to reassemble the sauce. Tatiana's barks came closer, accompanied by the thump of tennis shoes against carpet. There was the *skritch-skritch-skritch* of canine claws against the dining room doors. Quill pushed them open. Tatiana burst in, barks at an hysterical pitch.

"You did catch a mouse," Quill said. "Ugh. Good girl."

Doreen stamped in behind her. "That ain't a mouse. It's a hat. Your hat. And there's blood all over it."

CHAPTER 11

"Catch that dog!" Meg screamed.

"I'm tryin'!" Doreen thwacked the mop on the floor. Tatiana raced around the kitchen, the rabbit hat flapping in her jaws. Bjarne jumped, cursed in Finn, and leaped out of the way, a serving of squash soufflé held high above his head.

"Wait!" Quill commanded. She grabbed a leg of potted rabbit (despite Meg's agonized cries of "My dinner!") and crouched down on the floor. "Here, doggie, good doggie."

"Don't you dare give that dog my good food, Sarah Quilliam!"

Tatiana came to a halt next to the boot box at the back door. She sat down, the hat dangling from her jaws. Her little black eyes glared malevolently over the bedraggled rabbit fur. She growled. Doreen growled back.

"Don't, Doreen." Quill inched forward, the roasted rabbit held temptingly in one hand. "Gooood dog."

The back door opened. Tatiana whirled. John walked in. Tatiana leaped past him and into the night.

"No!" Meg, Quill, and Doreen yelled simultaneously.

"Good grief," John said.

"The hat!" Meg shouted.

All four of them dove out the back door.

The sun was setting in a modest blaze of pink. Shadows crawled across the snow-covered garden. The air was damp and still. The dog spun in circles on the snowy path, apparently chasing its tail. The hat sat in a sodden lump near a stalk of brussels sprouts, on top of a pile of cow manure. Quill snatched it up. "My hat," she mourned. "It's a mess."

"You shut up," Doreen said to the dog. "Get in there. Now!"

Tatiana considered this command for a long moment, her head cocked to one side, then followed the four of them back to the kitchen. Quill put the hat on the butcher block counter.

"That is a bad thing to do to a hat," Bjarne observed over Quill's shoulder. "Shall I give the little dog a treat?"

"You can give the little dog a kick in the butt," Doreen growled. "Here. Gimme that." She snatched the scrap of fat from Bjarne and held it out. "C'mere, you."

Tatiana sat down, scratched her neck ruff furiously with her hind leg, stretched, grinned, then accepted the piece of fat with a contemptuous air.

"Where did she find it, Doreen?" Quill took a long-handled fork and turned the hat over. "It's a mess."

"Outside somewheres." Doreen took a Kleenex from her apron, sneezed, and wiped her nose. "We went out for walkies . . ."

"For what?" asked John.

"Walkies," Doreen said impatiently, "so she could do her business. We went on down to the park and she run off in the woods and come back with this."

They stared at it. The hat was fashioned after the style

affected by World War II Chinese generals. The inside of the crown and the earflaps were lined with rabbit fur. The flaps could be drawn up over the top of the hat and fastened together with a button, or worn down over the ears and fastened beneath the chin.

It shed rabbit hair, continually.

"Why d'ya ever buy the durn thing?" asked Doreen.

"It's warm," Quill said defensively. "And I've never been all that fashion conscious."

"I know corpses more fashion conscious than you," Doreen agreed. "It sure is some mess." Snow, blood, cow manure, and dog saliva matted the hat from crown to chin strap.

"There's blood all along the inside," John observed. "The murderer was wearing this hat on the videotape, Quill? And in the cell block, when he knifed Dorset?"

"Yes. And I agree with you. There shouldn't be any blood inside the hat. At least, I don't know how it could have gotten there."

"Maybe it got knocked off in the cell block in the struggle with Dorset," Meg suggested. "You said he was bleeding pretty badly."

Quill shuddered at the memory. "It's possible. I couldn't see all that much. I didn't want to see all that much. But it's possible."

John threw a glance at the kitchen clock. "I've got to get to the dining room to seat the McIntosh party." He shrugged himself out of his parka, pulled off his sweater, and put on the tweed sports coat he normally wore throughout the day. "The van from the Marriott's out front with the overflow guests. I told the driver to come in here for some food." He poked at the rabbit hat with a tentative finger. "You might want to put this somewhere before he comes in to eat."

"I'll give Myles a call and tell him the dog's found it." said Quill. "Let's stick it in the storeroom, in the meantime."

"I've got a crazy suggestion," Meg said irascibly. "Why don't we try serving this meal in the meantime."

"Murders come and murders go, but food goes on forever?" said Quill. "Okay. Okay! You're right. John and I will get out to that rehearsal dinner and grin, grin, grin at the horrible senator."

Meg eyed her potted rabbit with satisfaction. "At least the condemned is getting a hearty meal. If you two are going to serve it, that is."

"You go on ahead, John. I'll just give Myles a call."

Quill dialed the familiar number from the kitchen phone. The sheriff, Deputy Dave informed her, was out, talking to some computer guy at Cornell about Nora Cahill's laptop. He'd be back around seven-thirty.

Quill left an urgent-please-call message with Davy, who said that he hoped there were no hard feelings over her recent incarceration. Quill said certainly not, and Davy, emboldened, offered the information that Bernie Bristol had resigned his justiceship in the wake of the unfortunate publicity surrounding Nora Cahill's death. The mayor, Davy told her, was practically on his knees to Mr. Murchison to return as justice, who had told him, the mayor, to go fly a kite.

"So there's a bare possibility," Quill said to John a few moments later in the dining room, "that Adela will get that justice job."

She smiled as Claire and Tutti walked in, and said out of the corner of her mouth, "And if she is elected, I hope her first job is to arraign Senator Santini. For murder."

Having caught at least her fiancé's name in this murmured speech, Claire said, "A-al's not *here* yet," in her nasal whine, and slouched over to the table by the window. Quill pulled a chair out for her and commented on the beauty of the rose garlands as Claire sat down.

"They're all right, I guess," Claire said listlessly. "Where's Mummy?"

"Still getting dressed, dear." Tutti beamed at the tablecloths. "Sarah, you have an eye. What do you think?"

"They're wonderful," Quill said sincerely. For whether or not Tutti was, as she suspected, the head of a large criminal organization of Italian (and Scot) descent, she clearly had taste. If not on her own, at least taste that she was willing to purchase. The tablecloths shouldn't have worked with the natural flowers and the mauve carpeting, but they did. The print was of brilliantly colored roses. They splashed across the tables; the pattern was tiny, the colors vivid. The heavy linen napkins were aquamarine, the china a creamy white rimmed with platinum. Claire sat in the middle of this splendor with a sallow face and a discontented mouth.

Meg came out of the kitchen and toward the party. She was dressed in her chef's coat, a specially made tunic that had been a present from Helena Houndswood, the celebrity chef who had visited the Inn two years before. The tunic was made of fine white wool, with full sleeves that ended in neat narrow cuffs at Meg's wrists. Her cheeks were pink from the heat in the kitchen and her gray eyes serene. Quill was swept with affection and then wondered, briefly, at her own emotions. She jerked a little in surprise: despite everything, the two bodies, her night in jail, the discontented bride in front of her, she realized that she was happy.

She took Meg's hand in her own and brought her to the table. "For those of you who haven't met her yet, this is our chef, Margaret Quilliam."

Polite applause swept the table.

"I'd like to welcome you to the Inn," Meg said. "Our partner, John Raintree, will be serving chilled champagne in a moment, so that Quill and he and I, in fact all of us here at the Inn at Hemlock Falls, can toast Claire and the senator, and wish them the very best."

"Hang on a second," said Marlon. "I want to get this on tape!" He took a mini-camcorder from the case sitting by his chair, then circled the table, the camera whirring. Meg straightened her collar uncertainly. Quill ducked out of camera range.

"But Al's not here yet!" Claire said.

Quill exchanged a glance with Meg. "Why don't I go upstairs and see if he's still in his room. I do know that he went out skiing fairly late. He may just have gotten back."

"Tell Elaine and Vittorio to come down, too, will you, dear?" Tutti, who was looking especially grandmotherly in pink lace over gray satin, gave Quill a decisive little nod.

"I'd like to tell you what we'll be serving tonight," Meg went on. "For the first course, I've developed a clear game soup seasoned with a combination of herbs we grow right here at the Inn."

Quill went into the foyer. The chair behind the reception desk was empty. Dina had left that morning to go home for the holidays. Mike had filled the Oriental vases near the cobblestone fireplace with fresh pine, and the scent filled this small area. Quill drew a deep breath. It was like being in the woods. The fire was low in the fireplace, and she bent to put a fresh log on it. The odor of burning apple wood joined that of the pine.

"It smells wonderful in here." Myles came in the front door. Snow powdered the shoulders of his heavy anorak and the heels of his boots. His face was red with cold. Quill went to him and put her warm hands on his cheeks. He kissed her. She put her arms around him, inside his jacket. She could feel his heart beating against her hands.

"Davy said you called. Is anything wrong?"

"We found the hat. Or rather, Tatiana found the hat. My hat."

His eyebrows drew together.

"Oh, it's Tutti's little dog. Apparently, Tutti dragooned Doreen into taking it, I mean her, for her constitutional in the park. The dog ran off and came back with the hat. I stuck it—the hat, I mean—in the storeroom." She looked around vaguely. "I don't know where Tatiana is. Doreen's stuck with her, I suppose. Anyway, the hat's there whenever you need it. How did the interview with Greenwald go?"

Myles's gray eyes narrowed. "The guy's slick. You're sure that no one saw him after you on the interstate?"

Quill shook her head. "Positive. The snow was awful."

"Greenwald didn't come right out and say it, but he intimated that a couple of witnesses could place you at Cahill's apartment."

"He's right. I wasn't very careful, I guess."

"Quill, you shouldn't have gone there in the first place."

"True, true, true. Sorry. I'll know better next time. It turned out to be useless, anyway. Greenwald practically blackmailed me into giving him those computer disks. As a matter of fact, he did blackmail me. He threatened me with impersonation and breaking and entering. So I gave him the computer disks."

"Hmm. It doesn't matter. You were right about Nora's hard drive. The computer boys in Ithaca found—"

"Sarah, my dear. Can you encourage my daughter-in-law to join us? We're waiting that delicious dinner on her and my son."

"Tutti." Quill pulled away from Myles's arms. "I haven't been up there yet. Have you met Sheriff Mc-Hale?"

Joseph Greenwald, his dinner jacket slung over his shoulder to accommodate his broken arm, appeared behind Tutti. Ed—or maybe it was Marlon—joined him and stood on her right.

"How do you do, Sheriff?" Tutti's eyes gleamed behind her glasses. "You've met my boy Joseph. And this is my boy Marlon Guppa."

Myles nodded and said, "Ma'am," which made Quill want to giggle.

"I'll be back in a minute with Elaine, Tutti. Myles, Meg's set aside some food for you in the kitchen. I think she put it in the storeroom."

Quill ran lightly up the stairs to the Adams suite on the second floor. She knocked, received no answer, then knocked again. She called out Santini's name, then took her master key from the chain around her neck and let herself in.

She turned on the overhead light. Doreen had been in to clean, and the room was neat. Quill and Meg had managed to save the chestnut floor in this particular set of rooms, and the yellow, striated wood gleamed softly in the lamplight. The suite was two rooms. In the living room, a Queen Anne style sofa sat in front of the small fireplace next to a wing chair covered in a Williamsburg print. The coffee table held a filled ashtray and a half-empty glass. Quill picked up the glass and sniffed. Scotch. So the senator had been in the room after Doreen had cleaned. She searched the small secretary that stood under the window. The stationery with the Inn logo was there, and a partially filled pack of matches, but that was it. No briefcase, no notes, no documents.

She went into the bedroom. The king-sized bed was covered with a wedding-ring quilt. The cherry rocking chair next to the four-poster held a crumpled envelope. Quill picked it up. It was empty. The return address was for the Golden Pillar Travel Agency. Typed on the front of the envelope were the words: "Enclosed, please find your ticket! Thank you for your business." It was addressed by hand to Marlon Guppa.

Quill opened the armoire: empty.

Maybe Santini'd stopped off at the Croh Bar in town after skiing and forgotten the time. She'd known quite a few Hemlockians to stop off at the Croh Bar and forget what day of the week it was. Except that he wouldn't take his suitcase, his clothes, his briefcase, and the contents of an envelope from a travel agency to go skiing, or drink at the Croh Bar, or go anywhere at all in Hemlock Falls.

Poor Claire.

Poor Myles.

She picked up the phone by the bed and dialed the kitchen. Meg answered, her voice impatient.

"Is Myles there?"

"I was just about to feed him. I will feed him and my twenty guests if you'll get off the phone!"

"Tell him it looks like Santini's skipped town. I'm in his room and everything's gone."

There was a short silence. "Wow," said Meg. "Sorry I snapped. Well, there's one good thing. At least I won't be serving a murderer."

Quill thought of Tutti and her two "boys." "I wouldn't be too sure about that."

The McIntoshes had taken a pair of adjoining rooms on the same floor as the Adams suite. Quill let herself out of Santini's room and walked down the hall to 246. She mentally rehearsed a few lines: *Elaine, Vittorio, I'm so sorry, but the senator seems to have skipped. Very probably with the cash from the murder of Nora Cahill in his pocket. And to avoid prosecution for two murders.*

She raised her hand to knock and heard the sound of angry voices; Vittorio's harsh and bullying, Elaine's soft and tearful. Quill turned away. She'd go downstairs and give the room a call from the front desk. Vittorio's voice rose; there was the sound of a blow. Elaine cried out.

Quill's reaction was instant and unconsidered. She whirled and pounded on the door. The voices within stopped, except for the soft sounds of Elaine's tears. Quill pounded on the door again. Vittorio jerked it open and pushed his angry bulk into the hall. "What the hell do you want?"

"Tutti was a little concerned and asked me to come up and find you. Dinner's waiting."

"Beat it."

Quill placed her palm against Vittorio's shoulder and shoved him out of the way. She walked into the bedroom. It was chaotic: clothes were draped over every available surface, cosmetics littered the small dressing table under the window, and three suitcases lay open on the floor. It was the bedroom of an untidy child.

Elaine sat on the edge of her bed, rubbing her wrist. She was in a silk full slip, pale pink. She looked at Quill with swimming eyes.

Vittorio came partway in and half-knocked, half-slammed the open door with his fist. He was wearing a dinner jacket. The smell of a heavy after-shave—*Polo*, Quill thought—floated across the room.

"You coming down, Lanie?"

She sat very still.

"Elaine!"

She stirred. "Yes, Vic. I'll be right there."

"You. It's Quilliam, right?" He jerked his head toward the hall. "I told you to beat it."

"I'll just give Elaine a hand."

He gave a short, unpleasant laugh. "Suit yourself."

"Close the door on your way out," Quill said softly. Elaine jumped when it slammed shut. Quill sat down next to her on the bed and gently lifted her arm. "This is why you wear the long-sleeved blouses?"

"He doesn't mean it," Elaine said, so quietly that Quill had to bend her head to hear her.

Quill touched her wrist gently. "That's already pretty red. And the ones farther up look old. It must have been going on for a while."

Elaine dabbed at her eyes with a Kleenex. "My make-up's a mess. And I've got to get down there to the dinner." She got up and crossed to the dressing table.

"Elaine, there're lots of people that can help you. There's even a group in the village, attached to the hospital. It's a shelter. The woman that runs it is terrific. Why don't you let me give her a call?"

Elaine dabbed at her face with a powder puff, then reapplied her eyeliner.

"Meg's good—um—friend is our local internist. He's a pretty good listener. Would you like to talk to him?"

Elaine picked up a red lipstick, set it down, and selected a gloss. She turned and went to the closet and took out a long filmy dress in pink. Full sleeves. High collar. She bent to step into the dress.

Quill's stomach lurched. She pinched her own knee hard, then managed to say lightly, "I didn't know Vittorio smoked."

A faint smile crossed Elaine's face. She pulled her

slip away from her chest and looked down at her breasts. "He quit for almost twenty years. This business with Al got him started again."

"What business with Al?"

She shook her head.

"Can I get you some antibiotic cream?"

"I'll be fine."

"You shouldn't let those burns go. And you shouldn't irritate them with cloth." Quill's voice rose; she was shaking with anger. "Why don't you do something to help yourself? And if you can't, let me. Does Claire know?"

"Oh, no!" Elaine turned pale. "Claire worships her father."

"I'll bet." Quill rubbed her face with both hands. "What about Tutti? Could she be any help? Now that's stupid. He's her son."

Elaine zipped her dress up, slipped into a pair of pink high-heeled shoes, and took up a pearl-beaded purse. She looked at herself in the mirror, then took a double row set of pearls from the top of the dresser and fastened them around her neck.

"What do you think?"

"Elaine."

She smiled. "He won't do it anymore. He promised."

"Elaine, every battered woman in the world believes that. You've got to do something to help yourself."

"Oh, no I don't. You don't know Tutti. She'll fix it. She'll fix everything."

Quill walked to the dining room with her. Vittorio was seated at the head of the table. The chair at the foot, near Claire, was still empty. Quill seated Elaine at Vittorio's right. She was afraid to say anything. Even to do anything. She'd heard that abusers took revenge when they were confronted—not on people like her, who would fight back, but on their original victims.

Tutti, at Vittorio's left, cast a shrewd glance at Quill, and said, "Doesn't Elaine look wonderful, Vic?"

"Yeah. Great. How long are we supposed to wait to eat?"

"I'm sure Al will be here any minute, Daddy." Claire crumbled a piece of bread between her fingers. "He's late all the time. And you said he had some appointments, Marlon, didn't you? With that little creepy person? The mayor?"

"Yes, Miss McIntosh. But he should have been back by now."

Quill let her gaze rest on Marlon for a long moment. His dark brown eyes shifted under her steady gaze. "The sheriff's in the kitchen right now. Why don't I ask him to put out a call? If the senator's in the village, someone should know where he is. Maybe he got lost on his way back to the Inn."

Marlon jumped. "Oh. Hell. We don't need to do that, Miss Quilliam. He'll show up sooner or later."

"In the meantime," Tutti said firmly, "I would like to eat. Your sister's prepared quite a meal for us, Sarah. I can't wait. The senator will just have to eat leftovers."

"I'll let the kitchen know." She smiled. She hoped no one noticed how strained it was. She resisted the impulse to whistle a few bars of "Flying Down to Rio." "Enjoy your meal, everyone. And let us know if there's anything else you need. . . . "

" . . . like a bridegroom," she muttered as she walked into the kitchen. Myles, Meg, and John were sitting at the counter, all three of them eating potted rabbit. Quill put her hands on her hips and glared at them. "Myles, I thought you'd be halfway to the airport by now. You're not going to let him get away?"

"What's this?" John asked. "I just got here."

"Santini's skipped. As in beat feet, left town, took a powder?" Meg said flatly.

John whistled. "Wow."

Myles swallowed a bite of rabbit and said calmly, "You're sure about that, Quill?"

"I don't know what other explanation there could be, Myles. His room's empty. His suitcase is gone. There's an empty airline ticket envelope. If you ask me, he took that blackmail money from Nora Cahill and just . . . skipped, and Tutti set it up. Why aren't you after him?"

"Wow," Meg said again. "Does Claire know?"

"No. And they want to start eating."

"Oh. Good." Meg hopped off the stool. "Bjarne! Guys! We're ready."

Quill took Meg's place at the counter and absently began to eat the rabbit. "This is just great," she said. "I'm so glad everyone's reacting to my hot tip. Myles. Are you going to put out an APB on Santini or not? He's probably halfway to Argentina now, or wherever it is that international felons escape to." She put her fork down. "I'm sorry. That sounded bitchy. It's just that this is so awful. Poor Claire's in there and I don't know which is worse, being jilted or being married to a murderer."

"There's no law or statute against refusing to get married. And the senator isn't our murderer. Santini couldn't have killed either Nora or Dorset," said Myles. "Santini was out with the mayor and Evan Blight the night of the murders, from about eight until well after midnight."

"When did you find that out?" asked Quill.

"This afternoon. One of the women involved in the—er—fracas with S.O.A.P. wanted to swear out a complaint against Blight and the mayor. It was a good opportunity to find out just what goes on at those meetings."

"What does?" demanded Quill.

Myles grinned. "Never mind. The alibi is supported by something else. Those computer files of Cahill's. It was a complete plan to sweep small-town America with a campaign called R.O.A.R., Return Our American Rights. You have the honor, Quill, of being the first candidate to kick this campaign off. Dorset, Bristol, and a number of other small town dignitaries from across New York State were involved."

Quill bit her lip. "So Santini didn't do it! Who, then?"

John got up suddenly, his face grim. "Your hat, Quill. Where is it?"

"The storeroom."

"Hang on a minute." John disappeared into the back and reappeared with the hat. He set it on the counter carefully, avoiding touching the bloody spot inside. "Take a look at this, Myles."

"Swell," said Quill. "Myles? Where are you going? You haven't finished your rabbit."

Myles stood up. His face was calm. "What you just told me about Santini being missing? It doesn't make sense. Tutti McIntosh was funding this whole R.O.A.R campaign. It was designed to put the senator back into his seat in four years. Al struck me as the sort of person who'd marry the devil herself for gain."

"Thanks for the pronoun," Quill grumbled. "So what do you think? Why else would Al skip out on his wedding?"

"We need Doreen," said Myles. "And that dog. There's hair, blood, and bone on the inside of that hat. And neither of our corpses had a head wound."

Quill's winter clothes were still damp from the day before. She drew on the snow pants, the ski jacket, and the knitted hat with a shiver. Doreen stamped impatiently outside the kitchen door. Her winter gear consisted of a leather flight jacket (courtesy of a former husband), several sweaters, stocking cap, and flannel lined jeans. For some reason, she'd stuffed Tatiana into a baby's sweater. The little dog pranced in the snow with more than its usual arrogance.

"She actually looks pretty chic," Meg muttered in Quill's ear. "You going to be warm enough?"

"I think so."

"Be careful. You, too, John."

Meg stood at the door until they reached the maintenance building. Quill turned and waved.

They set off on foot down the circular drive to the Inn and into the park near the Gorge. It was going to snow again, and soon. Clouds drifted past the moon like passing sailboats.

John walked with his head down, hands thrust in his pockets. Quill walked next to Myles, skipping occasionally to keep up with his long strides. Doreen zigzagged back and forth, once in a while throwing a snowball for the dog.

Tatiana was the happiest of the group.

"Right about here, Sheriff." Doreen took a sharp left and plunged into a grove of pine. The way was narrow here, the paths clogged with snow. Quill grabbed on to the back of Myles's anorak to help her keep to her feet.

The dog stopped. Raised its head. Sniffed. Broke into shrill barks and leaped forward, plunging through the drifts. John broke into a run. So did Myles. Doreen and Quill trudged along behind.

"I smell smoke," said Quill.

"S.O.A.P." Doreen said briefly. "They cooked that durn cow here last night. You shoulda seen it."

"Did you see it?"

Doreen turned her head in the dark. The whites of her eyes gleamed. She said with a chuckle, ''Me'n Marge? We follered that Elmer and Harland last night. You shoulda seen them guys. Half of 'em buck nekkid 'ceptin' that bozo Blight. He's too smart to jump around in a gol-durned blizzard with no clothes on. But there they all was, jumping and hollering around this big old fire, with this big old steer carcass a-turnin' and a-turnin' over the fire on this here spit.''

Which was where they found the body of Alphonse Santini, turning slowly over a dying fire, under the moonlit sky.

CHAPTER 12

"Thank the good Lord he wasn't skewered," said Doreen. She and Quill stood huddled together under the pine tree. It was cold and getting colder, but Quill would have had to be nearly comatose with the chill to approach the slow-burning fire. Myles and John kicked the slow coals away from the body. The remnants glowed like wolf eyes in the dark.

Myles squatted and examined the ropes that bound Santini. John knelt in the snow beside him. "You can see where the dog's scurried in the snow," said John. "Here and here. Do you think it was the head wound that killed him?"

"Most likely. Two shots behind the right ear. But I've been wrong before." He lowered his head in thought. Then, "Quill?"

"We're over here."

"You saw the videotape of Nora's murder what, once?"

"That's right."

"Think about it. Think hard about it. Pretend that you're going to paint the scene."

Quill edged nearer. Doreen bent and picked up Tatiana, who was for once silent. Quill closed her eyes.

243

"Anything you can remember about the figure in your coat and hat. The least thing, Quill."

"It was a man, I'm sure of that. His arms were longer than my sleeves. And he was my height, because the coat hit his leg where it hits mine."

"About five eight, then," Myles said to John. "Any idea of weight, Quill?"

Quill shook her head.

"Anything else?"

Quill went over the videotape in her mind. Nora getting out of the car. Nora bending over to brush the snow from her boots. Nora falling, her hands outstretched, her fingers spread in a final gesture of death. . . .

"Dorset. Dorset did it, too!" she exclaimed. "That must have been how he knew."

"Did what?"

"Nora spread her fingers like this." Quill stripped her glove from her hand and held it up. Her first two fingers formed a *V*. "Vittorio! Myles. It's Vittorio! It must be. That would explain what Elaine said. And all that crazy stuff about Tutti and the séance."

"The séance wasn't all that crazy," Doreen grumbled. "I think there's a lot to it."

"Tutti must have seen that videotape. Nobody knew about that hat. No one except me, Dorset, and the murderer. And Elaine told me—that Vittorio's scum, Myles, just scum—but Elaine told me that Tutti would find a way to keep him in line so he wouldn't beat her up anymore."

"Those long-sleeved blouses," John said softly, "I should have known. Damn him."

"Tutti's got the tape, Myles. She must have. And all that stuff that the senator said? About how it didn't matter where the money came from in that family, it was who had the control? It's Tutti. And the weapon she has over her son is the tape!"

"Jeez," said Doreen.

"Brilliant, Quill." John clapped his hands together softly.

She could see Myles's smile in the dark.

"You've got it, dear heart. John, we need some time. I'd like you to stay with the body. I'm going down the hill to get the deputy and to call forensics. Quill, I want you and Doreen to go back to the Inn. I don't want you to do anything, you understand? Just keep an eye on that whole party, Tutti in particular. I'm going to bring in some people to search the Inn; if Tutti's using the tape as a hold over Vittorio, it's got to be there someplace. If anyone tries to leave, don't stop them, but call me, all right?"

"Another storm system's moving in," John said. "Why don't you tell them you've heard Syracuse is blanketed and it's moving this way?"

"We'll be fine," said Quill.

"We're goin' back, then?" asked Doreen.

"Yes. And bring Tatiana." She reached over to ruffle the little dog's ears. "We'll find something nice for her supper. After all, she found the bod—OW! Dammit, Doreen, can't you keep her from nipping?"

Doreen carried the dog back to the Inn, which was just fine with Quill, since she was wearing half-boots that left her calves exposed. Back in the kitchen, Doreen set her on the floor, and she promptly fell asleep.

"Put her in the storeroom," Meg said callously. "With some food and water. Better yet, give her back to Tutti. Maybe she'll bite Vittorio."

"Are they still eating?" Quill peered through the swinging doors. Everyone at the table seemed to be having a fine time. Two of the Cornell students that worked as waiters in their spare time stood at polite attention beside the mahogany sideboard. Tutti was holding court. Vittorio was leaning back in his chair, genially smiling at Marlon Guppa. Elaine, sitting painfully erect, was chatting with Merry Phelan. Even Claire was smiling, flirting in a gawky way with Joseph Greenwald.

"He looks like a murderer, doesn't he?" Meg said into her ear. "Vittorio, I mean."

"Claire doesn't seem to be too upset that the senator's not here," Quill observed. "Didn't anyone say anything about it at all?"

"Oh, there was quite a bit of discussion," said Meg. "Claire finally went up to the Adams suite with her bridesmaid and found that all of the senator's clothes and personal effects were gone. They also found that envelope you did, from the travel agency. So they came back down and Claire cried that she'd been jilted and Joseph Greenwald poured her more champagne. After a second bottle of that Avalon Patriot's Red, Vittorio got up and proposed a toast. 'To the absent bridegroom,' he said. 'May he never return.' That got a big laugh, for some reason. Then Elaine started fluttering on about plumbing money, and about how the senator really wasn't their kind of people and good riddance to bad rubbish, and Vittorio told her to shut up. We should have known he'd done it the minute we saw him."

"But he hadn't done it then. Anyhow, I don't think anyone really looks like a murderer," Quill said in an uncritical way, "but Vittorio's going to get off scot-free if we don't find that tape."

"When will Myles get here with the search warrant?"

"Not for a couple of hours yet." Quill frowned. "I know the thing's here."

"Gol-durn it," Doreen exploded behind them. "You git!"

Tatiana whose brief nap seemed to have brought an unfortunate degree of vigor to her sixteen pounds, had jumped up on the counter and was worrying the rabbit hat. Quill turned around, regarded the dog, and pulled thoughtfully at her hair. "Hey, guys. I've got an idea. Meg? Can you ask one of the guys to bring another case of champagne?"

"For who? For them? Haven't they guzzled enough?"

"No," said Quill, "not nearly enough. Tell them this one's on the house Doreen? Can you keep that darn dog quiet?"

"Prob'ly."

"Good. I'm going to my office. Meg? When you give them that champagne, offer to videotape it. Get the camcorder from Marlon and bring it back with you. If he's drunk enough, he won't even notice that you have it. And then I want the three of us to go upstairs."

It took an interminable time for the McIntosh party to get through the extra twelve bottles of champagne. The Reverend Shuttleworth, who arrived for the wedding rehearsal, only to be told that the groom had failed to show, returned home in mild confusion. (Since mild confusion was a more or less permanent state of mind with Dookie, none of his family noticed.) Quill, Doreen, and Meg waited patiently on the second-floor landing for the party to wind down.

"They're comin'," Doreen said. "Hear that?"

There was a scrape of chairs, the kind of dismissive laughter that signals the end of a long party, a murmur of "good nights."

Tutti, Vittorio, and Elaine proceeded up the stairs. Meg moved the camcorder into position. Doreen set Tatiana on the floor. Quill stood at the head of the stairs.

"Now," Quill whispered.

"Git it!" Doreen roared at the startled dog. She held a mini-sized videocassette above Tatiana's head. The dog leaped for it. Doreen jerked the tape out of reach and ordered, "Git it! Git it!" The dog, irritated to a frenzy by the incomprehensible behavior of this bad-tempered human, barked like Joshua at the walls of Jericho. She leaped, and leaped again.

"They're looking up," Quill said from her vantage point on the landing. "Any time now."

Doreen let the cassette drop. Tatiana snatched it up with a triumphant "Yap!" Tutti, hearing the barks, cried, "Tatty! Come to Mummy!" Tatiana raced down the stairs, videocassette in her mouth.

Tutti caught the dog in her arms and grabbed for the tape. Tatiana wriggled and dropped it. Vittorio picked it up. His swarthy face turned pale.

"Goddammit!" roared Vittorio. "Ma! You told me you hid the goddamn thing."

Quill walked down the stairs. Doreen thumped down beside her and snatched the tape from Vittorio's hand. Meg followed, the camcorder rolling, the camera eye fixed on the group on the stairs.

"Give me that thing," Vittorio demanded. He swayed, caught himself with one hand on the banister, and blinked blearily at Doreen.

"Is it yours?" Quill asked sweetly. "I'm afraid the little dog went through your things when Doreen was straightening your room, Tutti. Where she unearthed this thing I don't know. It can't be yours, can it, Mr. McIntosh? It's marked, 'Property Tompkins County Police Department.' "

"Give it to me, you bitch!"

"Vic!" snapped Tutti. "Shut up!"

Quill took two more steps downward. "This is it, Mr. McIntosh? The videotape from Frank Dorset's hidden camera? The one that shows you killing Nora Cahill?''

''Yes, goddamit! Yes!''

Meg shut the camcorder off. ''Well,'' she said sunnily, ''I got it all. And the little dog, too.''

Quill surveyed the wreckage in the dining room with a sense of satisfaction. It was a shame about the roses, of course. But it had taken less than half an hour that morning to strip the walls and windows of the wedding finery.

Mike the groundskeeper poked his head in from the foyer. ''You want I should take the trash?''

Quill nudged one of the garbage bags with her toe. The scent of crushed roses was strong. ''Yes. Thanks, Mike.''

''I'll bring the tree in, then. You want it here?''

''I think so. Everyone's coming at eight tonight, so we have plenty of time.''

''No problem. I got all the ornaments down and I'll bring 'em in first. Meg having that oyster stew again this year?''

''And Marge is bringing the pumpkin bread.''

''Ahh!'' Mike patted his flat stomach. ''You didn't hear me say this, Quill, but I'd almost give up the holiday bonus for that pumpkin bread.''

Quill stripped the rose-patterned cloths from the tables, bundled them into a box, and replaced them with the red plaid she used for the holidays. She set out the buffet plates, the flatware, and the punch bowl, humming ''The Boar's Head Carol'' under her breath, then ''God Rest Ye Merry Gentlemen.''

Mike brought the tree in, a fifteen footer he'd cut from the woods beyond Hemlock Gorge. It filled the windows overlooking the Falls. It smelled of snow, of cold fresh winds, of pine tar. The two of them strung the hundreds of tiny white lights that Quill had collected over the years, then stepped back to view the result.

"It'll look great at night," Mike said. "You want I should plug 'em in?"

"Degradation!" Evan Blight bellowed, so suddenly that Quill nearly fell over. "Young man? Remove those artifacts of man's inhumanity to the arboreal immediately."

"Hello, Mr. Blight," Quill said. "Can I get you some hot chocolate? I'm afraid that breakfast is over."

"There was," he said a little pathetically, "a disturbance in the night."

"There was indeed. I hope it didn't keep you up."

"She most certainly did," he said with indignation. "Not to mention going through my personal effects."

"She?" said Quill. "You mean someone was in your room?"

"That . . . dog. That . . . perverse mutant of the noble wolf."

"Tatiana? Oh, I'm sorry. I guess in all the confusion last night, we sort of ignored her." Quill chuckled. "Tatiana isn't a dog that likes being ignored. But, under the circumstances, I hope you will forgive her."

"I understand from the Red Man that several guests were arrested."

Quill thought about this for a moment. "Do you mean John Raintree?"

"Yes! The Primal Savage. The nobility of him! It's a shame," Blight continued, "to see on him the wrappings required by our so-called *civil*-ization, although anything less civil . . ."

"Do you mean his clothes?"

"Why, yes. At any rate, I understand that the primal urge has been satisfied, the blood lust quelled."

"If you mean by that that Vittorio McIntosh has been

arrested for three murders, the answer is yes, he has.''

"And the motive. Lust, no doubt.''

"No doubt at all. It wasn't. He killed for gain. He killed Nora Cahill because she was blackmailing him over evidence she'd gathered of his organized crime connections. He killed Frank Dorset because Dorset recognized him on the videotape and also tried blackmail. And he killed Alphonse Santini because Tutti told Santini about the murders—to guarantee to the senator that she had Vittorio under her thumb, and that she would call the political shots—and Santini was ready to turn all the McIntoshes in to the police.'' Quill reflected a moment. "So I guess he died a better man than he lived. Or something like that.''

"*Cherchez les femmes,*" said Evan Blight.

"If by that you mean that women were behind Vittorio's downfall, you couldn't be more wrong.'' Quill, sorry that she'd lost her temper, asked if he would like some lunch before he checked out.

Mr. Blight ran his finger through his beard in agitation. He circled the dining room. His beard was even wilder and untrimmed than before. He'd exchanged the shapeless gray sweater he'd been wearing for two days to an equally shapeless brown sweater. "As you see,'' he said grandly, catching Quill's eye on him, "I have donned my holiday garb.''

"You were planning on staying over Christmas, then?''

The gray eyes blinked behind the fringe of tangled hair. "I would not be welcomed?''

Quill had the feeling, apropos of nothing whatsoever, that Evan Blight, world-famous standard-bearer for manly men, had nowhere to go. She sat down at the table she reserved for the Inn staff, and indicated the chair next to her. He shook his head warily, rather like a small goat approaching a large obstacle.

"Of course you're welcome," Quill said warmly. "We don't normally keep the Inn open over Christmas Eve and Christmas Day, but we'd love to have you join us. As a friend, Mr. Blight. Not a guest."

"The bountiful hospitality of Woman!" exclaimed Mr. Blight.

Quill held her hand up. "There's just one thing. Elmer Henry. Our mayor. And the gentlemen of S.O.A.P. You may not be fully aware of the—um—divisive nature of your beliefs, Mr. Blight. Especially now, at this particular time in the town's history. Perhaps you could soften your views, somewhat? I mean, in the spirit of the season. We need, Mr. Blight, to have the men and women of this town talking to each other again. And you could help, if you wished."

"Humpf."

"Humpf?" Quill sat back, frustrated.

"You would have me abandon a lifetime of beliefs? A value system carefully built up over years of study, years of effort, years of—"

"Bullshit," said Doreen. She marched into the dining room, clutching a pink, elastic object. Tatiana leaped beside her, jaws snapping for the straps dangling from Doreen's hand.

"Down, Spike," said Doreen.

Tatiana dropped to the floor obediently.

"Spike?" asked Quill.

"They was goin' to shoot her," Doreen said flatly. "On account of she betrayed that Tutti. And her name's Spike. Tatiana's no name for a dog."

Quill sighed. "Okay. I guess. But if she bites anybody, Doreen, that's it, do you hear me?"

"You'd think a lot better of this dog if you knew."

"If I knew what?"

"If you knew how she could keep this here Blight from wrecking our Christmas party tonight."

"The dog's going to do that?" Quill said, bewildered.

"The dog did it already. Look here." She thrust the pink elastic object at Quill. Beside her Evan Blight yelped. Spike yelped back.

"Good grief," Quill said. She unfolded it. "It's a minimizer bra."

"So it is." Doreen grinned in satisfaction. "Well, Ms. Blight. What you got to say for yourself?"

There was a long, long moment of silence. Blight tugged at her beard, pulled it slightly away from her chin, and winked at them.

"What do I have to say for myself? It's going to be a very Merry Christmas in Hemlock Falls."

"We'll wait to turn the lights on," said Quill. "Myles might be here soon."

Meg gave her a hug. "He'll be here."

"I hope so. He took Vittorio straight to the FBI office in Syracuse. But you know how these things go. He might not make it at all."

They came early, her friends. Marge and Betty, Miriam, Esther, and all the members of H.O.W. Elmer Henry and Adela, Harland Peterson and his wife, Dookie Shuttleworth and the patient Mrs. Shuttleworth, Kathleen and her brother Davy; it seemed as if the whole village gathered together in the warm and capacious dining room.

They talked, and laughed, and sang carols, and listened to Evan Blight talk about the harmony of love.

Meg brought hot stew from the kitchen. Andy Bishop poured hot cider. One by one the ornaments went on the tree; the flying unicorn that Meg had given her years before, the bubbling lights from Marge and Betty, the

beaded angel for the top of the tree from John's grandmother.

The sky grew dark. Snow began to fall, tapping
against the windows like the tips of feathered wings.

John's quick ears heard it first, the roar of the Jeep as
it came up the drive to the front door of the Inn. He
switched the tree lights on, and it glowed in the window,
a galaxy of stars, to welcome Myles home.

Claudia Bishop, a businesswoman, sold her company and retired to write full-time in 1992. She divides her time between the Finger Lakes in upstate New York and West Palm Beach. She also writes for television.

MARGE SCHMIDT'S
INCREDIBLE CHICKEN STEW

Marge has been very annoyed that her straightforward American cooking has heretofore been ignored in the Hemlock Falls adventures. Here is her recipe for the best chicken stew ever made. (*She* says!)

> one large, cheap old chicken
> two carrots, coarsely chopped
> two stalks of celery, coarsely chopped
> one large onion, chopped
> two medium bay leaves
> a tablespoon of garlic powder
> a few pinches of salt

Place ingredients in a large stewpot. Cover with water. Add one-half cup soy sauce. Simmer until chicken is tender, about an hour and a half.

Remove chicken from pot. Cool. Debone. Replace chicken in pot. Add one package Knox herb soup, three coarsely chopped and peeled potatoes, and one ten-ounce package of frozen peas. Simmer for one half hour.

Mix two cups Bisquick with one cup water. Drop the dough by large tablespoonfuls into simmering stew. It will make about fifteen dumplings. Cover and simmer for ten minutes. Uncover and simmer for another ten minutes.

Serves ten.